THE SWEET SMELL OF SUCCESS

Extended Edition

JET COLLINS

Inquiries and Book Orders should be addressed to:

Great Writers Media
Email: info@greatwritersmedia.com
Phone: (302) 918-5570

ISBN: 978-1-960939-49-4 (sc)
ISBN: 978-1-960939-50-0 (ebk)

READERS CHOICE

The format of ***erotica adult sex*** that readers will occasionally come across in this book, is no different, or any more sinister than the ***erotica adult sex*** that you would observe in a hundred million bedrooms in a normal civilised society.

Stella: Enjoy living the good life while you may.

There are dark clouds on the horizon, and they are heading your way.

FAMOUS HOLLYWOOD QUOTES

"It's not important as to how many men
have been in my life, but more importantly
how much life were in my men"
—Mae West

The old film star Victor Mature (died 1999) was told repeatedly by an army of fans that he was a great actor. He however felt that he should make it quite clear to them that he wasn't even worthy of being an actor, and that he had made 64 films which proved it.

`If you love me, tell me so, if not then slowly let me go`
—anonymous

`When I wake in a morning, I like to feel a new man`
—Jean Harlow

I suppose that's one of the ironies of life, doing
the wrong thing at the right moment.
—Charlie Chaplin

I never said `I want to be alone`, I did say `I want to be left alone` there is a difference.
—Greta Garbo

`How many husbands have I had? you mean apart from my own`
—Zsa Zsa Gabor

I'm a good housekeeper when I leave my men, I just keep their houses`
—Zsa Zsa Gabor

Life would be so wonderful, if we only knew what to do with it
—Greta Garbo

Most of the successful people in Hollywood are failures as human being.
—Marlon Brando

INTRODUCTION

As long as I live and breathe I don't think I will ever again come across a woman quite like Stella Delray. In fact I know I won't. Even before reaching double figures she already has had to suffer losing her parents in a hit and run, when crossing the road to get into their car. In her adolescent years and beyond, the cruelty of life was still hanging around when on holiday her grandfather got swept out to sea as a result of wandering too far out and ignoring danger signs. This left her and her grandma to look after each other. For the next seven years they did just that, but there were signs that her grandma was not quite the striking and authoritative woman she once was.

Sooner rather than later it was decided to move her to a hospice for Dementia sufferers. Stella still visits her whenever she can, but the simple fact is that her grandma has no idea who this girl is who keeps calling her grandma.

Now at the age of 21 and living on her own, she was always aware that life was not always going to be exactly plain sailing, especially after her family, one by one had been taken from her thru those tragic circumstances.

When a teenager she was tall and sexy looking with natural blond hair, she had boyfriends galore, but there was nothing ever serious that would develop from any of these short romances, simply because of her being a habitual cock teaser which helped to build up her confidence and ego, an ego that she felt was needed as she approached womanhood. She wanted life in some way or other to be much more exciting than getting tied down too early in probably some unworkable relationship, and to live just a humdrum sort of existence thereafter. She will however not accept that life is so cruel that a person cannot achieve their own private dreams.

On the contrary, looking on the bright side she instead believes that the strong feelings that she has are shortly going to take off, where a much welcome run of good luck is way overdue. Which in a way it is, but maybe not quite in the way she expected. Of course there would be good times, but the bad times could in fact be very dangerous. You may ask yourself, how can she survive?... does she survive? The story covers almost the entire globe, in its search to give you the reader a sense of adventure, the result is, you will laugh and you will cry. History tells us that a story in this genre needs sex, so with that in mind, ***strictly adult sex*** has been integrated into the story. Later in the book it is of no surprise that someone suggested to her that with all of the amazing experiences that she has gone thru in her life, that there was nothing whatsoever for her to ever come back for. Believe me the person who offered that remark knew only the tip of the iceberg. Me being your observer, you can join me and follow this long (but never dull) winding road, that has never ending twists and turns of a most energetic woman, who never gave in to achieve her dreams.

CHAPTER ONE

There is an old American idiom that has stood the test of time, "Being in the right place at the right time" it means that the lucky recipient of such an occurrence will as a result make some worthwhile benefit. I personally can never remember me being in one of those situations, maybe you the reader can remember one, if not… they will just turn up in our dreams then. One of those rare opportunities occurred to lifelong friends Susan Paxton and Stella Delray, when as usual on most Saturday afternoons they would meander thru the busy shopping centres of central London. Both girls are quite tall and slim, Susan with short auburn hair, and Stella having long blonde hair, which brought them a few wolf whistle's from the capital's busy traffic. However, on this particular sweltering summer's afternoon, they felt as though they wanted to escape the heat and the forever hurly-burly which the Capital most certainly is. Even if it's only for an hour, it should suffice. Being Londoners they had always intended at some time in the near future to visit the National Portrait Gallery, though they up to this point had never yet quite got round to calling in. So with it now being just around the corner, this was their ideal opportunity.

Now inside and admiring the paintings done by most of the famous artists of centuries ago was quite exhilarating; much more than they had expected. They eventually came across a Painting "You and Me" by Justin Mortimer (shall we whisper and say that it was just a little bit different) which with due respect could never be compared to shall we say a Rubens or a Rembrandt. Suddenly out of nowhere a tall and very smart, middle aged looking gentleman; who, sporting a carefully trimmed grey beard and moustache steps in between them, quietly asking them for their opinions of this rather unusual portrait. What followed after a convivial conversation between the gentleman and the two girls, was his polite invitation for them to join him for a coffee at the very posh teahouse "Cafe Mumbai" as well as a very important proposition to ponder? He has already introduced himself as Burford Maunder an American Film Producer, born and bred in Buffalo, New York State, but now living in Santa Barbara, California.

He momentarily stands a few yards away to study a painting by Canaletto, while the girls make a decision whether to accompany him to the Cafe. It doesn't take the girls long to realize that this supposed proposition could be either genuine or a hoax, but with nothing to lose they decide to accompany him, and to hear what the proposition holds for them. The three of them are slowly making their way towards the Exit, they would occasionally stop and point to other paintings and to discuss their meanings, along with other points of interest. Just a few minutes later a taxi has pulled up outside this old but immaculate Victorian building, where a very smart doorman opens the car doors. The party of three then enter thru the swing doors to a large most exquisite room, with marble tables and glittering chandeliers. It really looked impressive with waiters wearing neatly pressed shirts and waistcoats who were busy serving customers. Suddenly a waiter is waving to them to come across the large room as he had found a table and sofa for them. When they are finally settled the waiter said `Good afternoon Mr. Maunder how are you today?

`Very well thank you Cecil, and you?' `As usual rather busy, now what would you and the girls like to have?' Burford turned to the girls asking them what they would like, but their attention was elsewhere, they were still admiring the glam and glitz of something that they thought never existed until now. It just suddenly occurred to them that Mr. Maunder had asked them what they would like.

`Oh I'm sorry' said Susan `we were just miles away` which left Burford smiling to himself, knowing that he sees this kind of lifestyle every day, where the girls obviously don't. `Well' said Cecil 'you can have any tea or coffee that that is served anywhere in the world, as long as you know its name.' Susan and Stella look at each other and shrug their shoulders, Susan said she would like Indian tea, Stella agreed to have the same. `Would the ladies also like to have a slice of apple pie with cream?' asked Cecil, the ladies were now looking at Burford, `Go on then I cannot see that doing you any harm` so they agreed. While they were waiting Burford thought it was time to put his cards on the table as to why he had invited them. Leaning back on the sofa he tells them `Being a film producer I have created films all over the world, I also have the skill to know that when I look at people I can tell which character part they would be suited to in a film, whether they are film stars or even strangers, now this afternoon when I saw both of you I knew straight away that in a film that I will organise soon in the U.S.A. `THE

CONFESSIONS OF A LIFEGUARD` you two would be ideal.' Just then Cecil came with the coffee for Mr. Maunder, also with the teas and apple pie for the ladies, which looked quite delicious. `Obviously` continued Burford `the parts you have in the film are not big roles, but they could be important to you both in other films, providing that you listen and learn from the advice that is given to you by me and other experienced members on the set, so what do you think, would you be excited with the thought of becoming stars?' Susan and Stella are now looking at each other as though Mr. Maunder has spent the last five minutes telling them a fairy story, where actually, it could quite possibly end up being very real.

'Speaking for both of us` said Susan `It seems to be a golden opportunity that we simply do not want to let go, but we both have good steady jobs working in London, and if things didn't happen in the States, then we would not have a job to come back to` Burford now looking at both girls says `I am fairly confident that both your companies will allow you the three months that you will need to pass all the tests, "METROPOLIS" will give you a cheque that will cover those three months.' All of a sudden, the ladies were now looking more at ease because that guarantee would ensure a no loss of wages or jobs. After taking names and addresses they were now leaving Cafe Mumbai. he said he would keep to his promise to them, he then got into a taxi and returned to his hotel.

They without any further ado accept the offer from this apparently famous American film producer whose name up to now hasn't rang any (I'm sure I have heard that name before?) bells with them, whereas a name like Steven Spielberg certainly would have.

When the girls a week later receive their already promised plane tickets for California, that immediately puts to bed any hint of the offer ever being a hoax.

In a nutshell, during the following week Stella has eventually got permission from her boss at one of the big banks to pursue this golden opportunity in the U.S.A. although his thinking was rather sceptical, and that she would soon return and resume her job as a P.A to him. As regarding Susan working at a Solicitor's office, she ignored all the remarks from her colleagues that she would be just wasting her time chasing silly dreams.

Still with the feeling of being swept off their feet, and in seemingly no time at all, they are now arriving in Hollywood and meeting up again with Burford Maunder at "Metropolis" film studio. After spending those two months at the Acting Academy they have passed all the tests with nothing else but grit and determination.

It has now enabled them to have the two small parts in the Comedy/Sex film. If that too was a winner, it could lead to more parts in other films. Mr Maunder became a great and trusted friend to the girls who visited them regularly at the Metropolis owned luxury apartment that the two girls shared in Santa Monica.

Susan however had a confession to make to Stella, it was that she had fallen in love with one of the directors Michael Dawson at the Studio, and that the couple already had their eyes on a Mansion in Santa Barbara. Stella was very happy for her life-long friend, but at the same time rather surprised at the swiftness of her friend giving her heart away so fast. But they promised each other that there would always be that same close contact as before. The icing on the cake had come just a few weeks before Susan's confession, when they were both given a two year contract. A visit back to London was for them to leave their respective jobs straight away, and sort out any other loose ends, before returning to L.A.

Back to the present, and now in their new home, Susan and her husband to be Michael Dawson have decided to invite Stella to a weekend baseball game between Los Angeles Angels and Kansas City Royals, where Michael would introduce Stella to one of the Angels players Brent Osgood, who was a good looking guy who was single, and about the same age. After the introduction, Susan and Michael were both convinced that there was a chemistry between the two that needed no push or shove to progress. The couple were seen at Supermarkets; Restaurants, and Night Clubs. Occasionally the group of four were seen at Santa Anita race track; and various Casino's. One day Stella got a call from Burford telling her that the people upstairs wanted her to star in a remake of "Miracle in the Rain" and that she would have the leading role.

This was because Stella had excelled herself after having small parts in other films; displaying an ever growing talent and as well with an ocean of confidence that hadn't gone unnoticed by the people upstairs which really mattered. She was so excited that she gave Susan a call to tell her the good news. Susan was very happy for her best pal. A fortnight later and now in New York, a City she always dreamed of visiting even when a teenager, and with her now standing on top of the Empire State building made her feel quite rightly to be on top of the world.

However she had been warned by Burford before she left, that the Director was a man who used to shout at people if things were not to his liking. The one thing he didn't tell her was the description of this man, who apparently resembled one of those mad professors who had a mass of frizzy hair and coke bottle glasses. On the very first day he lost his temper with some stage hands and when Stella heard the shouting, she went to investigate, and was knocked over by this clumsy director Raymond Lustgarten, admittedly by accident. Stella had no idea that it was the film director and demanded that the man should apologise there and now for his bad manners.

He did but only in a low, hardly recognisable voice, which infuriated Stella who now told him `Next time be a man and let the world hear you say sorry, rather than be like a spoilt child and just whisper it`.

At lunch Stella asked Gary (her fitness guru) had he seen the director of the film yet. Gary replied that he has. `Are you sure it was Mr. Lustgarten?` `Yes I'm sure, as sure as I am looking at you now` Well how is it that I haven't seen him yet?` `But you have` `When? the only man I can remember meeting this morning was that creepy man with bad manners` `I am sorry to tell you this Stella but that was Raymond Lustgarten` Suddenly Stella feels sick to her stomach, and her expression resembled someone who had just witnessed a motorway pile-up. Unable to now eat her lunch she went to the window that looked out over New York thinking that after giving Mr. Lustgarten a severe rollicking, she would now be taken off the film and replaced by an understudy.

Amazingly when the director got all the actors and actresses together for the first time, there was no mention of that unsavoury incident. She found out later that he was one of the best directors in the U.S.

The one thing that Stella would never forget was when on the final day of shooting the film, Mr. Lustgarten went up to her, put his arm around her and told her that her performance in the film was terrific, and that hopefully they at some later date could work together again. Stella's eyes began to well up when she apologised for saying what she said to him all those weeks ago. `Believe me Stella when I tell you what you said to me, it made me realise what a selfish bullying bigot I have been, and I can only thank you for making me see life in the proper light` With that they had a quick hug and he was gone.

One of the workers who has worked on a multitude of films with "lusty" as he is known, told Stella that he had never seen him give the leading lady a hug before. Now on the plane back to Los Angeles, Stella was reflecting on the four weeks they were there in the "Big Apple" where they visited the: Niagara Falls; The Zoo, Statue Of Liberty; and the show Mama Mia on Broadway. Plus the fact that she and Mr. Lustgarten had forged a special friendship, which at one time looked so impossible.

CHAPTER TWO

Later when she had returned home and come back to normality, she thought a good idea was to find out what Brent her boyfriend was doing tonight, seeing as it was only 3pm. The machine told her that he was not available, and would she leave a message, she did. After having a bath and a visit to the Supermarket the time now was 6pm and as yet no reply. Maybe he has gone for a game of golf with his friends she was thinking to herself. So instead of chasing after him she made up her mind to settle down for the evening and watch television.

The following morning after a shower followed by breakfast and getting ready to drive to the Studios, she remembered to check her answer phone to make sure, but there was still nothing. When she got to Burford's office he was on the phone, but when he saw her he was waving to her to come in. As he put the phone down Stella noticed that he had a smile on his face as wide as the Mississippi river `You seem very pleased about something queried Stella. `You bet I am` he said `and it concerns you` `Who me`? `Yes you` `Why is that?`

`Because young lady somehow or other you seem to have turned Raymond Lustgarten from being a ferocious tiger into a big pussycat.

Not only that but according to him you turned in an excellent performance in "Miracle in the Rain". Stella shrugged her shoulders as though she was trying to say, `Oh it was nothing really` `Anyway' said Burford `I think the best thing to do is give you a well earned break`.

Stella is giving Burford with her body language the message that she doesn't relish the idea of doing just nothing. He reminds her that she has plenty of things to do till her next Movie. `I have been informed that you now have a famous baseball player as a boyfriend, so that will take up some of your spare time. There will be film premieres to go to where you will, just like your best friend Susan be asked questions about the film you have just seen. There is also your own film career which millions of T.V. viewers all over the world will now realize that as well as being glamorous you are also heading to the top`. Scores of people who I know in the film world are now beginning to ask questions such as `So just who is this Stella Delray` and such like, which is good news for you to know, because it means they are becoming interested in what they have heard on the grapevine of your progress.

Burford can see that certain sparkle in her eye of what the facts are, and what is expected of her and Susan in the near future.

He tells her also that there are functions to go to, such as: opening new Supermarkets; or Health Centres for the middle aged, plus play areas for the tiny tots.

She can also visit hospitals where people will recognise her, which will make them feel privileged when they shake her hand, `It's all there waiting for you. If you remember over a year ago in London you told me that you wanted to be a famous actress, is that right?` Straight away Stella said `Yes I did and I meant it` `Well

Stella Delray you are already a star, so go out and enjoy everything that goes with it`.

Burford and Stella were both smiling as they gave each other a hug. Just as she was leaving his office he picked up a sheet for her to read. He told her that on this piece of paper was a list of all the venues that he had just told her about that she could visit, if and when she would like to make a start? `Yes I would like to start next week, I will do one a week if that is okay?` `I knew you wouldn't let me down` said Burford` I will arrange one for Thursday so do not plan anything else for that day, and I will ring you later today and give you the details.`

After talking to a couple of workers at the studio, she was now making her way to her car.

Peter Clay one of the men who is a camera technician came up to her with a frown, asking her why she had dumped Brent Osgood? Suddenly feeling ambushed she replied `What makes you say that Peter, don't forget I have been in New York for the past month, I haven't even seen him in that time so how can I have dumped him?` now looking straight into his face she suddenly has dropped her car keys on the floor, due to this sudden accusation by someone who before was a friend and admirer. He picks them up and thrusts them back into her hand and starts to walk away, leaving Stella positively speechless with her mouth wide open. She calls his name. He stops for a moment with hands on hips, turns round and tells her that Brent Osgood is a hero to him.

`What I wanted was for the both of you to make a big splash together`. With a sudden retort, Stella is for the last time trying to make him understand the situation. `I'm telling you that I haven't dumped him, I don't want to dump him I really like him`! Peter is slowly making his way back to her telling her that he was sorry for losing his cool. `That's okay` said Stella and while they were having a little hug he suddenly remembers that with him being a big fan of Brent, he tells her `One night last week at the ball game I took some photos of Brent and who I thought was his new girlfriend, would you like to see them?` `You bet your life I would` said Stella.

Peter hurried back to the cloakroom for his wallet, leaving Stella with her brain doing cartwheels as to what was suddenly happening to her life.

When he came back he put the first photo on the car bonnet which showed Brent and this other girl in the main stand (he was not playing that night because of a septic toe) with their arms round each other's waist, cheering something that has just happened in the game. Stella turns round to Peter and says `All this happened last week you say?` `Yes just last week.` Peter laid the next one at the side of the other one which showed the couple having a kiss as they were about to get into his bright orange sports car. `I then followed them`. Stella was now looking at Peter rather curiously, and wanted to know why he had followed them around like a stalker does `I guess I just wanted to know where he lived, I'm not a weirdo, there are lots of people who would like to know where their heroes live`.

Stella is now smiling at him with understanding although at the present moment she feels like being sick. `So what did you do?' she asked him `Like I say I followed him in my car back to his apartment` at the same time pulling out the third and final photo and placing it at the side of the other two `Oh my God!' screamed Stella `What is it?`asked Peter nearly jumping out of his skin. `That is my god damn apartment not his! how could he do such a thing? bringing a strange woman into my house, very probably my bed as well,

I cannot believe he could do such a thing, I am going to fucking kill him!` As Peter was looking into her face which was now completely filled with disgust and hate, it seemed unreal that he had unwittingly sealed the fate of his hero.

Now looking at Peter for some empathy she says `Don't tell me that you still admire this kind of scum that is in our society, whether they are sportsmen or otherwise, everybody should be judged by their actions and nothing else`. Peter replies `I do agree with what you say, but you can't just stop admiring somebody simply because they have done something wrong, although I must tell you this, my estimations of the guy has really nosedived simply as a result of him hurting someone that I admire` `Who is that?` asked Stella `Who do you think silly, ...you'. Stella was now smiling again knowing that she and Peter were friends again. `Is it alright if I can borrow these pictures?` asked Stella `After what you have just told me you can have them`. After a borrowed smile she told Peter that she would see him later.

As she was driving home, the first thing she was going to do was to change the bed sheets `How could he?` she was saying to herself all the way home. `How did he get the key to the apartment? ` was something else that was going thru her mind, `I definitely didn't give him one, the son of a bitch`.

When she was back home and making a nice cup of tea for herself she checked the phone, she now heard his voice. `Hello honey, so you are back home, I have really missed you, and have literally been twiddling my thumbs while you have been away`. If it was possible for you to see Stella's face, it was quite red, and her eyes were like slits that were littered with contempt for this waste of space at the other end of her phone.

Accidentally on purpose she left him a message asking him to come round tonight as there is something she wants to sort out with him. In between now and when Brent was coming, she had a phone call from Burford asking her if she would like to open a new library in the district of Torrance on Thursday at 11am. She told him it would be a pleasure.

When she put the phone down, she thought to herself wouldn't it be a wonderful world if everyone was like her dear friend Burford Maunder. As she suddenly comes back to reality she knows only too well that life is full of hits and misses.

Tea time has come and gone and the adrenalin is beginning to flow as Stella looks at her watch. The Intercom is telling her someone downstairs wants to come up, after finding out that it is Brent she now presses a button for that to happen.

He has now entered and put his arms around her and is looking to give her a welcome home kiss, but she is resisting him. `What's the matter honey aren't you glad to see me?` `But of course I am` with a smirk on her face `So where is the kiss?` `There isn't going to be any kisses now or ever` `What the fuck has brought all this on?` he demanded to know. `I am now going to tell you, … better still what I am going to show you will be more preferable`. She reaches for her handbag. He has a look on his face that tells us that whatever she shows him he is going to have to have a watertight alibi, otherwise in five minutes he is going to be in the street (out on his ear, as they say). As the photos are now being placed on the coffee table in front of him, a cold shiver is running up his spine; with I think as well a sudden gulp. `Do you recognise yourself in these photographs?` `Well of course I do honey, they are of me` `Yes I know they are but who the fuck is this tart stood beside you?` `She was my girlfriend when these pictures were taken last year` `That is a lie and you know it is you scumbag, these were taken last week by a friend of mine, who incidentally was a fan of yours till today.

So are you now going to tell me as well that this (now pointing to his car in her allotted car space outside her apartment) was taken a year ago as well?` `Okay, okay so I got a bit lonely when you were in the big apple, I'm not the only one that does it am I?` `It doesn't concern me who else does what to whom, I only know that I personally cannot accept for one minute a person with your fucking devious scheming ideas okay!`

`No second chances?` `Not a snowball in hell's chance, oh and by the way just as a matter of interest where did you get the key to my apartment? I certainly didn't give you one`. Obviously Brent knew that the pretence had dissolved before his eyes. He was now laughing when he told her that he had taken some soft plastic to her apartment; waiting for an opportunity to make an impression of her key while she was having a shower or in her bedroom. That infuriated Stella so much that she went up to him and punched him in the eye. She immediately pressed a button that brought security into this very unsavoury situation, and had him removed into the street.

During the evening as she was watching T.V. she found it hard to relax as a result of today's torment and switched off. Playing soft music was a more relaxing alternative.

The following morning she gave Susan a call on the phone to see if she could visit her as she hadn't seen her for while. Susan told her to come for a few days if she wanted to, Stella told her that she would pack a small suitcase and see her within two hours. When she arrived Susan was sat on the veranda and in the shade keeping as cool as possible, they had a hug and a `mwah`. Susan told her to sit on the Veranda while she brought a gin and orange with ice out for her, finally they could now have a conversation about what has been going on in both of their lives. `Have you managed to get pregnant yet?` asked Stella. `No not yet, but it is early days and we are both confident that there will be the patter of tiny feet within the next year`. Both girls look at each other and cross their fingers. Susan asks Stella how she and Brent are getting on with their romance. Just as Stella is about to tell her, a little white Scottie dog jumps up on Susan's lap wanting attention. `What a lovely little dog` remarked Stella as she is now leaning over to stroke it, and says `What is your name?' Susan now comes to the dogs rescue, saying its name is just "Scottie".

`Where were we before Scotties interruption?` said Susan `Well thru a stroke of good luck, I have found out that Brent is nothing else but a two-timing creep and also a love cheat of the highest order` `Why what on earth has he done?` Susan's face has lengthened somewhat and at this moment all she knows, is that her best friend has had a raw deal at the hands of someone who was introduced to her by herself and her husband to be. After Stella told her the whole sickening story, Susan told her `I feel so guilty that this man who we thought was so respectable, has turned out to be so horrible, and I am glad at least he has felt your anger` `You must not take it out on yourself,` replied Stella `you were only trying to find a happy relationship for me` now putting her best friend's mind at rest. They now had a sorrowful hug for each other before they entered the house. After a tour of the house and gardens Stella was very complimentary by saving `What a beautiful house' `You like it then?' said Susan `Like it, I love it' replied Stella.

The house had five bedrooms all en-suite, a massive kitchen, big lounge, a more than adequate dining room with room for up to twelve guests, as well with a big swimming pool around the back. During her stay at Susan's beautiful mansion, they discussed any future films that were in the pipeline. Susan had been told by Burford that she had won the part of Mitzi Chantry in a violent gangster movie, where the location would be in Houston, Texas.

Susan wanted to know what was in Stella's film diary. `After the film I made in New York, the Studio has decided to give me a nice break, as I got myself emotionally upset`.

Susan was now looking over a furrowed brow at Stella with a serious concerned stare.

`How do you mean emotionally upset, why what happened?` Stella was now smiling nervously at her pal `Well it was on the first day of filming and this man who I had honestly never seen before, had barged straight into me, so I told him in no uncertain terms, to at least apologise and say sorry for his shameful action` `And did he?` `Well yes and no, he just mumbled some sort of apology that I could hardly hear, then he quickly left the set with his head hung low`. So just who was this man, did you ever find out? `Yes I did it was Raymond Lustgarten' Susan has suddenly fallen back onto the big plush sofa that must have cost a million dollars. `You are of course joking, Raymond Lustgarten the film director? I have heard rumours that he is very strict and a very unsociable man to get on with, but what happened after all the dust settled down?` `Well the first priority was to make this film "Miracle in the Rain" and any ill feeling between the two of us was thrown out of the window.

Susan was now picking up the drinks tray with the empty glasses and making her way to the kitchen area, but she wanted to know, that if she was in such a state how could she put her heart and soul into the film.

`Susan to be honest with you, I just do not know, but one of my group from Los Angeles named Gary gave me all my confidence back to finish the film, I am very grateful to him.` `Did Mr. Lustgarten say anything to you when the film was finished?' `Yes he did and I will never forget what he said to me` `I can't wait to hear this' said Susan. `He told me as he put his arm around me that my contribution to the film was terrific, and that he would at some point like to work with me again. He as well told me that he now saw himself in a different light, to when he previously came across as a selfish bullying bigot `My word Stella you certainly came out trumps in that one`.

When Michael came home from the studios in the evening, and even for the rest of her stay, Stella got the distinct impression that they were a perfectly matched couple. And she was happy that they were. Before Stella went home she wanted to know if her family were going to visit her and Michael. Susan replied that when the wedding was given the go ahead, they would be coming over to stay for a week.

CHAPTER THREE

When Stella arrived back home, there was a message from Burford on the phone replay, that he was going to visit her tomorrow morning (Wednesday) about a proposition. He told her it wasn't anything to worry about. Next morning after her early morning jog, shower, and breakfast she was now reading the local newspaper when the intercom suddenly let her know that Burford was here.

After his entrance and a hug from Stella, she asked if he would like his usual. `Yes please Stella`. As she was putting his drink on the silver tray, she asked Burford what this proposition is about `Well before I do that, I heard on the grapevine yesterday that your friendship with Brent Osgood has been terminated. I would just like to say how right you were to sever all ties with this so called boyfriend you had. Who by the way must be an idiot to treat someone like you in the way that he did, thankfully he got his just rewards now rather than later`.

As they sat down on the Sofa and chair respectively, Stella was quickly into her stride and had again to reiterate `So what is this proposition about Burford?` `What it is, seeing as you have no ties at the moment, how would you like to have an actress who is up and coming just like yourself, to share your apartment with you?` Stella suddenly had a feeling of being put under some pressure into a situation that may not work out.

`You have rather put me on the spot, and one of the main reasons is because I know nothing about her`. Burford was now opening his wallet where he had a photo of the girl in question. Stella was now looking at this young lady stood with her mother and father outside the studios.

Burford was giving her all the information that he had about her: `She is a year younger than you; she is a tall girl just like you, and she is a natural blond just like you; plus she has a younger brother, and is from Phoenix Arizona, where by all accounts she is going right to the top` `What if we do not get on with each other? I mean like me and Susan, we have known each other since infant school days, and there was never going to be a problem sharing this apartment with her`. `Do you remember said Burford, `when nearly two years ago I told you and Susan that when I look at my personnel I very rarely make a mistake when I make decisions concerning what is best for them?` `Yes I do` `All I am going to say` said Burford `Is that if you feel as though you want to be on your own that is perfectly okay, on the other hand if you feel as though a flatmate could give you a companionship that everybody needs at some point to rely on, and also to share in each other's thoughts, I strongly recommend Kelly Baxter, the choice is yours`.

By the time he had consumed his Vodka and Lemon with ice, Stella told him that she would welcome Kelly into her life. As he was now getting up from the sofa to leave, he told Stella that she was doing the Studio a great favour, as Stella was the only actress who was unattached and about the same age. `Are you in tomorrow morning Stella?` asked Burford `No, if you remember I have a new library in Torrance to open` `Yes of course you have, I had totally forgotten about that` `I will be here on Friday, you can then introduce us to each other?` `Yes I think it is better now than later, and don't be worried I know you two will get on famously` said Burford, with that so genuine and charming smile. On the Friday the two girls were introduced to each other by Burford. It was quite magical really, it was as if they had known each other for years, and the smile on Burford's face was wider than it was the other day. As they were getting on so well Stella cancelled whatever she was going to be involved with that afternoon. So now it was Stella who was going to show Kelly all around the area. Which included Zuma Beach where they would be showing their curves to all those heavily tanned volley ball players who took to the sand seemingly every day. Kelly had been given a car for herself, just the same as Stella's, only hers was a green one.

During the next few weeks Kelly had now moved in. "The Hollywood Film Awards" were very shortly going to hit town, and amazingly this year Susan Paxton has been nominated for best supporting actress for her role as "Eve Coe" in "Stranger's When We Meet". This is terrific news for Metropolis Film Studio's. Stella didn't know anything about her friend being up for this top award till her and Kelly went to the Studios one morning. Where Burford called her into the office to give her the good news. She now phoned up on her mobile to Susan, to congratulate her, and let her know that she was really happy for her. While she was on the phone she mentioned that `Burford wanted to know if I would like to share my apartment with an up and coming star?` `And what did you say?` `I told him that I would, and he introduced her to me at my apartment and that was about three weeks ago` ` How has it been since? `In that period we have never said an angry word to each other at all, and we complement each other with our acting, though I must tell you that she is a great actress for her age, she really is`. `I would very much like to meet her` `When are you down at the Studio's next?` asked Stella `It will probably be the day before they give out the awards`. `That's okay, me and Kelly will meet you at the studios`.

During the week before those awards, Kelly had to learn the script for a thriller that was going to be filmed on location in San Francisco. Which would be called "It's Never Too Late", in which she would play a big newspaper magnates daughter who is kidnapped.

Recently Stella has noticed that Kelly wants to be at her side in more or less everything that she herself is involved in. Whether it is shopping; watching T.V., or even visiting friends, but it's no problem to Stella as they love each other's company anyway. Last Sunday there had been a thunderstorm that arrived halfway thru the night, and Stella knew what was going to happen as it had already taken place on a previous thunderstorm, Kelly comes running into Stella's bedroom and gets into her bed with her head under the sheets and stays there till next morning. The following week at the studio, Kelly was waiting to meet Stella's best friend Susan, who tomorrow night was one of four actresses who were in the running for the Best Supporting Actress Award. Stella introduced Susan to Kelly who seemed to be overawed by the occasion of meeting an actress, who was now regarded as one of the best prospects in Hollywood.

Luckily Burford was there to give her confidence in herself, and within a few minutes she was more relaxed and chatting away and laughing just normally. At the Awards the following evening, Stella and Kelly both wore beautiful gowns along with their finery. All the big stars were there all mixing with each other: Stella was seen chatting with Wayne Flannery her screen hero. In the background Susan was in conversation with James Delph, America's top T.V. presenter about her rapid rise in the ratings. After two hours most of the awards had been given out, it was now time for best supporting actress award. The cameras caught a glimpse of Stella and Kelly smiling at each other and also with their fingers crossed.

The four contestants were: Jane Sobel—Karen Guest—Jackie Stenson—Susan Paxton. Guy Braddock who usually stars in war movies and westerns, has just opened the envelope and with a big smile (because he knows her well) says the winner is — Susan Paxton.

Everybody in the hall stands up and gives her a rapturous applause. She is now making her way on to the stage, she is turning round to the audience waving and blowing kisses. The camera has again focused on Stella who is now crying her eyes out.

Most of the movie world knows that Susan and Stella came over to America together over two years ago to fulfil their dreams, and who knows it could be Stella's turn next year.

Guy Braddock hands over the Oscar to Susan along with a smile and a big hug. Just then a middle aged gentleman has come on to the stage with his arms outstretched, with another big smile guaranteed. Susan is also reduced to tears as she can see it is Burford Maunder. She now runs to meet him and puts her arms round his neck, like a daughter to her father. I do not think that Susan had prepared a speech, and what she was going to talk about would be totally ad-lib.

First of all she thanked Burford for giving her a chance in life to achieve something that was always beyond her wildest dreams, it really was. Whenever she needed advice about something, he would be there. She has now turned around to smile at the man himself, who in return has smiled back. She thanks everybody at Metropolis Film Studios who have helped her in the last two years to achieve this wonderful honour. She also sent all her love to her family and friends over in London, telling them that they will have to come over shortly anyway, as she is going to marry Michael Dawson. The camera's follow Susan's finger as she points to him in the audience who is now stood up and turning round and waving. She finished her speech by saying that if anybody deserved an Oscar it was her very best friend Stella Delray, who had to put up with her ever since they were at nursery school together, who has now stood up waving.

There was the usual big party afterwards, and there were not many people without a drink in their hand. The biggest table was occupied by, going left to right: Susan and Michael-Burford and wife Valerie-Walter Ackerman (Chief executive of Metropolis Films) and wife Sybil-William Strauss (actor) and wife Debbie-and finally Stella and Kelly. Looking down on the table it seemed bizarre that Kelly the new kid on the block so to speak, was now sat in between her now best friend Stella and her favourite actress Susan.

Eventually the party broke up at about 4am. The following day straight out of the blue, Kelly asked Stella if she would like to visit her family in Phoenix.

`I would love to meet them, but what has brought that on, all of a sudden?` `Well` said Kelly `the reason is that in a fortnight I will be going on location to San

Francisco to make "It's Never Too Late" `Yes I did know `said Stella `So this would be the best opportunity we have, it's just that I want you to meet my family, I really do'. `Okay when are we going?` asked Stella `How about tomorrow?` `That's alright with me`. Kelly immediately got on the phone to her mother and asked her if she could bring her best friend Stella to stay for about a week, and would that be alright? Stella could hear her mother's reply that she would be welcome anytime.

Next morning they are now on their way in Stella's car; Kelly is telling Stella all about the area and what to expect. There is horse riding; swimming, a couple of Zoo's; and lots of other pastimes as well. After a five hour journey, they are now pulling up on the drive of this more than beautiful house, it really is. It reminds me of the houses you would see in the affluent district of Mayfair, London. They are now getting out of the car at the same time that Kelly's mother and father are coming out to meet them. After a few mwahs they enter the house, where wiping the feet is a must. They are immediately greeted by Ella, a black lady who is the maid. Her real name is Eleanor Hall, but her resemblance to Ella Fitzgerald is quite amazing, hence her nickname. She has now put Kelly and Stella's luggage into the elevator, which will be left outside their respective bedrooms. As they enter the massive lounge Stella is invited to sit on the settee which is facing the fireplace, where the mantelpiece is as tall as the two girls, it really is. Mr. Baxter asks Stella what would she like to drink, `A Gin and Orange with ice would be very nice` Kelly was now thinking her dad may have forgotten what drink she liked, and when their eyes meet he puts her mind to rest by saying `It's alright Kelly I don't need to ask, after five years I should know what your drink will be, a Rum and peppermint with ice.` `Yes thank you Dad` Bob was now looking over at his wife Sally, `Is it the usual for you darling?` `Yes please Bob` who was now muttering to himself `Vodka and lemon with no ice` `Did you say something darling?` asked Sally, `No, just talking to myself dear`.

So now Bob has brought the drinks over on a tray where he places it on a giant sized coffee table, which if it had a net going across the middle it would be ideal for a table-tennis match or something (it was that big). Just as they were all getting cosy, in walks their son Harvey who was 16 last week with his collar up. `Hello son get yourself a coke out of the fridge and join us` said his dad `Okay dad but I will have to go to the bath room first`. Ten minutes later he has now come back into the lounge with his coke, but somehow he looks different, in fact he looks a lot different, he really does, a change of clothes, and hair neatly combed. He has also brought into the room a pungent smell of aftershave which is now making everybody nearly sick, it really is. `Have you been helping yourself to my after shave?` asked his dad.

`You don't mind do you dad?` now sitting next to his mother on the settee and taking a mouthful of coke and swilling it around his mouth, like a mouth -wash before swallowing it. All this cool behaviour by Harvey is allowing Stella to think that he is trying to impress her, obviously he wouldn't be trying to impress his own family would he? `We would like you to meet Kelly's best friend Stella` said Sally, Harvey is now going across to shake her hand, at the same time he mentions that he saw her on T.V. the other night at the film awards, and can't wait to tell her `You looked gorgeous, you really did` `Well thank you very much` said Stella, Harvey felt as though he should also remind her `Even though you were crying a lot` His mother was now sternly looking at Harvey and telling him that it was a very emotional evening and that it is all part of the occasion.

`Didn't you see me on TV little brother?` asked Kelly `Yes I did and don't call me little brother you know I don't like it I really don't` at the same time looking across at Stella, with a speed of light glance. `What did I look like?` asked Kelly `Alright I suppose` `Mum is that the best thing he can say? `Alright I suppose` replied a disappointed Kelly `You have got to understand Kelly that he is only a teenager, and has a lot yet to learn he really has` at the same time pulling him into her side.

To change the subject Bob says to Stella that he hopes that she enjoys her stay here in Phoenix, so she might want to come back again.

`I'm sure I will` replied Stella. Just as the drinks were finished Ella came in to take the tray away, and to remind them that Dinner would be at 7pm. After she had left the room Kelly asked her dad what the main dish was tonight? `Have you forgotten what we have on Tuesday? it's "Radishes and dried Squid" after saying that he immediately looks over at Stella for some reaction and is instantly rewarded, with a look as though she has just seen a squashed cat in the middle of the road. Kelly comes to the rescue telling Stella that her dad is only winding her up. `Tell him he has done a good job he really has`. Between 4pm and 7pm both girls have had showers and are flittering between each other's bedrooms.

Kelly's bedroom has a TV but Stella's hasn't, but Kelly assures her best pal that anything worth watching can be seen on hers. Kelly is showing Stella all the family photos from years back, but she notices that Stella has tears in her eyes, and immediately closes the album and asks if something in the book has upset her. `No it's not the book it's just me`. Kelly is now looking mystified as to what is wrong, she really is. During the next two hours Stella has told her everything: that she was an only one, that her mother and father were killed by a hit and run driver; also that her grandfather got swept out to sea and that her grandmother is in a hospice with Dementia and doesn't know whether it is night or day` `That is awful, and I am not surprised that you were so upset I really aren't`. After a short while Stella was back to her normal self. Her final word was that `Time is a great healer of many bad things that happen in people's lives, and it is a good job that it is`. It is now 7pm and Ella looks forward every night to hitting the gong that lets everybody in the house including guests, know that dinner will now be served.

The dinner consisted of Soup and herb starter followed by Beef bourguignon with green beans and sautéed new potatoes, finishing with poached pear halves with hot chocolate sauce, and a red wine to wash it down with; the exception being Harvey who would have stilled orange juice or something. After the lovely meal Stella thought it would be a good idea to help Ella with washing all the dishes etc.

Kelly told Stella that Ella would be offended if she offered to help her, she would think that she was not up to her job and that she needed help or something. `How long has she been the maid?` Stella asked `It's about six years since her husband died, he actually was our gardener up to the time of his death, which left Ella living on her own which was the last thing she wanted. So dad offered her the maids job plus accommodation which suited her, it really did` Kelly's mum and dad relaxed in the lounge for the rest of the evening.

Both girls had a walk around Encanto Park where the people are obviously very rich, and live in beautiful houses, they really do. Which had Stella being rather inquisitive and asking Kelly what her father's profession is. `My dad deals in diamonds that are found in South Africa, he visits there quite often` `Does he go all around Africa looking for them?` asked Stella `I'm not so sure, but I know he spends a lot of time in Botswana because he took us for a vacation there, so I should imagine that is where most of the diamonds are found`. `Have you ever held a really expensive diamond in your hand?` asked Stella `Oh, many a time, if you want to see a really valuable diamond have a look around my mother's neck, she has a ruby in her necklace`. `I didn't notice it at the evening meal` said Stella, `No I think she only wears it when they are going somewhere important, but I will ask her to show you it if you like?` `Yes I look forward to that`. They now decided to sit down on one of the park benches and take in the view of these exquisite surroundings.

A short while later just as they were about to get up Kelly nudged Stella's arm for her attention. `What is it?` asked Stella `Can you see that big cream coloured mansion at the other side of the park, second from the end?`. `Yes, what about it?` `Can you see a young man washing that big posh car?` `Yes who is it, is it someone you know?` `Yes, his name is Garth Fosdyke and he is the most boring man in Phoenix he really is.

`Have you been out with him?` queried Stella `Once, and believe me once was enough`. `He was that bad?` said Stella. `All the time he would just brag about things like: the super powered motor bike he had, and for his birthday his dad bought him a speedboat to surf his way round the coast of Los Angeles.

He as well showed me a very expensive watch that his mother bought from Pratchett's the most expensive jeweller's in Phoenix. Stella interrupted her friend to say `If that had been me I would have told him that all this bragging was doing my fucking head in, and that I wanted him to order me a Taxi to take me home this very instant`. `Not only that`, said Kelly but the rest of the night he kept asking me at regular intervals did I want to know what time it was, and if I didn't respond he would tell me anyway, he is a proper asshole he really is`.

Stella has now burst out laughing at her friend's verbal attack on this Master Fosdyke. `Most of all` said Kelly `I blame his parents, they have fucking spoilt him rotten they really have'. `So where do his parents earn their living from?` asks Stella, `Who would you think gave me the information that his father owns three hotels, two in San Francisco and one in Los Angeles?` Kelly is now looking at Stella with a bored expression, waiting for the obvious answer. `Garth Fosdyke I should imagine` `Absolutely spot on` said Kelly.

They are now on their way home, but because her parents are as usual in the lounge on a Tuesday evening watching TV, Kelly suggests that they can go to her room and watch a quiz show. Soon it will be time to have a "Potluck" meal' which Stella has heard many times when in America. It is apparently another name for supper.

After the quiz show has finished, they are now making their way down to the kitchen. Stella asks Kelly `Have you any ideas what we can do tomorrow?` `How do you fancy riding on a horse thru the Arizona hills, or spending an hour or so in the pool, the choice is yours?` `Why can't we do both, we have all the time in the world don't we?` `That is a good idea plus we can have a meal out, and I know just the place`. Obviously going on horseback thru those rugged hills first, then having a meal at somewhere where Kelly knows, followed by a dip in the pool a bit later would be the best idea.

CHAPTER FOUR

Next day at the ranch all the horses are now lined up. Stella is a bit apprehensive about getting on to the back of this particular four legged friend, as it seems to be in something of a bad mood. Kelly who regularly goes on this trek has her own favourite horse. She also knows the horse that Stella will be riding (because the naughty girl picked it especially for her friend) tends to be a bit awkward at first and is well known for bucking. Stella has been given a leg up, but within 10 seconds she is now on the floor.

She notices that Kelly is laughing along with some of the cowboy's who work at the ranch. Stella at this moment is feeling rather aggrieved and is now going to wipe that fucking smile right off her friend's face. She asks for another leg up which she is given. The horse is again trying to get her out of the saddle once more.

Stella is now showing more guts and determination this time to stay on board. She has now been on the horse for at least half a minute she really has, and is now getting applause from the people who a few minutes ago were laughing. But the horse had the last laugh tossing Stella high into the air just when she thought everything was under control. She looked as though she had taken a nasty fall and was now laid flat out, but was actually only pretending to be knocked out. Kelly's face has changed from laughing to horror, as she is now running towards her best friend who lies motionless. Kelly tries to bring her round but is getting no response, the ranch doctor is sent for but he also can't make her conscious either. Kelly is now beginning to cry as she feels responsible for what has happened to her companion. After a few more minutes of anxiety for Kelly, Stella suddenly opens her eyes and winks at Kelly, who suddenly now feels the fool `You bitch there was nothing wrong with you after all was there?' Stella was now getting to her feet and saying `No but I think you knew that fucking horse was bad tempered, and you and your pals were already having a good laugh at my expense`. Kelly goes up to Stella and puts her arms around her asking for her forgiveness.

Stella gives her a big hug, and tells her that it's alright. Kelly told her that if she ever lost her friendship she would want to die. The rest of the morning (Be Be) that is the nickname of the horse, short for "Bucking Bronco" has behaved very well, and after the ride Stella gives it some friendly pats on its neck.

After dusting their jeans down the girls are now going down the freeway. The time is now 1pm and they are feeling quite hungry they really are.

Now Kelly has a surprise lined up for Stella. They are now turning off the freeway and making their way down a dusty track towards something that resembles a cafe. Stella quizzes Kelly` What the fuck is this, we are driving up to?` `A cafe` replied Kelly, `Well to me it looks as though it is going to collapse at any moment` `Anyway he makes a good meal and that is why I come here` `Is he a friend or something?` `Rodney is a good friend of mine and he looks forward to me coming`. `Is he a young man that you might have your sights on?`

Stella quizzes again, only this time with a wry smile. Kelly now has a big smile on her face as she says `I don't think so, he is about 65 years old, and I think he has about six grown up children`.

When they pull up outside, there are two cars and two wagons stationed in some makeshift parking lot. Before they go in Kelly tells Stella that he is a film fanatic and that he has pictures of all the famous stars of today and yesteryear around the walls. As they are now entering there is a red carpet laid down leading from the door to the counter.

It would appear as though it has just been put down for some reason. The carpet has obviously seen better days, as there are plenty of worn patches along it, there really is. Suddenly a small elderly man with a pinafore tied round his waist and a baseball cap on that says "Scottsdale Scorpions" is quickly making his way to greet them.

He has welcomed Kelly like he always does, he is now looking up at Stella in total admiration. `I cannot believe that you are stood here in my little cafe` Stella has been totally overwhelmed by the attention of this seemingly quite friendly person who she has never met before. She is now looking over at Kelly (who has the broadest of smiles on her face) for some possible explanation as to why all of a sudden she is the centre of attraction. Some of the customers are now looking at a full blown picture on the wall, of a lady that resembles the lady that has just come in, Stella. Rodney is now escorting her down this apology for a carpet followed by Kelly.

Rodney is now pointing to the poster of the lady herself. Stella, who in return is now speechless to think that somebody like him is quite clearly a big fan of hers. `Do you mind if I give you a big hug?` asked Rodney. `Of course I don't, and then I will give you a big hug back` but she had to bend down slightly as he was only about 5'6 tall. As it was now quiet after a busy 12—1pm stint, the three of them are now sat at one of the tables to talk about films. First Kelly had to tell Rodney that they were starving, he immediately jumped up and asked them what they would like.

After taking the order into the kitchen for his eldest son to prepare, he came back and sat down next to Stella, who felt as though she had to ask what did he find so interesting about her, was it: her acting; her looks, the way she walked; or the way she talked. `My dear Stella it is everything about you that I like, it is just something that happens, there is simply no explanation. It's a bit like Marilyn Monroe a lot of people loved her and a lot of people didn't. When I took my wife to see "Miracle in the Rain" it was the first time I had ever seen you, and to me you made that film come alive you really did, you made acting look so easy`. Stella is now putting her hand on his and thanking him. Kelly asked Rodney if he had seen Stella in "Strangers when we meet". He replied that he hadn't but would eventually, even if it meant getting the DVD next time he went into Phoenix.

He was now saying `I understand in that particular film you were acting with another English girl .... err Susan Paxton and I have heard since she won some actress award`. Kelly told him that both she and Stella were big friends of hers. Their meal was now brought out, so Rodney got up and went into the kitchen area and left them in peace.

`What a lovely meal that was` said the girls as Rodney came to take their empty plates away `You know` said Rodney looking at Stella `I was just thinking that things could have been so different' `How do you mean?` said Stella, with a questioning look. `Well if I had been born say forty years later than I was, there could have been the possibility that I could have met you somewhere, we could have then got married and had children, and eventually you could have been helping me in the cafe, wouldn't that have been nice?`

He now has his hands clasped across his stomach with his head on one side with a very contented smile. He is now winking to Kelly. Rather than burst out laughing Stella used her inner decorum by saying `Well you never know Rodney it could easily have been that way` Moments later his son came out with a camera to take a picture of the three of them together, with the girls towering over Rodney in between them. Anyway it was time to go, and they now were slowly making their way down that infamous red carpet to the door.

As they said their goodbyes Stella turned round and gave Rodney a quick kiss on his lips. Rodney shouted after her `I will never wash my face again!`

As they were on their way back to Phoenix, Stella mentioned to Kelly `I got the distinct impression that Rodney knew that we were coming today` `How did you work that out?` `Well I think that apology for a red carpet was laid as we were seen getting out of the car, and I think somebody told him that we were coming` `Well I can't think who` said Kelly now trying to keep her face straight. `I have a very good idea who it was` looking out the corner of her eye in the direction of Kelly who now realized that the pretence had gone and admitted that it was her. Kelly now leaned over to the best friend she had ever had and gave her a kiss on her cheek `I only did it because he has had this poster of you on the wall for months, even before I knew you, and I remember him telling me that he would love to meet you, so I arranged it for him to meet you`. `Well to be honest I am glad that you did, because I found him to be a lovely man, I really did and I will send him the DVD of "Strangers When We Meet" when we get back home`.

Towards the end of the week they had a day out at the Zoo, and Craig who had a schoolboy crush on Stella wanted to go with them. On that day it was hot and humid, and after going half way round Harvey decided because of the heat he would have to take his leather jacket off, although he didn't really want to because he thought that with it on, he resembled Marlon Brando in the film "The Wild One" which he thought would impress Stella that he was a cool dude. Whether Stella saw him in that light, I very much doubt. So now the jacket has been transferred to around his waist.

Everybody seems to be walking round in some sort of slow motion replay, due to the oppressive heat. Kelly is walking a few yards behind her brother and best friend, and has already come to the conclusion that one of them is besotted with the other, and that the other has taken the responsibility of being totally understanding to this teenagers crush. While walking thru this maze of animals with all its fine greenery, Kelly was beginning to get annoyed with her brother. The reason was because at various parts of the Zoo, as they were walking he would put his arm around Stella's waist, at the same time she would put her arm over his shoulder making Kelly feel like some fucking gooseberry or something.

Harvey although only sixteen is almost as tall as Stella, and anybody who didn't know the situation would have assumed that they were just another young couple in love. They called in at a cafe to get some ice cream and as they were sat outside, Craig suddenly had to go to the boys room. Kelly now told Stella that he had never put his arm round her waist when walking thru a park when they have been out with their parents. Stella told her `He is going thru that age when it is so easy to get these crushes, and with me living at your house for a week that is what has happened, I mean when he puts his arm around my waist I can't just shove it away can I?` that would be cruel`.

Kelly tells Stella of her immediate thoughts, `If we had been stopping for another week, I'm sure he would be asking you for a date`, Stella started laughing but at the same time giving Kelly an example `Just supposing that if you and I fell into a deep lake, and neither of us could swim, and Craig dived in but could save only one of us, who do you think he would save?` `Obviously you` said Kelly with a downcast expression` Of course he wouldn't, he would save you, simply because you are his sister and no matter what you think, deep down he loves you to bits`.

It was now Sunday morning and it was time to say goodbye, Kelly's dad was putting their luggage into the boot. Even Ella had come to the door to wish them a safe journey home. Craig ran up to his sister and gave her a kiss on her cheek and whispered something in her ear. He then went up to Stella and after giving her a kiss on the cheek told her, that the next time she came he would be bigger and stronger than he is now. `Well I will certainly look forward to that`.

The last goodbyes came from the parents who told Stella that whatever happens she would always be welcome to come back. As Stella was getting into the car, Kelly was giving her parents a big hug and a kiss also telling them she would be giving them a call when they get home.

During the long drive home, Stella asked Kelly what her brother Harvey had whispered in her ear before they had set off. `He told me that although he and you had forged a special friendship, he said that he loved me more than anybody in the world` `That was a wonderful thing for him to say to you, but if you remember I told you the day before, the same thing didn't I?` `Yes you did`. After a few more stops they are now back home, and it isn't long before they are back in their beds and fast asleep. Monday was going to be a busy start to the week as Kelly would be going to San Francisco on the Tuesday to star in the film "It's Never Too Late", which if successful would be a big boost to her acting career. Meanwhile Stella has been given the main role in a remake of the film "Yellow Sky" where she plays a gold prospector's daughter, who both become isolated in a ghost town where six misfits who are on the run, decide they want to take all of their gold. So that means the girls won't see each other for a month, except for phone calls.

We will fast forward to when each film has been completed and they are now back in L/A. Quickly they are getting back up to speed into the normal routines of : Rubbing the suntan cream on each other's back, down on the beach; Supermarket shopping, watching T.V. and playing music; were their pleasures. As regarding housework Stella always did the cooking; just like she did in London when she lived on her own. Whereas Kelly had always relied on Ella or her mother for her meals back home in Phoenix. So Stella would make sure that Kelly would keep the apartment nice and clean.

One night when they were watching T.V. Stella had a brainwave. `Why don't we now go on a tour of

Europe?` `That is a very good idea it really is` putting her arm around her pal's shoulder and playfully pulling her towards herself. Kelly wanted to know more. `How long would we be away for? ` `I reckon we could see all the big cities inside a month?` `I can't wait' said Kelly.

`First thing in the morning` said Stella `I will ring my agent Christine and ask her if she will arrange the: Flights, hotels; etc in London, Paris; Rome and Malaga`. During the following week the vacation was all arranged. Christine had now set up that, instead of the girls staying at Malaga, Greg Cornwell who is a major star at the studio, would be happy to accommodate the two girls at his luxury villa, where the Mediterranean Sea was just outside the back door. Getting permission from Burford to go was easy, he was such a wonderful understanding person, he really was. Within seven days they were in London: looking around the Tower, and later it would be Buckingham Palace; Trafalgar Square feeding the pigeons, St. Paul's Cathedral; and the London Eye.

These were all the places where they had their pictures taken together, also getting a couple of shows in. Staying a few nights at a 5 star hotel which faced on to the river was exciting, especially to Kelly on this her first ever visit to England.

Christine had also arranged for the girls to visit Arsenal football club and watch a game on Tuesday night and to meet some of the players after the game. Which included an American player Doug Jones who lived just an hour's drive from Phoenix and who was the same age as Kelly. After a good win they met some of the player's in the lounge, including Doug who was captivated with Kelly's beauty and intelligence. For the next half hour the two of them seemed to be enjoying each other's company, which could lead to a reunion maybe next spring back in the States?

Wednesday morning they were now leaving London for Paris, where the main airport is in the heart of the city. Apart from the hotel, "The Louvre" was their first port of call of the day; It is the home of the "Mona Lisa" and also the "Venus De Milo". Later the girls were walking up the "Avenue des Champs Elysees" with all the magnificent shops; apartments, and hotels, which must make it one of the major streets in the world. At the top is the "Arc de Triomphe" which Napoleon had commissioned after one of his famous victories, but who died 15 years before it was completed. So that was more pictures for the album. Their hotel was looking across the river Seine towards the Eiffel Tower, where they would reach the top of tomorrow.

Kelly had noticed that the streets in the Capital were very condensed, that just went on and on forever.

Where in London you could at least escape the hustle and bustle by sitting in many a tree lined square or park. After four nights in Paris they were now on their way to Malaga, where Greg Cornwell would welcome them into his Villa for a week.

On arrival at Malaga they were met by Greg's gardener come handyman Bruce Streelman who looks after the mansion all year round. He is a divorced man, but has two teenage sons who are living with his ex-wife in Atlanta. He is in his early forties, 6ft tall, good looking with a very athletic body which hasn't gone unnoticed by Stella. Greg is on the steps of his mansion to welcome them. `What do you think?` asks Greg `It looks a fantastic place especially with it being next to the beach` said Kelly. `How many bedrooms are there?` asked Stella as she was now looking over her sunglasses at Bruce bending over to get the girls luggage out of the boot. `Seven, all of which are en-suite' replied Greg. After a welcoming drink at his private bar he tells the girls which are their bedrooms. `Kelly I have put you in number six where you will be facing the sea, and you Stella in number three, which has a four poster bed`.

When they are making their way up the staircase Bruce is right behind carrying four suitcases. `Goodness what did you have for breakfast?` asked Stella as they had now reached the landing, Bruce just smiled. After taking Kelly's suitcases to her room, he was now taking Stella's to the far end of the landing where her bedroom was. `Just the kind of bedroom I like` said Stella as Bruce was now putting her luggage next to the bed. He was now smiling at her displaying his perfect white teeth.

`What is so special about this bedroom?` he asked her `Well it has a four poster bed which has curtains that can be closed, where all the sounds can be shut out and there is total darkness`. `All beds are the same to me, they are just for sleeping in` replied Greg with a cheeky smile. `What does your wife think of you, just using your bed for sleep?` Stella's face lit up when he told her that he was divorced. `You mean you are a single man?` as she is now looking up into this man's blue eyes which are nearly covered by his longish jet black hair. `I liked to be tucked into bed at night, is there a chance of you doing that for me?` `If you want me to I will` he was now smiling again. `Where is your bedroom?` asked Stella. `Next door to yours, so when you are ready just knock on the wall` `I will` she said at the same time trying to control her hot and sexual tendencies. After a long soak in the bath Stella went back downstairs to tell Greg that she and Kelly were now going for a stroll on the beach. `Dinner is at 7pm so don't be late!` warned

Greg `We won't` said the girls. As the two of them were throwing pebbles into the sea, Stella told Kelly that she was smitten with Bruce and that she was hoping to get him between the sheets tonight. `Yes` replied Kelly `but is he smitten with you?` `I have a feeling that he is and I will soon find out`.

After dinner there was a cosy evening chat with Greg and his gorgeous wife about his own film career, and even about his favourite sport... tennis. Plus did he have any films lined up? `I think there is one in the pipeline, and I should know in a few days`. Greg now looked at his watch and suggested that a good night's sleep would do them all a world of good. As the girls were going up the staircase Kelly asked her friend rather sarcastically `Will you be having a good night's sleep?` with an inquisitive stare. `I hope not, it depends if Bruce decides to share my bed`. Kelly gave her a hug and warned her that she was going to sleep with a man that she hardly knew. `Don't worry I will be gentle with him`. Shortly after Stella is in bed naked, where the bed curtains are now surrounding it.

If it was hopefully going to be a night of heavy sex she didn't want her hair all tangled up by the following morning, so she put a white headscarf round the top of her head. She is now tapping on the wall, after 5 minutes she knocks again and shortly after she can hear her bedroom door open and close. Suddenly the bed curtains are drawn back and Bruce is now looking down at this beautiful woman laid on her back smiling up at him. His beautiful and powerful body, covered by just his sexy pyjama bottoms is allowing her more than passionate feelings to take over, where she will allow him any kind of sexual pleasure he wants. She notices an ever increasing size of something quite large in his crutch area, that is making her lust for him more intensive.

With his body and arms covered in hair, his face full of sexy stubble, what more could a woman want? As he momentarily sits on the side of the bed, she now reaches up and their lips meet, intentionally she now reveals her breasts which are now draped over the top of the bed sheet.

Now she has got him in bed, she has only partially closed the curtains, as she not only wants to see their bodies joined together, but also the pained expression on his handsome face as she squeezes his balls, also when she drives her tongue down his throat, plus many more pleasures that she has in mind now that he is at the side of her. Now in a semi darkness there is an intensive exploration of each other's body. Bruce has made sure that his protection was in place. Their open mouth kisses were getting to be more frenetic. Stella could feel his stubble scratching her face which made her lust for him even more aggressive. The bed sheets as a result were getting more and more disturbed. At one point Stella was concerned that Bruce's extra large violin might not fit into her violin case? After push came to shove she was eventually now more than satisfied. Stella knew that here was the man of her dreams whose strength was so strong that she would be powerless to stop him doing anything that he desired anyway. After all the exertions of the last hour they were now ready to melt into each other's arms and go to sleep.

During the night Stella's sexual desires had got the better of her, so she gently awoke him from his sleep as she wanted to feel that wonderful warmth of his penis entering her body yet again. Which would release more of his energy.

CHAPTER FIVE

Next morning at 9am she began to slowly awake. She turned to her right hand side to find that Bruce had gone. When she was having a shower she was reflecting on last night, and that she had received total sexual satisfaction from a man she hardly knew. Even though one of his muscles was much larger than anticipated.

Now she was getting dressed, and she could hear a grass mower in operation. Looking out of her bedroom window she could see that Bruce was cutting the grass on the private tennis court with just his jeans on. She opened the French windows and called his name. He was now looking up and waving. `How are you feeling this morning?` he shouted `I feel great thanks to you` he smiled again and said `I'll see you later`. She now joined Kelly in the kitchen for breakfast. Kelly was now looking at Stella in apprehension when she asked `Well, did anything happen last night?`

Stella turned round to her friend with both thumbs pointing to the ceiling and with a smile as wide as a washing line. Kelly now with her mouth wide open said `You mean you slept with him after all?` `Kelly let me tell you that it was like being in heaven, I cannot think of anybody on this planet that could come close to giving me better satisfaction than Bruce `So what happens now?` `If he were to ask me to marry him tomorrow I would` `You surely don't think that he would do, do you?` `Of course I don't I am only dreaming that's all`. Greg came into the kitchen.

`What are you two beauty's going to be doing today?` Stella was now looking at Kelly saying `I think we will spend most of the day on the beach and relax, what do you say Kelly? `Yes that's fine by me` 'Don't forget` said Greg you can always come back up to the house and Antonio our cook will make you something up` `Do you know Greg` said Stella `I am really enjoying this opportunity of staying in your beautiful Villa`. Kelly is now looking at Stella from across the kitchen with a smile on her face as though she is thinking `Yes and don't we know why`.

Later as the girls are on their sun beds Kelly asks Stella `Have you had a word with Bruce about the rest of the week concerning you two?` `No not yet but we are going to meet after dinner tonight`. At the dinner table that evening was Greg and his wife, Stella and Kelly and Bruce, who for a change had shaven and looked very smart with a shirt and tie. The meal was perfect but some of the anecdotes were a bit of a bore.

After dinner Stella and Bruce went for a stroll on the beach. Stella wanted to know what had gone wrong with his marriage. `Well I owned a paint warehouse in Atlanta and I had ten people working for me. So I was able to buy a nice home for my family. We also had some good vacations down in Florida in our vacation home, when suddenly Supermarkets started to sell paint as well as food. Which meant that our customers could now buy both food and paint at one place in the same day, which lowered our takings by a half'. `So did that put a big strain on your marriage?` asked Stella `Well with not having anywhere near the same income that I was used to, I sold the business. I got a substantial amount but with me not having a job, the money just frittered away`. `So what did you do?` asked Stella `I got depressed and turned to drink which was the last straw as regarding my marriage`. `So she left you then?` `Yes, and in a way I don't blame my wife for leaving me. She met a man whose wife had died a year before, which left him with two young children to bring up'. `Is he a good man?` asked Stella

`Yes he is because my two sons who went with their mother told me he was alright, but not as good as me`. Stella and Bruce were now smiling at each other. `Certainly I was in no state to look after them`. `Obviously you were allowed access to them?` `Me and my wife had agreed that before she left, that would be no problem, I still see the kids once a year when I visit the States`. `How is it that you came over here to live in Spain?` `I have known Greg Cornwell since I was 20 years old. We went to the same dance halls in Atlanta.

Both him and me are also "Atlanta Chief" fans. As well we both decided to go to Drama school. Anyone could see that he was going to make the big time. He was just so naturally gifted he really was.

I knew in my heart of hearts that I didn't have anywhere near the talent that he had, and it kind of put me off. So I dropped out, that is when I started to get into the Paint business.

In the meantime Greg was now making a name for himself in the Cinema. Originally they were just ordinary films but his presence in the films made them good. On me and my wife's first date we were watching

Greg in one of his first films. I didn't dare tell her that we were best mates because she would look at me as a flop she really would.

After my divorce I would write many a letter to him asking if there was any work out there in sunny California? but before sending them I would screw them up as he would think that I was begging. That is one thing that I would never allow myself to do, I really wouldn't. Nevertheless I was happy for him, I wasn't jealous. When I sold the business I obviously hadn't much to do during the day so I joined a fitness club, that is when I stopped drinking, I had never smoked anyway. Something told me to get myself fit which I did and have been fit ever since. Amazingly Greg paid a private visit to Atlanta to find out whatever happened to me. Someone told him that I was now a fitness fanatic and could reach me at "Buster's Fitness Centre".

I got the surprise of my life when he tapped me on the shoulder. My initial response was `My god what are you doing here?` `I used to fucking live here remember? ` he replied with a wide smile. We embraced each other and when I got changed, within a short while we were at his hotel, and to my shame that night I have to admit I got sloshed`. Now looking at Stella with total honesty he is telling her that from that day to this, he has never let himself to be drawn to drink (apart from Christmas). We also discussed how our two lives had gone down different roads, his meteoric rise to fame and to the debris of mine.

The one thing he asked me for before he left was for my phone number, because he was going to find me a job out there. After a fortnight I got a call, he told me he was making an action packed movie, and a stunt man was urgently required and was I up for it? I just replied that `I was on my way` and for the next seven years I was the man, and I never once let him down. He became a top box office star and he bought this beautiful Villa and invited me to come to Spain. He asked me to keep it nice and tidy for when he had important visitors`. They were now nearly back at the Villa. `So don't you ever want to go back to the States and settle down?` asked Stella.

He came back with the answer that she didn't want to hear. `No Stella I want to spend the rest of my life in this house, where I can enjoy doing what is natural to me`. Stella went back to Kelly to tell her that Bruce has no intention of returning to Los Angeles. `Maybe it's as well` said Kelly `Why?` `Well just because you two had a sexy night together doesn't mean that you could be automatically happy living together does it?` Stella is now looking decidedly miserable when she has to admit `Yes I think that you have a good point there`.

Later on Greg said he would take the girls around the bay in his yacht on the day before they set off for Rome. When on his yacht Stella told Greg that Bruce didn't ever want to go to California again and that he is very happy here? `You bet he is' said Greg `You seem to be very sure?` `Because my dear as you must have noticed he is like the proverbial jam pot where all the flies try to enter.

When I have single young women or even middle aged women staying here, they want to share their bed with him`. He is now looking straight at her with his eyebrows raised (all of a sudden Stella feels slightly embarrassed and uncomfortable to say the least).`Me and Bruce have been mates a long time but in life I was lucky and made good` (he is now looking to the heavens with gratitude).`I already know that Bruce a few years ago had life a bit rough, and being a big mate of mine I felt as though I wanted to help him if I could.

As a result he is now one of the most contented men on the planet`. Bruce who was also on the yacht, suddenly shouted `White shark starboard` Greg got hold of Stella's hand and took her to look at this fearsome monster that was close by. Kelly was now moving towards Stella her constant friend for safety. Just like she does when they are at home when there is a thunderstorm.

The yacht was now on its way back to the harbour ably assisted by Bruce in his white cropped t-shirt that was blowing in the breeze, revealing his bulging stomach muscles, plus his shorts, which allowed the girls (especially Stella) to observe his tree trunk thighs. Kelly noticed Stella almost having an orgasm watching this Adonis, `Aren't you ever going to get this fucking man out of your head?` asked Kelly pulling her sunglasses down and now looking over them towards Stella. `To be honest Kelly at the moment I can't, but when we go to Rome tomorrow I am hoping that my infatuation for him will eventually fade away`. `What about the other night will that just fade away as well?` Now a smiling Stella turned to Kelly and told her `That night I can assure you will never fade, never`. Kelly has now returned to her magazine with her head moving from one side to the other. Later that night as Stella was putting on her negligee, she thought she heard a tapping on the wall, after a few moments it was there again. `My God does he want me to round to his bedroom?` she immediately thought, after a quick refurbishment of makeup she was tapping on his door. `Come in` a voice said. When she went in he was totally naked, laying on his side and leaning on his elbow with the bed sheet almost down to his "bits".

He was all smiles as he suggested that they should say goodbye in the proper way. He was now moving to one side of the bed so that she could join him.

In less than a minute they were now heavily engrossed into the much steamier side of sex, where oral sex was now very much in evidence, as she was now in full flow extracting with her mouth as much semen as she could from this man's super fit body, before later having a few helpings of intercourse, in what turned out to be a long night. The following morning as Bruce was getting dressed, Stella herself was now waking up with a quick fire question `Are you sure that you don't want to come back to California?, with him now leaning on the closet he replied `No I am sorry Stella; but as much as I love you as a bed partner I cannot see anywhere else in the world I would rather be than here, as well Greg relies on me to manage his Villa which is of prior importance to me`. After breakfast Greg was ready to say goodbye to the girls, after Bruce had now got their luggage tucked away in the boot of Greg's B.M.W. `When are you next at "Metropolis studios? Stella asked Greg `In another month they have a jungle adventure film on the Amazon River lined up. Where we make friends with some hostile natives, but in the meantime there are a lot of poison darts coming in from all directions.' Kelly is laughing saying `It sounds like a lot of fun`.

After a few hugs from Greg the car is now leaving the courtyard, Greg shouts `See you in a month`. Stella is in the front seat next to Bruce who is driving. Kelly who sat in the back seat can see them talking and laughing with each other. Though she can't hear what they are saying, as he has the window open and the traffic is making it too difficult to pick up. She can tell by their body language that they are obviously very happy in each other's company. The circumstances as they are will prevent any continuation of what could have been a great relationship. Now at the airport the car has been parked, the luggage is on the conveyor belt and all that is left is the goodbyes. A kiss on the cheek for Kelly who is now leaving the scene so Stella and Bruce can be a little more intimate. Kelly is eventually joined by Stella who needless to say has a few tears coming down her face. Kelly now puts her arm around her best friend in sympathy and tries to console her.

It's not long before the plane is airborne. Malaga airport and beautiful Marbella are slowly disappearing from view, as is Stella's dream man Bruce. Rome with its: Spanish steps; St. Peters square, and the Coliseum; were places of special interest as the photographs will prove later. Throwing a coin into the Fountain with as well a wish could be beneficial to the girls. Maybe Bruce will change his mind and start a new life with Stella in California. Maybe Kelly will become the big star of next year's awards which seems quite likely anyway. Trips into the Italian countryside and lakes were memorable especially when the girls were caught in a torrential downpour where one willing villager was prepared to also risk a soaking to take their picture. So after a five night stay they were now on their way back home. After a week's rest they were now ready to find out what was going on at the Studios, and were they in for a big surprise? Stella's film "Yellow Sky" was going to be better box office than expected, and Kelly's film where she had star billing "It's Never Too Late" looks also like being a block buster which would elevate her quite high in the ratings.

Metropolis Film Corporation has recently promoted James Walsh one of the corporations up and coming executives from the parent company in Boston. Now he will be the top Liaison officer at the Los Angeles studios. His first priority is to get all the company's personnel data on to a fact file which includes information of each individual, such as: Have they got any long term illnesses? have they been prosecuted for a motoring offence; or drugs, have they any health or drinking problems etc.

One day while browsing on the computer file, he came across a former work colleague when they were in Boston, his name is Michael Dawson. One small section of the fact file states, "Living as a partner with Susan Paxton in her Mansion in Santa Barbara, with the intention of getting married and starting a family." Now alarm bells have started to ring in James's head, because something isn't quite adding up? He is now referring to a few years ago back in Boston, when James's wife and other ladies sometimes had a night out together which included Michael's at the time wife Angela. James remembers his wife coming home one particular night, telling him that she now knew why Angela Dawson had no children after four years of marriage.

Apparently one of the other ladies had asked her why they hadn't yet started with a family. As it was late at night and Angela had already gone over the top with drink, she now staggered up from her seat and blurted out to all and sundry `I have been asked, when am I going to start with a family? My answer to that is ***fucking* never!** because firstly my husband is always too busy going out with his mates, and secondly he is **bloody impotent!**` `Now if that is true, James is thinking to himself why on earth is Susan going to be wasting valuable years, with a man who cannot ever give to her the thing she wants more than anything else, and that is children.

He is now looking on Susan's fact file for her phone number. He is as well checking his watch to make sure that she is still not in bed. It is now approaching 10.30 am so there should be no problem. James is also aware that Michael is at this moment in the studios. As he is waiting for her to pick the phone up, he realizes that he is going to have to approach this rather emotional situation very carefully. The call has now been answered by Susan `Hello Susan this is James Walsh at the studios` `Hello James what can I do for you?`

`Would it be convenient for me to visit you this week?` `Yes come tomorrow morning if you like…….. why is there a problem?` `Sort of but I can't tell you over the phone` `Can't Michael help you?` `I'm afraid not, this is about you, and by the way do not mention anything to Michael, this is strictly confidential` `Okay see you in the morning` Susan is now slowly putting the phone down with a rather furrowed brow. Next morning at 10am James was now wiping his shoes on Susan's front door mat before being welcomed into her lounge.

`Would you like a drink first?` asked Susan `A port and lemon would be nice thank you` he is now making himself comfortable on the sofa `You don't look very happy` said Susan as she was handing him the drink. `Put it this way I am very concerned about something I found out yesterday` Susan decides to sit down, as she is suddenly feeling very uncomfortable in herself. `It concerns me you say?` `Very much so I'm afraid'. She now takes a sip of her Brandy and now takes a deep breath and says `Go on James give me the lowdown` `According to the company's Fact File, you and Michael have now acquired a house` he now stops and as he is looking around him, he tells her `And what a beautiful house it is, if I may say so` `Thank you very much` replied Susan `So anyway, hopefully you will eventually have children is that correct? `Yes it is` `Have you been trying to get pregnant before you get married? `Yes we have but with no luck yet` `So you would be upset if you were told by a gynaecologist that there was no chance of you two being parents to your own children?` `It would be very upsetting` `I can understand that` replied James `We are going to a gynaecologist friend of Michaels next week for tests to maybe get some answers`. James is now scratching his head what he should now suggest. Suddenly he says to Susan `After those test results have come thru will you tell me, and I will come to see you, whatever you do you must not say anything to Michael, okay'.

There was obviously something afoot that Susan should know about, that was presumably quite serious.

Being patient and having to live in the same house with someone, who possibly had some dark secret or something to hide, was not the ideal life she was trying to build for a happy marriage. As well trying to be casual and not giving any indication that underneath she was profoundly worried, and that it would also be like a severe test of her acting abilities to hide her true feelings. Which could seriously be the best acting performance of her life so far, but at least it would bring out the truth. About a month later Susan was now sending a text message to James telling him that the results had now come from Dr Newlove (the friend of Michael's) at the hospital, but she hasn't got the courage to open it. He rang back a bit later to tell her that he was now on his way. Before he went he had to make sure that Michael was in the Studios before he set off. James is now looking out of his office window and sees Michael's car in the parking lot. On arrival at Susan's house (which incidentally is her house, as she was naturally earning a lot more than Michael was).

She was now stood at the door waiting for him to arrive. They now went into the kitchen where the letter was on the table and had been for the last two hours. Now looking at Susan he said `Are you ready?` `Yes` said a nervous Susan, he now opened the letter and read what he had suspected all along. It told him that the test showed that Susan was infertile and would never be able to have children of her own. Also according to this letter, the test on Michael showed that he was potent and that he could be a father to his own children.

James suddenly feels anger that this Dr. Newlove has risked his career by getting paid presumably a large amount of money, to clear Michael of being the obstacle that would prevent Susan of ever being pregnant, which would point the finger then at Susan being the unsuspecting culprit. Leaving her with the inner guilt that their married life would be now childless, when it could be exactly the opposite. Before he handed Susan the letter he told her that `Not for one second believe that what you are about to read is true.

This letter is going to be the main evidence to get a custodial sentence for both of these men`. After Susan had read it she said `But what if it is true that I am actually infertile?` James now went up to her, put his arm around her shoulder and said `I am willing to put my job on the line, that this letter is clearly a fabrication of the truth. If you do as I say we will prove that it is' `So what do you want me to do?` asked a now worried looking Susan `Would it be possible for you to get a photo copy of any payments of over a few thousand dollars, that Michael has paid to anybody in the last 2 months? secondly I would like you to see a specialist that I know who is obviously totally unbiased, and he will confirm I am sure that you are fertile and that you can have children whenever you like` `What about Michael? ` asked Susan `We will get lawyers to make Michael have another test, and I will tell you now that your husband to be, is the one that is infertile and not you` `I wouldn't know what to do if it turned out that he had been so deceitful to me?` said Susan. `You would do one of two things: you could totally forgive him and live a normal married life, but without your own children. Or you could remove him from your life and find somebody who is not deceitful and selfish, who will give you what you want and that is children`.

Susan is now borrowing a smile already knowing which path to choose. While James is finishing his coffee, Susan has gone to the study to get a photocopy of Michael's recent transactions. After five minutes she comes back out with her face looking rather ashen which James has also noticed. `You were right` she said pointing to the photocopy, he paid Francis Newlove $100,000 dollars two weeks before we went for that test` `I knew it, I just honestly knew it` said James who is now consoling her as she is beginning to see Michael in a different light, a light that she at the moment cannot possibly accept. On his arrival home Michael was told to leave the house until there was a conclusion to this nightmare. The look on his face, as he packed his suitcase gave Susan the notion that he had been rumbled.

A week later after a further test on Susan, she was given the all clear to have as many children as she wants. `Look` said James `why don't we go for a meal to celebrate our success of finding out people who are deceitful and also selfish?`. Susan agreed entirely with what he said and felt now that a heavy burden had been taken off her shoulders. As well she wanted to get her life back to normal. They are now pulling into D'Arcy's an exclusive restaurant just outside Beverly Hills.

After a very nice meal they are now sitting comfortably in the lounge with two port and lemons, 'What have the Studio got lined up for your next film?` asked James `As far as I know it's an adventure film set in Alaska, but I haven't read the script yet, it sounds interesting though, it's always been somewhere that I wanted to visit` `So who will be your leading man in the film I wonder? `asked James smiling over at her `I will have to ask my dear friend Burford`. She is now looking into her glass reminiscing. `What are you thinking?` he asked her `I am just going down memory lane, when two years ago in London, me and my best friend Stella were approached by Burford to appear in a film "Confessions of a Lifeguard". James was quick to remark `I remember seeing that film on DVD it was actually quite funny, where you had a fight with another girl over this lifeguard` `Well that girl was Stella`. ` I didn't know that?` said James laughing, `all I remember thinking was, what are these two stunning beauty's fighting over that wimp for. Now here I am lucky enough to be sat with one of them` `You do say the nicest things` said Susan. James was now pulling his wallet out to pay for the meal and drinks. He feels Susan's hand on his sleeve. `I will pay, it is only fair after you have gone out of your way to help me when it wasn't even your problem`.

`Yes, but it is my problem, it is why I was given promotion, to get everybody at Metropolis into the fact file, your problem actually is the first I have been involved with and it is an obvious success. As regards the meal I want to be able to tell my kids that I once had a meal with the best actress in the world Susan

Paxton, and do you know what, they probably wouldn't believe me`. Susan is quite amused and quipped `I can only hope that they do` showing in the present circumstances a rare genuine smile. `I have a camera in the car` said James and within the next few minutes the waiter was taking a picture of them sat in the restaurant.

If we forward a week where Michael Dawson has give Susan a call to try and patch up his unforgiveable act of deceit and treachery.

He was asked by Susan to come clean about his wicked intention of trying to prove that she was infertile when it was him all along, and that he had also implicated Francis Newlove a gynaecologist into this rather sordid affair. Also by putting $100,000 dollars into his bank account to verify that the tests resulted with good news for Michael, but the opposite for Susan, when it was all a wicked lie. Michael now feels terribly guilty for what he has done, and the only chance to be forgiven was to now grovel and to tell her the truth, and that he only did it because he thought that she would leave him as he couldn't fulfil her dreams. Susan told him `It breaks my heart to see you like this, but what else can I do, the damage is far too great to be repaired`. Later during a phone call to James, Susan told him that Michael had told her that he was ashamed of himself, and was there any chance of reconciliation? `I told him that there wouldn't be, but he could use the garage to keep his belongings in till he had found other accommodation`. James could hear her sobbing on the phone, but told her that at the moment it probably hurts like hell, but it will eventually subside into insignificance.

What eventually happened later in this very unhappy episode was that Michael after a meeting with Susan that lasted two hours, where he begged forgiveness for doing what he did. Although she was heartbroken seeing him with no job (Metropolis Films had no option but to sack him) she knew that their relationship could never be the same again. He got a taxi and took his belongings to a rented house downtown.

Susan had a reprieve for Michael, that after consulting with James she decided to drop all charges against him and Francis Newlove. The gynaecologist though was struck off, which they thought was about the correct amount of punishment. The last thing that Susan wanted was to see a broken man stood up in court, a man that she had once loved. A fortnight later she was informed that Michael had taken his own life by inhaling exhaust fumes in a garage.

CHAPTER SIX

There was a written note that had been left for Susan's, attention, which Burford would now send to her in an envelope. As she read it she was overcome with grief, it read-

`My Dear Susan

`I am sorry for the hurt that I have caused you, but I only did what I did because I thought that you would leave me for somebody else, who could give you something that I unfortunately couldn't. I really did love you, and maybe if we ever meet in another life, we could make a fresh start

Love Michael

Susan was now on her own for the first time in her life, apart from George her butler, who although getting on a bit at 62 has a flat at the side of her mansion. Who is a source of companionship if she hasn't any visitors staying over (which is quite rare). He cooks and cleans and even does the shopping. As regards any washing, he takes it to a company that will not only wash it, but iron it as well. Susan is aware that Stella and Kelly have been to Europe on vacation and should be back home now. She gives them a call to see if they would like to spend a week with her. Stella replies `You bet we will` and they arrive the same day. As Susan is showing them to their bedrooms.

Kelly says to Stella with a smile `There is just one thing that is missing here` `What is that` `Bruce` `If only` said Stella with a heavy sigh. Walking just in front, Susan turns around to Stella and asks her `Who is this Bruce then?` `Just a man that I met at Greg Cornwell's Villa in Marbella` . Kelly feels as though she wants Susan to know more about this man. Stella looks a little embarrassed as Kelly tells Susan that her best friend was besotted by this hunk of a man that she slept with twice. `Oh my goodness what have you been getting up to?` asked Susan who told her that she could be now pregnant. `I hope I am' answered Stella, `because I am sure he would stand by me?` Susan and Kelly are now looking at each other with a `I am not so sure about that` expression. Later in the day there was plenty to catch up on, including this tragic episode of Michael. At first, both Stella and Kelly couldn't believe that he would resort to such measures, such as to put the blame down to Susan, just to get what he selfishly wanted for himself.

Stella remarked `It just seemed so out of character, whenever I bumped into him at the studio he was always so accommodating and seemingly quite happy`. Susan is beginning to wipe her eyes again while saying that her heart wanted so much to forgive him, but alas her head had the last word. They agree to change the subject and to talk about their next films. Kelly tells Susan that next week she is going on location to Kenya to star in a remake of "Beyond Mombasa" `Burford has also arranged for us to go on Safari during the shooting of the film, and guess who I hope will be my companion out there?` she is now looking at Stella with a smile, `Who me?` said Stella with her mouth open in astonishment .`Of course You, I would feel so alone with you not being there` she is now going over to Stella and giving her a kiss on the cheek, and at the same time putting her arm around her waist.

As all this is going on, Susan who has known Stella literally all of her life, even when they were in junior school, they were always known as the inseparables.

She would never have thought that another girl who almost the same age could replace her. Now with the affection that Kelly shows towards Stella, and as well Stella's affection to Kelly it has actually happened. Susan is not at all feeling envious that the two girls love each other's company. In fact she feels tremendous happiness for them both, and as far as she is concerned long may it last. Kelly is now asking Susan if she is about to make a film soon, `Yes while you are away in the sweltering heat of Africa.

A month later I will be in the much cooler Alaskan mountains` Kelly looks around at Stella and says `Do you think that we could go to Alaska next summer for our vacations? I have only ever seen films and photographs of that part of the world. `I can't see no reason why we shouldn't` said Stella. Susan told George that he wouldn't need to go shopping this week as she and the two girls would do it instead, as his choice might not be quite to their liking.

During the rest of the week the three girls enjoyed themselves in the pool. Also a trip on to the beach where Stella was telling Kelly that this was the beach where she and Susan had that fight in the film "Confessions of a

Lifeguard" their first film. Although Kelly is listening, she has now turned around to see Susan struggling with the hamper and immediately runs back to help her. When they have now found a spot on the beach, Stella now confirms with Susan that this was the beach where they had that fight two years ago. `Yes' said Susan now looking at Kelly `She gave me a lot more bruises than I gave her. Kelly and Stella were now laughing. After a game of "Frisbee" and the small picnic it was now time to get back to the mansion.

Meanwhile George had made them a tasty looking salad with a white wine that Susan had asked him to specially prepare, `Which she thought the girls would like`. On the day that the girls were going home, Susan had noticed that Kelly had kept admiring the Oscar that Susan had won on that special night the other year. At one point when Kelly was holding it, Susan went up behind her and put her hand on her shoulder, and told her that one day in the near future she would as well be the owner of her own Oscar.

Kelly turned around and they gave each other a big hug. Earlier in the day Susan had asked Stella if she would like to come back and live with her, and that it would be just like old times.

Stella had replied `Yes, I would love to, but what about Kelly she would be on her own in the apartment?` `Wouldn't Burford get another young actress to take your place` `He probably could, but that is not the point, we have a friendship that will never die, just like yours and mine, and to say goodbye to her would break my heart, it really would `said Stella. Susan's reply was `It was just an idea that suddenly came into my head, and I should have realized that there is a very special bond between the two of you'. Stella now told Susan

`In normal circumstances I would jump at the chance of me and you being together again but certain things happen in life where you can't always do what you had originally intended to do` `Luckily` said Susan `I have friends that I visit or they visit me, plus my family that come across twice a year.

Otherwise now that Michael has gone I think that I would go crazy living in a big house like this on my own`. Stella is now nodding in sympathy. `The only reason that I got this house was because I could see me and Michael with our children being very happy living here`. Eventually the time has come for the girls to go back home. Stella and Kelly thank Susan for a lovely week, Kelly and Susan wish each other good luck with the films that each other will be making shortly. Not long after, the two girls are back in their own apartment where there is a happier atmosphere.

We will now fast forward to when all the personnel are now assembled at a location five miles outside Mombasa in Kenya, for the making of "Beyond Mombasa". The weather is terrific, but quite hot. Just a few hundred yards away is a cascade of water that meanders into a small lake which gives all the personnel making the film a welcome relief from the hot temperatures. The first weeks filming has been completed and everything has gone to plan. The week after sees the Safari now in progress.

The jeep with Stella and Kelly in has been buffeted around after being charged by a Rhinoceros a few times, scaring to death its occupants especially Kelly who is holding on to Stella for dear life.

Later they see: Giraffes eating off the top of 20ft trees; some of the elephants are rolling about in the mud lakes, also the massive herds of Wildebeest are a sight not to be missed. There have been plenty of pictures taken of the girls, one of which showed them holding two young chimpanzees. The next morning was just as hot as the day before. The Safari had been a great day out that would always be remembered, but now it was back to business. Kelly and her co star Jed O'Brien had now to do some scenes in Mombasa.

So with the director and film crew they travelled the 5 miles in an open wagon. Kelly wanted Stella to come as well, but on this occasion she couldn't make it as she had an in-growing toenail that was giving her a lot of pain. She couldn't be seen by the studio doctor till after lunch.

After a full day in Mombasa filming, Kelly feeling tired and thirsty told the others that she had seen a supermarket in the next street, where she now made her way towards it. She had picked up an assortment of orange juice and a few beers for the crew. As she was now about to be served, suddenly two hooded men with guns burst in and started to take money out of the tills. The police had earlier been given a tip off that a robbery on the supermarket was imminent, and had followed them in to arrest them. Before anybody could escape the melee, there was now a shootout between the robbers and Police: Bullets were going in all directions, where a couple of bystanders were hit with stray bullets.

More police were now rushing in, where one of the robbers has now been shot dead. The other robber is now in a panic and in desperation grabs hold of Kelly around the shoulders and pulls her towards his body. This results in her now being a human shield for this American hoodlum with the name Clyde Fallon, who was on the run from his own country, after already killing two shopkeepers in separate incidents in downtown Philadelphia. As the local police are slowly moving in to get their man, Fallon warns the police that unless they get a car to the back exit for his escape he will have no option but to shoot his terrified hostage Kelly. They agree to let him have his way providing she is set free before he gets into the car. Slowly making his way backwards to the exit, he suddenly trips over the outstretched arm of his now dead cousin Sylvester Fallon which releases his grip on Kelly who is now suddenly making a dash for freedom. However not before this fugitive has wickedly shot her twice in her side. With Kelly having now slumped to the floor, suddenly he has lost control of the situation and as a result there is a barrage of gunfire aimed at him. As he now crawled into a corner the police emptied at least a dozen bullets into his already dead body.

Ambulances are now at the scene and quickly get the injured including Kelly to hospital, who undoubtedly by far has the worst injury. Meanwhile a couple of streets away, the Director and crew have heard the firing of shots and the commotion that is going on.

Suddenly they realize, that was the direction that Kelly went. Most of the crew and director are now running towards the incident, but there is no sign of Kelly. The director is now getting worried and asking people if they have seen a young white lady. Most of the people are black and don't understand what he is saying. One of them comes running up to him saying in only just recognisable English, that he saw a white lady put into an ambulance with plenty of blood on her clothing.

Straight away he is now on his mobile phone to Base which is five miles away, telling them that there has been a shoot out in a supermarket, and it looks like Kelly has been badly injured and is now in hospital.

Bob Dyson who is in charge of operations has told the director that they are coming straight away to the hospital. Bob is now telling Stella what has happened and they are now quickly on their way. Stella is beside herself with worry, her stomach is tied in knots, and the anxiety is making it hard for her to breathe. Eventually they arrive in the parking area of the hospital, where they are met by the film crew who have already located where Kelly is in the hospital. So Stella and the others have now entered the Intensive Care unit and are met by a black doctor who tries to calm them down. Luckily he can speak reasonable English and tells them that Kelly is badly injured, and that everything is being done to save her life. `Can we see her?` asked Stella, he tells her `At the moment she is unconscious and needs to be watched every minute for any alteration to her condition` `Do you think that she will pull thru?` asked Bob Dyson `Well I would very much like to say yes, but at the moment I honestly don't know, but I am confident that she will regain consciousness fairly soon`. So Stella and the others sit down resigned to a long wait. One of the crew gets tea and coffee for them out of some old machine that has seen better days. After a two hour wait, the doctor came out to say that she has now regained consciousness. So if they would like to see her, now is the time as she is still very ill.

Stella who knows her better than anybody on the planet is first in and is literally torn apart to see her best friend just laid there not moving, drips and all those sort of things are doing their best to keep her alive. As Kelly's eyes open she can see the film crew around her bed including Bob Dyson and Stella who is someone who means everything to her. As the crew one by one come up to her bedside they are touching her hand and whispering to her that she must get better, she must. They are now outside the Intensive Care unit leaving

Kelly and Stella alone, Kelly is now holding Stella's hand who is now continuously crying.

Kelly is finding it hard to talk, but she is able to tell her best friend to be brave, and that she will always love her even after death. Stella is beginning to realize that something is about to happen for the worse, something so terrible that she will never be able to come to terms with it` `Please don't leave me Kelly!` `Stella you must know that I will never leave you`, and as her hand slowly lost its grip with Stella's she had now slipped away. Stella ran out of the room and out of the hospital and sat on a bench absolutely heartbroken. She was quickly followed by Bob Dyson who put his arm around her trying to comfort her the best he can but it is almost impossible. Eventually she is persuaded to get back into the car. `What about Kelly?` she asks `I will see to all that, and I don't want you to worry any more than what you already are` said Bob.

All the way back to base she is still crying. Later in the day after getting in touch with the President of Metropolis Film Corporation, Bob has been told to scrap the film and come back home. When back in L/A Stella is unable to get any sort of relief or control over her grief. She has now been taken back to her apartment in Santa Monica by a staff member Troy, who after getting her luggage up in the elevator, comes back down to see her still outside and looking up at the entrance. He can't think of anything to say that will make her feel better, so he gives her a long, long hug and a kiss on the forehead. As he is driving out of the gates he turns around to see her still stood looking up at the entrance. Somehow to her it just doesn't look the same, it used to look so full of happiness and laughter. Now it looks so drab and miserable as if it is sharing with Stella this tragic loss of a dear friend. She now enters the apartment, she just drops the two suitcases on the floor one of which topples on its side as though it has also got feelings too.

She makes her way slowly to the window, as she is looking down onto the street she can see Kelly with her arms full of shopping, looking up at her and laughing.

Stella would willingly give everything up if that could be reality. As she slowly walks around each room, everything she sees is bringing back memories that are stabbing her thru her heart. She falls on to her bed, the same bed Kelly used to jump into whenever there was a thunder storm. Stella has now fallen asleep, an hour later she has now woken up shivering and making a meal for herself is going to be difficult. Somehow she is telling herself that she must pull herself together and realize "that life has to go on" she can almost hear Kelly telling her the same.

She gives Susan the bad news over the phone. Stella can hear that Susan's voice is also letting her know that she is deeply disturbed by this catastrophic news. Stella tells her that she can't live in the apartment any longer, because of everything that is in the flat brings back memories followed by tears. Susan tells her to get all of her belongings together and bring them to her house, because she can understand what she is going thru. A day later she was back with the friend that she had known all of her life. As they sat and talked about this tragedy, Stella could tell that Susan was genuinely very upset as well, because she and Kelly were also getting to know each other so well. Susan told Stella that she wanted to go to the funeral, and that she would take her if that was alright. `Of course you can, I was hoping that you would want to come anyway`.

Susan had just remembered that Burford had rung earlier to ask Stella if she would call in at the studio's to see him. `I think that I had better go now because knowing Burford he will make me feel a lot better`. When she arrived at the studio's everybody that she came into contact with were full of sympathy for her, knowing that the two girls were best of friends and inseparable. It's only a few days ago she was crying her eyes out, but now with grit and determination she was able to get some sort of control of her feelings once more. When she entered Burford's office he came from behind his desk and gave her a prolonged hug. He whispered in her ear that he was also overcome with grief when he was told the terrible news. Which now brought a couple of Stella's tear drops on to Burfords shoulder. Stella let him know that she wouldn't be going back to the apartment again because of all the reminders of their great friendship would always be evident, and which also would be too painful. Also that Susan would give her accommodation for as long as she wants at her home. `I think you have made the right decision`. He also told her that he had been in touch with Kelly's parents. `As you can expect they are having great difficulty coming to terms with it as well`.

Stella told him that she had stayed with her and her family the other month and quickly realized that they were a very close family. `They wanted to know how you were taking it` said Burford `and I told them that you were taking it very badly` after a pause Stella asked `Have any funeral arrangements been made yet?` `Yes the funeral has been arranged for a week today in Phoenix. I will be taking Walter Ackerman (President of Metropolis Film Corporation) who thought very highly of her as a future megastar in the film world`.

Before she left she gave Burford a kiss on his cheek and told him that because of the severe body blow that had recently happened in her life, she was contemplating putting her acting career on hold and returning to London until she had sufficiently got her mind sorted out.

Which could be a year at least. Burford told her `I can see in your eyes that you are tormented by what has happened, which leads me to believe that you probably do need a complete break, I am also confident that no matter how long you are away you will one day return to the studio`. On the way back down the freeway to Susan's house, she was observing all the traffic going in both directions, whose occupants were totally oblivious to other people's misfortunes. Which to her is quite acceptable as they themselves along with the whole human race, will at some point be in this same situation as she is now. Stella is going back in her mind to her own family where her mother and father were killed by a hit and run motorist, her grandfather drowned by the incoming tide, and her grandmother who has dementia and who doesn't know the difference between night and day. She has now arrived back at Susan's house.

The following Tuesday is the day of the funeral. There is a massive turnout of People in the City who although they didn't actually know her, they were aware that she was a gifted actress and that she was a credit to the city. Her family and all her many friends were at the service. "Stella before entering the church notices somebody calling and waving to her from the crowd....it was Rodney who owned the cafe in the middle of nowhere. He always thought of Kelly as a truly wonderful friend whose laughter and appreciation of life would never be shared ever again. Stella has now shoved her way thru the crush towards him, hardly a word was spoken between the two as they gave each other that very long special hug that said everything."

Minutes later, Stella was sat behind the family, just sitting there and looking at the coffin which could hardly be seen because of all the flowers that surrounded it. Knowing that someone so beautiful and so special would never be involved in her life again, was at this moment breaking her heart into a million pieces. After the ceremony all the family including Stella (who the family specially wanted to attend the private burial) were now stood around the graveside. Harvey, Kelly's brother was stood next to Stella and as the priest was conducting this brief service, he was searching for her hand to hold, which Stella now gave him, that gave them both a special bond that would be there forever. A special function afterwards with at least two hundred family and friends were celebrating her short life. Burford Maunder and Walter Ackerman were seen talking with the Baxter family, while Susan and Stella were sharing a joke with Harvey. Gradually the sorrow of the occasion seemed to take a back seat, where a more relaxed atmosphere now entered this sad event. Which is the way Kelly would have wanted it to be. Mr. Baxter and his wife went up to Stella, and after a special hug they told her that she must visit them whenever she could, as she would always be welcome.

Stella once again was close to tears when she promised them she would. Even Ella the maid wanted to hug Stella and to tell her that Kelly had at some private moment told her that she, Stella was the priceless jewel in her life. These were wonderful things to be told and treasured, but they were making Stella more and more tearful. Eventually like anything in life, things have to come to an end and although it will always be remembered, it will unfortunately have to be now put on one side as the normality of life will have to be resumed.

As Susan and Stella are on their way home, normally they would be talking about something and everything but not today. Susan knowing that Stella had been subjected to a very distressing day, decided to let her be in her own thoughts, and hardly a word was spoken till they were home.

In the course of the following week Susan told Stella that while she would be away in Alaska making the film "A Town Called Trouble" (incidentally the film is set in the 1850s) George would look after her, and anything she wanted he would get it for her. If she wanted to cook her own meals, George would quite understand. Now to Monday morning and Susan is all packed up and ready to go. Stella warns her to be careful and watch out for those grizzly bears, looking at her with a serious face. `Don't you worry I will be careful`. The month that Susan was away it gave Stella plenty of time to put her life into perspective. For one thing the studio which had a couple of films lined up for her had now been given to another actress, due to the trauma she had suffered. The people upstairs reckoned her exceptional talent would be impaired by recent events, which would interfere with her concentration.

After another month goes by, Susan is almost ready for coming home, just one more scene to do which requires her to escape on a raft from a murderous gang who on horseback were after her gold. Unfortunately the Director of the film was unaware that it had been raining quite heavily during the night. So when Susan was now going down the river on the raft it suddenly hit a stretch of water where it suddenly became dangerous.

It smashed into a fallen tree that was now blocking the river which resulted with Susan being thrown into the air, and into the raging torrent.

Her long dress had now got caught on one of the branches and was now holding her head under the water. Luckily there were three of the film extras stood at the side of the river. One of whom dived straight in without any hesitation. This man had to swim about 20yds against this surge of dangerous water to reach her, he managed to hold her head above water till he got his breath back.

The immediate problem was that if the fallen tree broke free and carried on down the swollen river, they would both be sucked below the surface and facing certain death. Eventually he released her from the dress which was now too heavily tangled up in the branches.

What seemed like an eternity, he had now pulled her into the side by putting his arm under her chin.

Another man used his mobile for the film director to suspend any filming for the day, and for medical assistance which came as quick as it could, and although the hero was reasonably conscious, Susan was very much the opposite, and both were now taken to hospital. A few hours later Stella gets a phone call from Burford telling her that Susan had been in an accident on a river. `My God is she alright! `From what I have heard she is now in hospital and conscious' `Do you think I should come up` `No, you stay where you are, for one thing it is too far and another is that I am sure she will be back home within a couple of days`. When Stella put the phone down, George was now nervously rubbing his hands together and curious to know what had happened to Miss Paxton in his own quiet polite voice. `There is nothing for you to worry about George she will be back home in a couple of days, putting her arm around his shoulder. The following day in the late afternoon Stella hears a car being driven up to the door. As she is looking out of the window, Burford is helping Susan out of the car, as she appears to have a heavy bandage around her ankle. Stella and George are now stood at the door as Susan slowly makes her way in with Burford's assistance. George is now getting the luggage out of the boot, as Stella is putting an extra cushion on the settee. `What on earth have you been doing to yourself?` Stella was asking her. Susan is now accusing herself of being an idiot. `I should never have allowed myself to get on that bloody raft!` At this point George is stood in the background waiting for instructions to make a hot drink for them or something. Susan now turns to George `Be an Angel and get us all a drink, I will have a Brandy and Soda`, he already knows what beverage Miss Delray will have, but has forgotten what Mr. Maunder has.

Burford can see that George is struggling to remember so he politely asks for a Vodka and Lemon with ice. After George has now left the room Stella would like to know who was the man that saved her friend from drowning?` `I think you are going to have to join the queue Stella because I would like to know as well` added Susan. `Somebody must know who it was` said Stella who is now looking at Burford who is shrugging his shoulders as he doesn't know either.

George has now returned with the drinks. As they are now sat comfortably (except for Susan who is in pain with her ankle). Burford tells the girls that he will find out who the mystery man is tomorrow, as he needs to be rewarded as he had risked his own life to save a person that he didn't even know. He is now looking at Susan for her to agree, which she wholeheartedly does. (Incidentally the river scene was filmed again the following day, but this time with an actor in women's clothing). The end scene in a saloon would be completed in the Studio with Susan after she has recovered. Susan breaks the silence by saying `I am absolutely starving' looking at her watch which says 4pm. She is now looking around for George again, (as she is totally ensconced on the settee and at the moment cannot move) he now comes in to take their glasses away. `I know its short notice, but is there any chance of you cooking a dinner George?` he replies that it has all been prepared and in 15 minutes will be ready for serving. `Excellent` said Susan who is now looking at Burford when she whispers `I just don't know what I would do without him, I really don't?` Burford nods his head in total agreement. Next day in the afternoon Burford rang Susan to tell her about the man who saved her life. `So what is his name?` asked Susan `Well according to his fact file, Daniel Peterton is a thirty year old father with one child`.

`His wife must be very proud of him?` `Well she probably would be if she was still with us` Burford replied. `You mean she has died?` `Yes I am afraid so, she apparently got salmonella poisoning when on vacation two years ago` `I am very sorry to hear that`. After a slight pause Burford explained to Susan that `Daniel was an extra in the film and was needed to be in the area where you got thrown into the river, and the rest you know about` `Is all this information on his fact file?` asked Susan `Yes, and it states that he joined us to get extra money to pay for his daughter's operation` `Operation for what?` asked Susan `Apparently there is a bone in her right foot that needs to be straightened out quickly otherwise she could be crippled for life` `What kind of money does he need?` `The file says that he needs $40,000 dollars` Burford now tells her. Susan for the moment reflects on the incident again, `All I can remember is that at one point, I thought that I would never be able to get out of that river alive, there was nothing to support me from going under, all my muscles were going numb with the freezing water. When suddenly there was this figure putting his arm around my neck, next thing I remember was laying on my back in the hospital` `How much would you like to meet this man?` asked Burford `Very much, why can you arrange it?` `Of course I can, then you can thank him yourself can't you?` `You bet I will`! A few days later Susan had another call from Burford to tell her that he had organised a special party for the making of "A Town Called Trouble" so she can meet her hero. Where there would be a gathering of people, rather than a meal for two at a restaurant which might turn out to be rather difficult for them both. As Susan arrived (her ankle now fully recovered) with her friend Stella for this special party she was looking for Burford so he could reveal who this brave gentleman is, but he hasn't arrived yet. Both girls are given a table nearest to the orchestra and a waiter has brought drinks for them. As Susan takes a sip of her drink she is looking at people sat at tables around the dance floor to see if there are any strangers (men of course) that could possibly be that special person.

She knows most of the people who are here, as they are nearly all into show business. She notices two men stood together having a beer or something and one of them is tall, very good looking, nicely built and dark hair. In fact she nudges Stella's arm and whispers to her that she hopes that the man stood over there is the man. Stella whispers back that she hopes it is as well.

CHAPTER SEVEN

Burford has now arrived with his wife and are now making their way towards them. `Have you seen him yet?` asked Burford `No, the trouble is Burford I have no idea what he looks like, I mean I can't go up to a stranger and say excuse me but did you save me from drowning the other day, can I?` Burford is now laughing. `Of course you can't` Burford is now looking around the room and eventually whispers in her ear `I have just seen him` `Where?` `Over there`. It turns out to be the very man that had caught her eye a short while ago` I will go and bring him over` said Burford. Stella is telling Susan that she thinks he looks real cool, and Susan can't wait to be introduced to him. `Susan this is Daniel Peterton I believe you wanted to have a word with him` she now stands up and gives him a kiss on his cheek. He gives her a kiss back, she tells him that he was extremely brave to do what he did, `Anybody would have done the same` he replied `I do not think so, but put it this way I'm glad you did` and that got them laughing together. As the night went on, surprisingly Susan and Daniel were in each other's company all the time.

They even danced together with the music being played by the small orchestra. Stella was rather fascinated by this unusual liaison between an actress who won best actress award and just a film extra. Nevertheless she was crossing her fingers that there could be romance in the air. Even now as Stella was having a dance with Burford she could see at the back of the hall that the couple were perfectly relaxed in each other's company, standing together near the wall with drinks in their hands.

As the evening was coming to a close, Daniel was seen helping Susan on with her cape, and she was smiling as he whispered something in her ear. Burford with his wife and Stella were now leaving the hotel just behind Susan and Daniel, they noticed that Susan gave Daniel a kiss on the cheek. Daniel now made his way out of the entrance and got into a taxi. Which now left Susan with Burford and his wife and Stella, who wanted to know if anything had materialised as they had been together all evening. `Well` said Susan `I think I am in love`

Stella is now looking into her friends eyes and saying `You are obviously joking you hardly know the man!` `Yes I know that!` said Susan, `But if I remember correctly wasn't there a man in Spain that you fell in love with, that you hardly knew?` `You mean Bruce?` `Yes that was him` Stella is now looking at Susan like a naughty girl looking at her mother after being put in her place. Now wanting to get back on the right side of her friend again, she says `Yes well maybe you have in a way fallen in love with him,...... are you seeing him again?` By now Burford and his wife have decided to leave the two girls to sort out their love lives, and they have suddenly disappeared in another taxi. The girls are now walking across the parking lot to their car as Susan tells Stella that Daniel is taking her to some Rock n Roll evening somewhere. Stella looks across at Susan and says `Hey that's good, I told you earlier that he looked cool`.

They are now being friendlier with each other and are laughing as they drive home. The following morning at breakfast Susan was telling Stella that she would like to know more about Daniel's daughter who is having great difficulty in walking. `Best thing to do is to ask Burford who can probably find out if and when Daniel's daughter is going to have the operation` `Yes I will do that` said Susan. A few days later, there was something else to get excited about there really was, it was her first date with Daniel. He came on time which was a good start, but his car wasn't getting any younger and was getting nearer to ending up on the scrap yard every time he used it. It seemed strange to see a personality such as Susan sitting in the front seat of what they would call years ago as an "old banger". To its eternal credit it got them to the Rock n Roll extravaganza ten miles out of town. It became obvious that they both were into that kind of music. At one point it was noticeable that Daniel had his arm around Susan's shoulders while she had her arm around his waist. Finishing the evening they called in at one of those fast food outlets and had a beef burger each, washed down with a coke. They were now holding hands across the table and looking into each other's eyes. As they were getting ready for leaving, Daniel went out first so he could get the engine started, as sometimes it took five minutes to get it warmed up. Susan had to go to the ladies. When she came out the manager was stood smiling at her. `You are Susan Paxton aren't you?` `Why yes` now showing that special smile that had made her lots of fans. `Would you mind if one of my staff takes a picture of you sat at the table, and me smiling down at you, as if I am serving you one of our favourite dishes?` `Of course I don't mind` `I think it will be good for my business` he hastened to tell her. The picture had now been taken and as she was leaving, the manager came running up to tell her `Your husband has left his mobile phone behind` She was going to tell him that it wasn't her husband, but after a few seconds of thought she just thanked him.

When she eventually got to Daniels car, he had only just been able to get it going. After an hour he was now stood outside her house telling her that he had enjoyed every minute of her company, and she told him the same. After saying goodnight with a kiss on her cheek, she was slowly walking to the front door purposely, he suddenly shouted `Susan!` When she came back to him he put his arms around her body and brought her into his, and with a special kiss that was to seal from now on a long and lasting affair. Stella who was looking down from an upstairs window, had now been witness to something that would shortly turn her own life completely around. There was some more tragic news in the following weeks. Susan and Stella have been informed that their dear old friend Burford Maunder had died. Apparently he had been working in his greenhouse when he started to have chest pains, his wife immediately called for the paramedics, but before they got there he had passed away.

So now the very man who was instrumental in the girl's success has now left the scene. At his funeral the Church was filled to capacity as expected. During his time at Metropolis Films he had turned ordinary people into household names, because of his skill of noticing talent in its early stages.

Life at the moment is falling apart for Stella it really is. Losing her great friend Kelly, as well there was the Michael Dawson shock, the man who loved Susan, who had chosen the wrong way to solve a major problem, and had committed suicide, of course not forgetting dear Burford. Finally Metropolis Film Corporation putting two films that had been lined up for her on the shelf, because quite rightly they were worried that after all her recent troubles, it would not let her so natural talent show thru. There is as well the growing possibility that Susan who is now in a serious love match with Daniel will want to share her home with him, which would make it very awkward for Stella to still live there, although Susan would never ask her best friend to leave. So Stella is going to have to sort out what she will do. Within the week and after deep thought she decides that she is going to make a new start.

The place she has chosen is London, she feels as though a complete turnaround is the only way to get rid of all the gremlins that are hanging around her life at the moment. So with deep regret and the understanding of what she is going thru, Metropolis Films are releasing her (temporarily they hope) from her contract. Susan is visibly shaken with her friend's decision to leave the U.S.A. and return to her roots, even though at the moment everything in her life has gone pear shaped. The girls have promised to keep in touch with each other. So now a week later she is back in her home town. As regarding money she got a good payoff from the studio, as well she still had money from the sale of her London home three years ago. Trying to find friends from years ago turned out to be a bad idea as they were nearly all married with children, or had left the area. She booked into a 4 star hotel till she found accommodation which she quickly soon sorted out.

Although it wasn't exactly the kind of property she had been accustomed to for the last three years. Just a semidetached bungalow in Northolt Park was to be her next home.

She was hoping to keep a low profile as she didn't want people to know, especially those who she would come into contact with, such as neighbours, new friends or anybody else for that matter to know that she was a Hollywood actress. People, she thought would be asking questions and telling her that she was a fool to walk out of the film industry, when most people would give their right arm to be in it. These were the very things that she wanted to escape from, which would keep reminding her of the recent turbulence in her life.

Getting some sort of job was a priority, only because it would keep her mind occupied. She could afford to be choosy as the money wasn't the issue at this point. She went into the City quite frequently, to look around the shops, go to coffee bars and the like. Firstly though she always called in at Newell's Agency that catered mostly for office staff, and on this particular day she was in luck. A large company in Wembley which manufactured light bulbs etc, needed someone to be the personal assistant to one of the Directors. During her interview she was asked the normal questions, one of which was what was her last employment, which she said was being the personal assistant to one of the film directors at Metropolis Film Studio. The personnel officer said to her with a smile. `Looking at you I would have thought you were one of the star's` Stella answered with a smile and comment `I wish`. She got the job offered to her later in the week as she had all the qualifications that were required.

Now she had this job it should give her confidence a boost. On her first day she was introduced to her new boss James Danvers a 35 year old married man with two teenage daughters. He also had an interest in formula one motor racing. Well that is what he told Stella as an introduction as to what made him tick. To Stella he was a good looking guy, with slightly greying hair at the temples and what looked like a good physique (but not as good as Bruce's).

A month has gone by since Stella started her new job, and as well as enjoying her new role. She had also made a few friends who are already married, but had managed to leave their husbands at home on Friday nights, which allowed her to join them. One night all the girls were sat around these two tables that had been brought together to accommodate them all, to laugh and tell stories. One of the girls whispered to the others `Look who has just come in?` as they looked around Stella was surprised to see James Danvers going to the bar. Clare, one of the girls who obviously knew the family well said `He has probably come to get out of the way of his wife` `Why what is wrong with her?` said another, Clare replied that `She has never been the same since she got an extensive driving ban for speeding while under the influence of drink two months ago`. As the time is now 11pm nearly all the girls have now gone home for the weekend.

Stella had just come out of the ladies room to get her coat on, when James came over with his pint of beer, `Why are you going home so soon?` he was quick to ask `Well everybody else seems to have gone home` `Let me buy you one, and we can share a taxi home` `Go on then` said Stella. As they sat down James told her that with him being so busy recently he hadn't any spare time to find out much about her. `All I know is that you are single and that you have been living in America for the last three years and that you are beautiful` `I have heard that you say that to all the girls` `That isn't true Stella, I would only say it to girls who are beautiful, and believe me that is what you are, beautiful` `Mr. Danvers what would your wife say if she saw you chatting me up?` `Well the way she is at the moment I don't think that she would be too bothered` `Why is that?` `She blames me, why I don't know, because it was her that got caught speeding while over the limit, I wouldn't mind but I wasn't even in the bloody car`.' Stella is now standing up for her Boss by saying that `She is obviously being a very unreasonable woman` `You are the first person that has been on my side` and is now leaning over and giving her a kiss on the cheek. Meanwhile the bell has rung for "Time gentleman please" Stella has now stood up and is trying to get her coat on, but James is there to help her on with it. As they go outside there is a taxi just about to drive away, but the driver winds his window down to tell them he will be back in ten minutes.

As it is now early October when the nights are darker and longer and there is that certain chill in the air, all you want to do is get home to that fire and put your slippers on. That is what is going thru Stella's mind, but at the moment James is stood right behind her shielding her, she can feel the warmth of his body. There is also that comfortable acceptance of each other's company, even when there is a prolonged silence. The taxi has now arrived back and they both get in. James instructs the driver to drop Stella off first. As the car pulls up outside her house James gets out and opens the door for her where she is now returning his kiss. James looks out of the taxi window and shouts `See you Monday and don't be late'.

On the Saturday night as Stella is sat on her settee watching T.V. with a few chocolates and her favourite drink Gin and Orange with ice. She can hear some sort of squeaking noise coming from outside. She looks out of the window and apart from the wind and rain, there appears to be nothing there. On settling down it's there again. So this time she goes to the front door, as she opens it, a black and white kitten is looking up at her, the cat is wet thru. She has now brought the kitten inside and got an old towel and dried it in front of the fire. After a while it stopped crying. So what was she going to do with it, hand it over to Animal Trust to take away or keep it for herself? The toss of a coin decided that she would keep it. She had thought of a name to give the kitten after looking for evidence that it was a male, it would now be called "Burf" after her great old friend Burford Maunder. Every Sunday was Supermarket day and she would now get cat food for her new lodger.

Monday was now here and when she went into the office, she noticed that James was in a no happier mood than he was last week. When the office was empty except for those two, Stella asked `Have you and your wife settled your differences?` `Not really because she now doesn't want to go to the German Grand Prix next weekend.

She says that she is sick to death of looking at cars especially now that she has been disqualified, and that I would have to go on my own for a change.` `Yes you told me that you like motor racing` `The thing is I had booked a hotel a month ago for me and her`. `Do you want me to ring the hotel and see if I can change your twin bedroom to a single? Stella now asked him. James after being deep in thought tells her `No just keep it as it is` `Do you like wasting money Mr. Danvers?` `Please Stella I think we know each other well enough, where you can now call me James` Stella is now smiling as she says `That's fine by me James` `Now where was I` said James. `Something to do with booking a room I think James` `Oh yes I was going to say, what's money anyway, you can't take it with you` Stella has an idea what he is going to say next she really has`. `I have a great idea` said James `What is that?' said Stella who is now leaning back on her chair with her arms folded `Why don't you come instead, I promise that you will enjoy yourself". Stella decided to play him at his own game, `Do you mean that we will have to sleep in the same room?`

`Yes, but I promise that I won't look'

`Look at what?`

`You know`

`No I don't know`

`I will turn off the light before you get undressed`

`I would like the bed nearest the window`

`Okay that's fine`

`There will be two beds won't there?`

`Yes I think so, why would a double bed worry you?`

`Depends`

`Depends on what?`

`Whether I will be allowed to get to sleep or not`

`Why shouldn't you?`

`I don't know it's just a feeling that I get`

`I promise you will be sleeping before 3am`

`Okay I will come`. This week they would both need to be cautious. James didn't want anybody to be aware of his infatuation for Stella, and she didn't want any of her new friends to know what was happening next weekend in Germany. At 5.30pm on the Friday the pair of them board the plane separately, but have seats next to each other as James had booked the flight at the same time as the hotel. Now an hour or so later Stella and her boss are now going up in the elevator to their hotel room. When James had put the key in the door and opened it, Stella was still coming down the corridor.

He quickly came back out into the corridor with a look of (supposedly) sheer disappointment to tell her that there weren't two single beds, but just one big double bed. When she got inside the room and closed the door, she told him in no uncertain terms `You knew damn well that it would be a double bed, didn't you!?` he was now stood like a naughty schoolboy in front of his teacher. `Yes I have to admit that I did know, because I rang the hotel later to change it to a double bedroom, I was just hoping that you would want to sleep with me that's all` `Well I do want to sleep with you but I hope you know that if your wife finds out, you know that you will be a dead man walking don't you?`

`I will just have to take that chance won't I`, she now puts her lips on his and gives him a gentle kiss, telling him he is a brave man.

After the evening meal and a few drinks they are soon in bed, after a few passionate kisses Stella is now taking James's pyjamas off.

Her naked body is now underneath his, one of her hands is running thru his head of hair, while the other one is first making sure he has protection in place, and secondly making sure he has a full erection so that she will shortly achieve the satisfaction she desires, and hopefully his as well. Mission accomplished they now fall asleep in each other's arms. If at this point you are worrying who is looking after Stella's kitten "Burf". I can tell you that it was arranged that her neighbour 83year old Mrs. Gibbs would look after it.

On the Saturday morning the two of them were doing some window shopping in Hockenheim city centre, with Stella linking arms with James and calling into a few coffee shops. Last night must have been a night to remember as they stopped a few times to share a kiss.

They bought some bread and were now making their way to the lake in the park. Where they would soon be surrounded by a million birds scrambling round looking for all the crumbs. When the bread had all gone, the birds slowly began to leave the scene. That left them both another half -hour just talking to each other, at one point James was now putting the now empty bread wrapper into the bin at the side of the seat, he said to her `I have been meaning to ask you since you came to work for us` . `What have you been meaning to ask me?` asked Stella as she was looking into his hazel eyes. `It's just that I have seen someone somewhere that looks very much like you, but I cannot recollect who it was, or even where, you haven't got a twin sister have you?` `No I`m afraid that I haven't, but probably one day you will find out who it was and where` `Well I hope so because it's really bugging me`. She is now resting her head on his shoulder just gazing at the ripples on the lake, and thinking to herself how people's lives can change ever so quickly, like hers has done. It was only a few months ago that she was in Kenya with the friend that she loved to be with, where they shared each other's lives along with pure affection for each other. Then almost at the snap of a finger it all dissolved in a most horrible way. And that now at this moment she is having a naughty weekend with someone she hardly knows, sat on a park seat at the side of a lake somewhere in Germany.

CHAPTER EIGHT

They were now making their way slowly back to their hotel, where they would have a drink at the bar and go back to their room. James wanted a shower, but meaning as a joke, he suggested that they had one together looking at Stella with a cheeky grin, surprisingly she was all for it. So for over 10 minutes they were as one in that soap splattered cubicle doing what comes naturally. After the evening meal they got talking to a couple in their fifties, who had travelled from Yorkshire for the race.

The couples had met each other on the Friday when they were checking in. Now sat in the hotel lounge they came across as a decent couple and who were very knowledgeable as regarding the statistics of formula one. They were even coming out with statistics that even James wasn't aware of. Now to Stella it was all very boring, in fact watching hens lay eggs would have been more interesting, it really would. Realistically she was just a guest of James, and she would be the first to put her hand up and say that she knew nothing at all about racing cars.

When the middle aged couple retired for the evening, both James and Stella breathed a sigh of relief and immediately sank back into their nice easy chairs. After a short pause Stella was now telling James that `I saw the lady looking at the ring on your finger and then looking at my left hand, where there was no ring. So I think it is pretty certain that she knows that we are not married to each other, and as well realising that I obviously didn't know anything about racing cars which must have seemed a bit unusual`. Well that is their problem, not ours` said James. `I suppose you are ready for bed now are you?` asked Stella as she snuggled up to him at the same time looking for a kiss, which he gave her. `That was the best night's sleep I never got' said James as he got out of bed the following morning leaving Stella still in bed hugging a pillow, trying to tell James that she wanted to stay there till lunchtime. He jumped back into the bed took the pillow off her and gave her a passionate kiss, which suddenly brought her back to reality. Although she tried to be accommodating to the excitement that James was building up to for the race this afternoon, unfortunately it wasn't going to work for her. She would now have to rely on the fact that this was just simply a weekend away with her boss, that would let them both know that they were made for each other. Even for the fact that he loved motor racing and she didn't. After the race James asked her what part of the race did she like best? she replied `When the driver's were squirting each other with champagne'. Not surprisingly James is now shaking his head from side to side. When they arrived back in London James thanked her for her company, and was sorry that she didn't quite like the motor racing, but everything else was wonderful, giving her a wink and a kiss. Stella told him that she couldn't have been with anyone better. She went in one direction and he went in the other, home to his wife.

Back in the office on the Monday morning he comes in and says good morning to Stella and a few other girls that work in the office.

At 10am he emerges from his own private office and asks for Miss Delray to go into his office. She takes her pen and pad, when inside James asks her how she is after her trip. She answers `To be honest James after the weekend and not getting much sleep, I am tired out, I really am.` `Do you want to go home and catch up?`

`If that's alright with you I will` `Of course it is, I feel a bit the same way but the company needs me here I'm afraid` `I will make an excuse that you have a tummy bug` `By the way was your wife happy to see you back home on Sunday? did she have your slippers in front of the fire waiting for you?` James is looking at her as though she must have forgotten who she was talking about. `No I am afraid that she is still giving me a hard time, because I can drive my car around but she can't`. On her way home Stella felt sorry for James having to put up with someone, especially his wife who apparently, when anything went wrong he would have to take the blame. She was quite sure in her own mind, she herself would never be aggressive quite like that.

During the next few weeks the same ritual of this relationship continued. Where nobody at work would get the slightest inkling that there was anything going on between the two of them. During the week their meetings were usually on Tuesday, and Friday's when instead of playing in the work's dart team, and on Friday's when he would normally be down at his local. He instead would now be at Stella's house.

One Tuesday when he came, his face expression said it all. `Has something happened at home?` asked Stella `She has been at me again saying that I was stupid when I put a valuable dish in the oven, and it cracked because of the heat` `So was it an accident?` `Yes it was but she said I was useless and so as a result there was another argument` after a short pause he looked at Stella like a man downtrodden and said `I really want to leave her` `What about your two daughters, they need you to be there till they are of age to make their own decisions?` `Yes you are right but would you be willing to wait another three years?` They sit down in the living room to talk about this problem. Stella tells James that she doesn't want to be the woman who has come between a man and his wife, all because the wife is going thru a phase in her life where she is very agitated and aggressive.

He is now asking Stella `How long is she going to be like this?` he is looking at Stella for some comforting words. `I wouldn't even like to hazard a guess, she probably doesn't even know herself, but if you have been married for sixteen years I think you should give her more time for her to get back to normal...... certainly more than you are doing'.

James is now gazing at a picture on the wall, he isn't studying its meaning, but just using it as an object to concentrate on a big decision in his life. After a few minutes he tells Stella that he thinks that she is right, and that deep down he doesn't really want to leave his wife. Also that not seeing his daughters on a regular basis, would be a big body blow to him. Looking at Stella he said `I thought that you and me got on really well together?` `We do and if you were a single man I would be there for you without a doubt, but I am not prepared to carry on being your mistress even so` `Do you think we should finish our relationship?` said James with a big sigh `Yes I am afraid I do because I have a life too, and I eventually want the same as you, a family including at least two children` James was now seeing the positive side of life, rather than the negative. Usually a relationship like what they had, meant that someone was going to be eventually hurt. So James is now putting his coat on, and is now giving Stella a big hug before he left, as well having a borrowed smile and telling her not to be late tomorrow.

The rest of the week in the office was just as though nothing had ever happened. Nevertheless she felt as though there was now nothing left but just a brick wall between the two of them.

It might be better to move on as there was never going to be that same chemistry again.

On the Friday when all the other office girls had gone home, she stayed behind on purpose. As she went into his office he was tidying things away for the weekend, she just felt so sorry for him and even for herself. He looked up and saw her, he suddenly gave her that same wonderful smile that he had regularly given her in that special month that they had shared together. Now he saw the sadness in her face, and suddenly his lovely smile had gone. A few seconds later he came round from his desk and as he was now hugging her, he said `You are not coming back to work next week are you?` she now pulled away from him to look into his tear filled eyes. In the nicest possible way she said `No I won't be coming in again` he pulled her in close again as though he wanted to hold on to her as long as he could. Although she was basically feeling just the same as he was, she told him that she would have to go now. As she opened the door to leave, Stella turned around to wish him all the best for the future, and as well hoped that he and his wife would find again that special love that at the moment was missing. He asked her if she would just stand still for a few seconds for his mind to absorb this beautiful woman who played a small but significant part in his life. She did and then she was gone.

So if we review Stella's life up to the present moment. It's almost two months ago that she came back to London from the U.S.A. she didn't come back because she was fed up, on the contrary she loved it over there. It was just that everything seemed to go wrong all at the same time (which we have already gone into). Which in her mind meant coming back to her roots and hopefully rerouting back to the top. She is at the moment looking out for another job that might help her to achieve this. Although she isn't short of money by any means that is not the problem. What she wants is to meet new friends. Being in London is and always will be a terrific place to live, but to be happy and having friends is the key. It is now Friday afternoon Stella has decided to spend a day in London, so taking the car would be a bad idea it really would. So getting an Oyster all day train pass was the best choice. She had an Interview at 11.30am at a manufacturer of spectacles, where she had got into the last two.

As she left the interview at 12.15pm she was quietly confident.

After looking at some of the latest fashions at various fashion houses, she had her lunch at a top department store. While having a soup of the day she noticed that the time was now 1.15pm she was now wondering what Susan would be doing at this moment in Los Angeles.

She was thinking of giving her a call, because she promised that she would keep in contact. Now suddenly she can't do that because she has just realized that the time in Los Angeles is now 5.15am, and Susan would still be in bed. A few thoughts were now entering her head, is Susan still in a relationship with Daniel Peterton, who dramatically saved her from drowning? Or would their romance have now fizzled out by now? This was something that she would like to know, but she is saying to herself that if she doesn't make the effort she will never find out. As well she wants to give Susan her phone number so they can communicate, as it is nearly two months since they were last together. When she emerged from the store she felt an icy blast, after all it was the end of October and the pavements were littered with leaves. She was walking down the Edgware road and came to Marble Arch. A nice quiet stroll thru Hyde park to see all the trees now beginning to show their true colours, a rusty green appearance was very evident.

There was a man stood near the Peter Pan statue, he was holding his hand out with what looked like nuts, and amazingly the birds were taking their turn of eating out of his hand. Someone who could see that Stella was astonished by what she had seen, went up to her and told her that the man had been doing this procedure for at least ten years. She could tell just by looking at his face that he was just a happy man in his own little world.

Stella was now making her way to the Ring, a bridge that spanned the Serpentine lake, that would lead out onto Knightsbridge. With the weather being rather chilly there were not many people about. As Stella was in no particular hurry, she noticed a middle aged lady getting out of her car with her handbag and a white poodle at her side. Presumably for their daily walk. She was about 25yds in front of Stella and going in the same direction.

Stella had now stopped to look over the wall of the bridge at some swans, that had now assembled on the grass below her. A few moments later she heard someone behind her coughing, a rather nervous cough she thought.

As she turned around to see who it was, she saw a tall youth with a sporting track suit on. He suddenly started to walk quite quickly, continuously looking round as if he was assessing the situation around him. Maybe with Stella stood still she wouldn't be in his calculations. He has now put his hood over his head and is now running towards the woman with the poodle. Stella now realising that something rather nasty is about to happen, has as well started to run and at the moment is about sixty yards behind the hooded youth. Just before he makes a grab for her handbag, the lady has realized what is about to happen and is now holding on to her bag tightly. She is now screaming for help which has now got Stella running flat out. The youth is determined to take possession of her bag, and is not going to allow this old woman to deny him.

He has now forced her into a precarious position where she has had to release the handbag. At the same time she has lost her balance and has now fallen the 20ft into the lake. Stella is now almost there, she sees that the hoodlum is now in full sprint down some steps and will soon be out of view.

There is no time to think, she has now taken off her scarf, coat and leg boots and put her handbag under her coat, and has now jumped into the freezing lake. At the same time hitting her arm into the stone support of the bridge, which is suddenly very painful even before she hits the water. The sudden coldness of the water has suddenly taken her breath away. She remembers from her schooldays that when a person is drowning they surface twice, and when they go down again for the third time they stay there.

At the moment Stella is flapping her arms and kicking with her legs to stay afloat waiting for the lady to surface, which by now surely must be her second time. There is a splashing of water to her left, she makes a grab for the woman and gets hold of her collar. Stella's arm is killing her as she slowly manipulates her to safety. By this time there is a small crowd cheering and clapping from the bridge, and about four men are ready to help them on to dry land. Two caring motorists have gone to their cars to bring blankets to wrap around them, another man has assured Stella that an ambulance is now on its way. Both women are shivering uncontrollably, they really are, of the two women Stella amazingly seems to have come out of this the worst. Within the next ten minutes they have been driven by two ambulances to the hospital, where they are rushed thru the corridors to the Emergency department and attended to straight away. Someone who was in the small crowd had put Stella's belongings into the ambulance which enabled the police to find out who she was. So who was the other lady? Could it possibly be her mother? there was just nothing that would tell them. They couldn't ask either lady at this point as they both had hypothermia, especially Stella who as well had a bad injury to her arm. Meanwhile the husband of the older lady is at home frantic with worry, as his wife should have been home an hour ago according to his watch that he has referred to a dozen times already. Normally she always walks into the house at around 3.15pm it is now almost 4.20pm. Their maid comes into the lounge with a very worried look and is also wringing her hands to prove it. He has been trying to get her on her mobile phone but to no avail. He tells Mary that he now is going to Hyde Park, as that is one of her favourite walks when she takes "Sugar" her poodle, which is about two miles away.

He quickly gets in to his Limousine and is now making his way there. He knows that something bad must have happened, and there is no shortage of possibilities going thru his mind. It isn't usually like him but he was now banging on his steering wheel as the traffic lights have turned to red. He knows where she normally parks her car. He gets a short relief of the mental torture that he is going thru, as he now sees in the distance her white B.M.W. parked on the bridge. After getting out of his car he is now running towards her car, but not as quick as he would like (he is over 50), he tries the doors all of which are locked. The short relief he had a few minutes ago has now gone back to panic stations, which at his time of life he can do well without. He is now just stood there with his hands on his hips looking in all directions. His breathing is now laboured, it's not that he is unfit it is just that his adorable wife is out there somewhere, and he wants to know where and quick.

As a last resort he is now leaning on his wife's car bringing out his mobile to ask the police if they had any information, relating to a middle aged lady being taken to any of the hospitals in the vicinity in the last two hours. He was now put on hold till they had checked. They came back that at the moment there was nothing coming thru to their call centres concerning this lady. As soon as there is they will contact him straight away. It is getting dark now and a few degrees colder as he gets back into his car waiting for that vital information. Something else that has entered his already troubled mind, is that the dog is not anywhere to be seen either.

He always remembers his father telling him that whenever and whatever goes wrong in your life, the world will not stop and give you sympathy, (apart from the family) in other words if you have a cross to bear you will have to carry it yourself. For the first time in his life he is now extremely worried as he is sat in his car, being in the dark and looking at buses going past, where workers and their mates are laughing and joking on their way home for the weekend.

As well people in cars who give him a quick glance as they speed past his parked car not knowing, or seeming to care that the man who they are looking at could be possibly about to be given very disturbing news. Suddenly his mobile was playing one of those silly tunes that yesterday was acceptable, but today it isn't. Like a greyhound out of the trap he now had the phone up against his ear, his heart is now beating quicker than a machine gun dispatching bullets. His concentration is so intense that his eyeballs are moving in all directions, as if a fly was trying to find a way out of his car, and he was watching its every move. `Is that Mr. Ogden?` a ladies voice said. `Yes it is have you any news?` `Yes we have, we think that it is your wife that was admitted to St. Mary's hospital at 3.15pm today along with another lady, could that possibly be her daughter?` `We haven't got a daughter` now looking at the phone as if it's just bitten a piece off his ear. `Mm rather strange` said the lady, `but anyway good luck, I hope that they are both okay` he is now looking at the phone and saying to himself` — `Daughter, what the fuck is she on about?` Within 10 minutes he is now stood in the reception of St. Mary's hospital patiently waiting in a queue for information that will take him to his wife's bedside. At the moment there is an old lady moaning to the young receptionist about her bunion, that is giving her pain along with the most boring details of how the fucking thing started to flare up, at the same time not realising the long queue that had built up behind her.

Mr. Ogden was thinking that his wife could be at death's door for all this old woman knows.

Eventually another lady receptionist had come to the desk to help out, which quickly brought Mr. Ogden to the head of the queue. She informed him that his wife is in ward 18. `In which direction do I go?` `Straight down there`, pointing to a long corridor with her recently manicured finger nails, turn left and you can either use the elevator or the stairs, you are then aiming for the second floor and ward 18` `Thank you very much` said Mr. Ogden. She gave him one of those meaningless smiles that we all get, which even in the present circumstances are still comforting nevertheless. `At last` he said to himself as ward 18 suddenly came into view. As he entered, a nurse with a folder held close to her chest asked `Who have you come to see?` `Martha Ogden` `Oh Martha follow me` as they were approaching her bed he didn't know what to expect he really didn't. He certainly didn't expect to see her smiling at him, but she was, it could be a genuine smile, or it could be a borrowed smile which would let him know that she was far from well. He was now taking his coat off and pulling a chair up to her bedside. He gave her a kiss on the forehead and was now holding her hand. Looking into her eyes he could tell that she wanted to tell him what happened, but at the same time there were a million questions that he wanted to ask her. Obviously she was in no fit state to answer them.

One question she had to ask him was `Where is my "Sugar" have you found him?` The last thing he wanted to do was to give her the extra worry that her beloved poodle had gone missing. Though he feels as though he should, and indeed he now tells her the truth `It looks as though the dog has been frightened by what happened and has now run away`. But he did promise her that before she comes home it will be found, and looking into his eyes she believed him.

It was now time to go, and after putting his overcoat on, he gave her another kiss on the forehead and slowly made his way out of the ward. As he was about to get into the elevator, he was joined by a policeman and a detective. `Is it Mr. Ogden?` `Yes it is have you come to see me about my wife?` `Yes we have` The elevator has now arrived at the ground floor. As they get out, the detective invited him into a quiet room of the hospital.

Within a few moments they were sat around a table. `Would you like a coffee Mr. Ogden?` `Yes please but no sugar` `Coming up` said the policeman. `Are you aware that your wife was within a whisker of dying this afternoon?` Mr. Ogden is now looking horrified, `Why what happened?` `Your wife was the victim of a mugger, who after a struggle managed to snatch her hand bag, which unbalanced her and she fell into the lake` `My wife can't swim` now looking at both men in quick succession. `Well luckily for your wife, there was a young lady who could swim, and she jumped in after her and managed to pull her to safety` `My god I didn't know this, my wife never said anything` `Yes but you must understand that your wife at the moment isn't quite at the races yet is she? it will all come back slowly to her eventually` `Who is this young woman? I must see her to tell her that I feel indebted to her for the rest of my life` `Well that is I am afraid impossible at the moment` `Why?` `Because she is in intensive care at the moment due to complications affecting her breathing, as she injured her shoulder diving in to save your wife's life`. Mr. Ogden is now looking towards the window with tears in his eyes. The detective isn't going to say anything else till Mr. Ogden gets control over himself.

After a minute or two of wiping his eyes, he looks away from the window to the two policemen and says that `If anything happens to that poor girl I will never have peace of mind again`. `By the way did your wife have a white poodle with her when this attack happened?` Now with a look of sheer relief he says `Yes she did, why have you found it?' `Yes` `Where was it?` `It was sat at the side of a white B.M.W car` `That is my wife's car` `Another witness said he saw the dog running away from the incident after your wife had fallen in the lake` `Oh I am so glad that you found it, because it would have broken my wife's heart to have lost it`.

After finishing their coffee's, the three of them were now leaving the room with the detective putting his hand on Mr. Ogden's shoulder telling him to go home and get a good night's sleep, and when he comes in tomorrow there may be some good news about his wife and also Miss Delray.

CHAPTER NINE

Next day he got a phone call from the hospital, to come and pick his wife up. Mr. Ogden must have told Mary last night when he got home, that `It was a young lady that had dived in to the lake to save her life, and that the girl is now in Intensive Care`. `I pray for that poor girl and hope she makes a full recovery` said Mary looking at her employer with a sad face. On arrival at the hospital the first thing he wanted to know was `How is Miss Delray in intensive care?` `The consultant has just let us know that there is some improvement, but it will be another week at least before any decision is made to release her from hospital` `I so much wanted to see her before I go` `Go where?` `I am going to Turin tomorrow to organise a big Fashion show for a top fashion designer from Italy and I will be gone for a fortnight with my wife, as we are also hoping to have a short skiing vacation for a few days, depending how well my wife feels`. `Sounds like an exciting business to be in?` said the nurse. `I am the managing director of a company that organises fashion shows all over the world, and I have some of the best models in Europe on my books`. Mr Ogden asked the nurse if any of Miss Delray's family had been to see her yet` `The police have made enquiries to see if she has any relatives, the only one she has is her grandmother who is in a hospice suffering from dementia, who told us that she has never heard of anyone called Stella Delray.

So at the moment I am afraid that she is on her own` `What about a boyfriend?` `All I can say is that she doesn't have any rings on her fingers` `Anyway when I get back in a fortnight, when she has hopefully been released from hospital, me and my wife will arrange to meet her and say a big thank you`. `Well I certainly do hope that she pulls thru so that you can see her` `So do I, very much so`

During the following two weeks Stella makes a welcome return to full health, and has been discharged and is now back home with her cat "Burf". Who for the last fortnight has been looked after by Mrs. Gibbs next door. A few days later she gets a call from the hospital telling her that `Mr. Ogden and his wife have now returned from their vacation, and have asked us for your phone number so they can give you a call to arrange a meeting, is that okay by you?` `Yes I look forward to that` said Stella. Two days later Mr. Ogden gives her a call and he asks her to meet them in the lounge of a five star hotel in Leicester Square at 8pm. Stella tells him that she looks forward to meeting them. Moving on Stella has now arrived at the hotel at 7.50pm and goes to reception to ask if a Mr. Ogden and his wife have arrived yet. The receptionist is now looking towards a certain table and chairs which at the moment are unoccupied, and tells her not yet. Stella has now got her favourite drink, and is stood talking to a young man who she recognises from her schooldays, and who is employed by the hotel.

The Ogden's have now arrived at the hotel, they order some drinks as they are taking their coats off. They are now sat at their usual table, and after getting comfortable they start to look around for Stella, who although they don't know what she looks like, they have built up a picture in their own mind as to what she may look like.

At the moment there seems to be no one here that does. Martha is looking at this particular young lady who has been talking to this waiter for a short while. She is now nudging her husband's arm, who has been watching a football match on the hotels sports screen `What is it dear?` he asked, feeling rather annoyed with this sudden intrusion.

`I have just noticed a girl over there talking to that waiter, she is tall and very beautiful, how would she rate up against your models?` After looking at her he said `I would think that she probably is a model already, especially as you say with her being tall, nice figure and a beautiful face. If she isn't a model already she should be`.

He turns around quickly to look at the screen because a goal has been scored. Martha went to the reception to ask for a menu, as she was browsing thru it, the receptionist is now telling her that a young lady was asking if you had come in yet. Martha was looking around the lounge quite excitedly asking at the same time `Where is she, is she in the room?` `Yes` `Where?` `The tall girl who is talking to the waiter. She went quickly back to Graham and took the drink out of his hand. `What are you doing now!` he snapped. `I want you now to look at the girl who saved my life` `Have you found out who she is?` `Yes I have` at this point Graham is now very eager to know. `Go on then quickly show me` `It's the tall girl I showed you earlier` `Are you winding me up, who told you?` `Reception told me that she had been asking for us`. By now Stella had got rid of the waiter who was pestering her to go out with him, but she had noticed a wedding ring on his finger. So she told him that she would, but only if it would be alright with his wife and kids.

That was why after looking at her watch she decided to put her coat on as it was obvious at the time of 8.40pm that the Ogden's were not coming.

She was now walking towards the entrance. She had to walk past the Ogden's who were now stood up. Martha called her name `Stella!` who had now turned round and saw this lady with tears in her eyes coming up to her with her arms outstretched. Martha now knew for certain that she was the stranger that had come into her life at a very critical time, and that her bravery would allow her to live her full life thru. Even Graham was full of tears now.

Stella and Martha must have been hugging for five minutes, as Graham was waiting patiently to also show his emotions by getting in his hugs as well. Graham suggested that they should have a meal at the hotel and celebrate with champagne to hopefully have a long and lasting friendship.

During the meal and observing from a distance, you would think that Stella must have known the Ogden's for years. In their conversations it turned out that Graham was 52 and Martha 50, we are all aware that Stella is now 26. They have three sons, Terry married with two sons and a daughter living in Chicago, Charles 28, married with one child living in South Africa, and Brian who is 22 single and has an apartment living in London. Stella tells her new friends that she and her best friend went to live in Los Angeles over three years ago, and for the moment that is all she will say.

She has told them that one day they will hear the full story. Stella is now looking at her watch it is now

11.45pm and the night has simply flown by. She tells them that she will have to run to the Tube station, or she will be very late getting home. Graham has told Stella with the full backing of Martha that she will be staying at their home in Knightsbridge, and that he is not going to take no for an answer. Martha puts her arm around this beautiful girl letting her know that they have really taken to her, almost like a daughter which they were never blessed with. On their way home in a taxi, Graham was sat in the front while Stella was falling asleep on Martha's shoulder in the back. Getting out of the taxi Stella was now wide awake and looking at this beautiful house, which was the home of Graham and Martha. Later in the kitchen Martha was making cocoa for the three of them, she also brought Stella one of her many robes to wear, in which she looked quite stunning.

With it being a six bedroom house and each with its own en-suite, there wasn't going to be any difficulty in finding accommodation for her. The following morning at breakfast Stella was introduced to Mary, whose immediate reaction was that she was overwhelmed by the elegance and beauty of this girl, whose hand she was now holding. She told Stella that what she did that terrible day was braver than the brave, and that the total commitment that she gave was for a stranger and not herself. Stella thanked her for her kind words.

Later in the morning Stella was shown around the house and gardens by Martha, while Graham was on his computer doing business which extended around the world. Stella was told by Martha that her husband owned the biggest model agency in Gt. Britain, after Stella had been wanting to know what kind of business that he ran, to substantiate a house of this size especially in such an affluent part of London, which Knightsbridge is. As they were now going back into the house, Martha took Stella into the lounge where Mary was waiting to bring them coffee. `Make that three Mary!` as Graham now entered the room and sat beside his wife. `So Stella, what do you think of the house?` asked Graham. Stella was now smiling showing her immaculate white teeth. `All I can say is that this is one of the best houses I have ever stayed in, and I have stayed in a few nice ones` Graham and Martha are now looking at each other as much as to say `Who is this intriguing girl in our midst who has been in similar homes to ours?` `Can you elaborate on where some of these houses were?` asked Graham.

`One is a friend of mine who won an Oscar for best supporting actress last year` They are now looking at each other again probably thinking how has she got to be friends with movie stars. Graham is now clicking his fingers trying to remember who it was that won that Oscar. Stella tells him that her first name is Susan, `Of course I now remember it was Susan Paxton, how on earth did you become friends with her?` `We went to school together and grew up together just down the road from here in St. John's Wood` `You mean she is English?`

`Of course` `Well I never knew that, I thought she was an American`. After a brief pause Martha asked `Where was the other house?` `Marbella in Spain which Greg Cornwell owns, which leads out on to a wonderful beach` `Yes I have heard of him, I do believe he is a bit of a heart throb, were you and him friends as well?` looking now at Stella with a wry smile. `Very much so, but I got more infatuated with his best friend, but only for a week though.

`A week is that all, why what happened?` Stella at this point didn't want to say anything else, because she knew that if she carried on it would bring Kelly into the story, which in turn would only bring tears.

Martha realising that she had touched on something tender went over and put her arm around her shoulders, just like a daughter who has had a nasty fall and is now comforted by her mother. Graham thinks it would be a good idea for him to go back to his computer room, rather than be embroiled in matters of the heart.

Martha is for a few minutes comforting this beautiful girl, by straightening her hair gently, and giving her a kiss on her forehead.

Martha is beginning to understand that there is a sad part of Stella's life that she wants to hide away, and hopefully when the time is right she will tell her. Stella is slowly coming back to her normal self and apologises to Martha for being a big softy. `You don't need to apologise, it seems to me that you have been thru enough just lately'. Graham had now come back into the lounge and went straight up to Stella put his arms around her, looked into her face and told her, that from now on, any troubles she has will be their troubles as well. `Do you feel as though you want to go home now?` asked Martha. `Well yes I do because I have a kitten to look after, for instance last night because I was meeting you, or even when I am away for a few days, Mrs. Gibbs next door looks after it in her home`.

Stella, after getting her things together is now asking if they are ready to take her home? `Of course we are darling, we wouldn't in any circumstances let you go home on your own` going up to her and giving her a hug. Anyone can see that the couple especially Martha is besotted with Stella. For some reason Martha doesn't like the idea of Stella living on her own, she would rather have her live with them. When they arrive at Stella's house they are invited in for a coffee.

When Graham and Martha are sat comfortably in this nice but rather small lounge area, Stella tells them that she will go next door for her cat. After a few minutes she is back with it in her arms and puts it on the rug. Graham is playing with it and it suddenly scratches him and runs behind the settee. Stella is now going thru the post and tells them that there is a letter from the company who make lenses for spectacles, and is now confidently opening it. Graham and Martha are looking at her face for a happy reaction, but suddenly her expression changes from a smile to a frown, which tells them that she has bad news. `What has happened?` asks Martha, Stella passes the letter to Martha who is now getting her glasses out to read it. `Oh dear it says that you just failed to get the job, and wishes you good luck for the future`. `So what will you do now?` asks Graham, `Well` said Stella suddenly feeling rather uncomfortable says `Me and a friend went on a night out with some other ladies a few weeks ago.

A week later one of the ladies told my friend that she was going to offer me a job being a model for her agency, but my friend told her that because of a serious injury, I would be in hospital for a fortnight.

So the lady said she would wait until I was better, so I will phone my friend to let the lady know that I am now well again. Now we have a situation where Martha is now looking daggers at Graham, as he obviously isn't getting the message that Stella hasn't now got a job. Martha asks Stella if she would like to come to a party at their house next Saturday. `I would love to` said Stella as she was finishing off her coffee `It's for one of Graham's longest serving employees, who is retiring and going to live in. Mallorca` `I will buy a new dress for the occasion `There will be a few important people there` said Martha. `You will be the belle of the ball `remarked Graham as he was now putting his coat back on to go home. After giving them both a hug they were now leaving. Stella was waving to them as they were driving off.

On the way home Martha was absolutely livid with Graham, `What have I done?` suddenly feeling the wrath of his wife. `It's what you haven't done that has really annoyed me!` `Why what should I have done?` `That poor girl is out of a job, a girl that I think of as a daughter that we never had, also the most important thing of all is that she risked her life to save mine, and I already think the world of her` `Well I also think that she is a wonderful girl, and I always will for what she did` replied Graham. `Yes but the point is that you yourself said last night that you thought that she must be a top model by her elegance and her looks`

`Yes I did and I meant it` `Well in that case the opportunity presented itself, for you to ask her to join your company, and the bottom line is that you indirectly refused her !` After a few moments thought he turned round to his wife and said `Yes I can now see that I have been a complete idiot, and I will on Saturday tell her that as from Monday she will be one of my top models`. `Well if you don't I can assure you that you will be sleeping in another bedroom and I'm serious!`. Saturday was now here and Stella had been shopping in Bond Street, and bought a sparkling blue gown for the special occasion at the Ogden's tonight. As she was driving up to the house, there were dozens of cars outside, with people milling around the front door. So she went to the back of the house where she found Martha arranging with Mary and a few other caterers how they should present the food. As she went into the kitchen Martha turned around. `Stella what are you coming into the back of the house for?` with a smile `Well I thought that people would be looking at me and wondering who I was` `Yes, well you did the right thing because I don't want anybody to see you at the moment, that is until everybody is about to enter the dining room so that I can introduce you in the best possible. way`.

So now Stella is taking her new gown on a hanger up another staircase to the room that she slept in last week.

Like most film stars she loves the opportunity to flaunt herself, and this was going to be one of those occasions. When she was ready she looked a million dollars with her slim line body, a long blue sparkling dress with a silver necklace that she had bought today from a top jeweller in the City.

Martha had now assembled all the guests at the foot of the main staircase, before they went for their meal. She started by saying `As most of you are aware I am a very lucky person to be stood here, and being able to tell you about someone who entered my life at a very critical moment. A day when the weather was cold, where someone snatched my handbag, and as a result I ended up falling into a freezing lake. As I cannot swim I was now sinking into the murky depths of the Serpentine. I can assure you at that time my past life was flashing before my eyes. Unbeknown to me there was a young lady who was already near to this dreadful incident, who dived the 20ft, almost fully dressed into the lake without any consideration to her own safety. Somehow she managed to bring me to the side of the lake. As a result she almost lost her fight for life in a hospital bed, due to severe hypothermia and a damaged shoulder.

Anyway I now want to introduce this young lady to you all, "Miss Stella Delray` Everyone is looking to the top of the staircase where Stella is now walking slowly down to clapping that is almost deafening. Both Graham and Martha are clapping, where tears from Martha are quite noticeable. Once at the bottom all of the guests are now flocking around this not only beautiful, but also a very brave girl, and wanting to find out more about her. Graham and Martha look at each other as though they were the proud parents of a daughter that they always wanted, but never achieved.

The rest of the night was a complete success where Stella was still the centre of attraction. Bill Atkins did receive his retirement cheque for many years of loyal service.

Eventually all the guests had now gone home in taxis or by their chauffeur driven cars. As the caterers were removing all the dinner plates, beer glasses, wine glasses etc. most of which had lipstick on; Graham, Martha and Stella were now sat on various sofas around the rather untidy looking lounge. Graham asked Stella `How did you like your big entrance?` `I really enjoyed it, I felt just like my friend Susan when she won the "Best Actress" award` `You certainly looked like a film star anyway`, added Graham `Why thank you Graham` giving him a big kiss on his cheek and now going over to sit at the side of Martha, putting her arm around her, then giving her a well earned kiss for making it a wonderful evening. As they looked into each other's eyes there was that special feeling of affection between the two women. The time was now 2am and Stella was now making her way up the staircase, she suddenly turned around and said to them both `I have just remembered I have some good news` `What is that darling?` asked

Martha `I got that job that I was telling you about last week, where a lady wanted me to join her agency as a model, and that it was a certainty that I would get plenty of work offered`.

Suddenly, Graham has dropped his wine glass on to the wooden floor with shock, where it has smashed without having any consideration for the cream coloured rug where the red wine has now splattered onto it. `Please don't tell us that you have signed an agreement?` asked Graham `Yes, of course I have why?` They have both now come to the bottom of the staircase and the expression's on their faces has now turned to horror` I was going to ask you tonight to join my company to be one of my top models` `Why didn't you ask me last week, and I wouldn't have bothered applying to the other agency?` Martha is now looking at Graham as though she could kill him, as of now. `I just thought nothing would so quickly materialise from the other agency, especially within just a week` said a now under attack Graham.

`You can't blame me` said Stella, `I was out of work as you know when I showed you that letter; I was hoping and praying that you would give me a chance, but you declined, which gave me the impression that I wasn't quite good enough for your company`.

Martha is now crying uncontrollably. Stella has now come back down the stairs and is trying to console her. She is now telling Stella `I wish now that I had drowned, at least I would be at peace with myself, but now I feel sick to my stomach`. `Don't say things like that dear` said Graham `Don't you dear me, you have managed to build an empire out of nothing, and yet you are so stupid to allow a girl that I love to be snatched up by an unknown agency, which is probably so small you probably wouldn't get a table and a couple of chairs in it`. Graham looks and feels as though he wants to crawl under the carpet and die. `How long have you signed up for?` asks Graham `Two years` Graham is now putting his head into his hands and looking down on to the floor. Stella is now taking Martha up to her bedroom nice and slowly. When she reaches the top Martha turns round to Graham who is still sat in the same position. She tells him to go to one of the other bedrooms tonight and also for the foreseeable future. An hour later he makes his way up the staircase, he suddenly stops and is now staring at the lounge clock, where you can almost read his mind, he is wishing that he could turn the clock back.

The problem is that millions of other people throughout history have wished the same, but unfortunately it is not possible. Next morning in the house it is as though there is a funeral about to take place, everyone is miserable even Stella who certainly didn't wish for this to happen. But she knows that she did the right thing, to look for opportunities to make her life come alive again. Martha is getting no solace from this predicament, and has now told both Stella and Graham who have got their faces stuck into the Sunday papers, that she is going to tell this other woman to cancel that agreement or else! Graham is now looking over his glasses and his paper and says `How do you mean **or else**, you can't go round threatening people because of mistakes made by others.

I know I have been a complete idiot, but there is not much that I can do about it now is there?` `Well I am still going to see her and tell her to kindly tear up the agreement`. Graham is now shaking his head from side to side. Stella is keeping out of this debacle which shows no signs of calming down. Sunday evening and Stella is now back home. Monday morning Martha has got an appointment to meet a Miss Cheryl Dempsey aged 33 who apparently was married, but her husband turned out to be a bigamist. She has since insisted that she will never marry again, but having an affair was okay. She is now living alone in a four bedroom detached house in Chelsea. She invites Martha into her office, which incidentally has a lot more space than what Martha assumed earlier.

`Is there a problem?` asked Miss Dempsey looking over her glasses, with as well a straight face.

`Yes there certainly is`

`What is it?`

`You have quite recently signed up a young lady as a model`

`What is her name?`

`Stella Delray`

`Yes I have why?`

`I have come to ask you to cancel that agreement, because my husband was in the process of signing her up, but he did genuinely forget to`

`What is your husband's name?`

`Graham Ogden` after a quick look on the computer Miss Dempsey mentions `Your husband has the largest model agency in the U.K.`

`That is right he has`

Miss Dempsey now replies with all guns blazing, `The point that I want to get across to you is, that if he has forgotten to give Stella a contract, then that is unfortunate, but at the same time he must realize that we live in a world of opportunity, and if you want something you have to move in quickly to get it`.

`I will agree with that` said Martha.

`Stella did tell me that you and your husband were her friends, but it was from another source that I learnt she had apparently saved you from drowning, is that correct? `Yes, she did, and that is why I love her so much, and I don't want to lose her`. 'In which case he should have immediately given her a contract knowing she was out of work. Obviously for some unknown reason, it being either that his brain cells had a malfunction, or that he was letting Stella know that she must realize that getting into his elite model agency cannot just be given at the drop of a hat, and that she must have to wait like other models for their chance, in which case I'm afraid makes him a Bigot, and he has now thrown his chance away`.

`So you will not relent?`

`I am afraid not, Stella Delray is a beautiful girl, she certainly has the best credentials to make herself and my agency a lot of money. When I went to her house she told me she had no family and also that she lived alone. Now I myself live alone in a four bedroom detached house in Chelsea. I told her that it would make good sense if she sold her house and came and lived with me in my house for a small rent, which would give her bank balance a boost`

`What if you two don't get on with each other?` asked Martha

`What I have noticed is that Stella's outlook on life is similar to mine, she also has a nice nature and I think that eventually we would be very close friends` `Did you get the impression that she would very much like to make the move?`

`Yes I think that she is all for it, she did say that she would visit you and your husband whenever she could`. Miss Dempsey is now looking at her watch and telling Martha that she has booked a meal for her and Stella to cement her move to Chelsea.

If we fast forward a month, Stella has now sold her house, given her cat "Burf" to Mrs. Gibbs next door where it will get all the attention it wants. She has moved into Cheryl's house (Miss Dempsey) and that they are getting on very well together. The bookings that the agency are receiving for Stella's modelling assignments is of a big financial boost.

CHAPTER TEN

Cheryl has booked a ten day vacation for her and Stella in Bermuda. It is a reward for Stella as she has put a lot of effort into getting the agency more profits and recognition. First there is a contract to do for a big chain of shops that sell ladies latest fashion, the location is in the sweltering sand dunes of Alexandria, in Egypt. There will be four models going along with a camera team who will make the video, it will take about five days to do the shoot. Which means that Cheryl will be without Stella's company on the Saturday, when they normally spend all day in and out of coffee shops and the big stores. It is now Saturday and the plane has now landed in Alexandria.

The girls are now taken to their hotel where from the roof of the hotel, you can see in the far distance the Western desert. In the evening the girls are sat around talking about things that women talk about (you know what I mean).

The one thing that they are not talking about (which nobody seems to have told them yet) is the fact that six young women tourists have gone missing over a period of two years who are now presumed dead. The police just do not seem to have any clues as to who is committing these crimes, only the obvious conclusion that somebody, somewhere **is.** After the filming has finished, the Models and the camera crew are glad to be going home because of the heat. Stella has told one of the other models to let Cheryl know that she will come back on Friday. The reason is because Stella has taken to this old City and is now going round all the Bazaar's and shops in the narrow alley ways looking for trinkets and suchlike. It is just up her street, but which will take another day to go around. It is another hot day in Alexandria, Stella has chosen to wear a turquoise silk, hanging off the shoulder blouse which is halfway up her body and hanging loosely, minus her bra due to the incessant heat. Instead of a skirt she has on a pair of jeans which have been cut with scissors to the top of her thighs, also with a buckle belt. While walking round the streets she calls in at an outside Cafe for some cold refreshment.

While she is sat there an Englishman has now come and sat close to her, he introduces himself as David Stanton Linder from Oxford. As they are talking about the comparison between the heat of Egypt and the cold of England, Stella is looking at his hairy muscular body, where his white shirt is open to the top of his trousers and his sleeves are rolled up to his armpits, plus his particularly good looks. If he asked her to meet him tonight she most definitely would, especially now that he has told her that he is single He was telling her of his house which is just outside the city boundaries, in the beautiful surroundings where the desert is literally outside the back door. It is as well so quiet you could even hear a fig drop. He tells her that as you look up into the dark sky at night you can see millions of stars. `It sounds like a really nice and romantic place` said Stella `Well you can be my guest, and if you like you can either stay the night or I can bring you back later tonight, it is just about ten miles from Alexandria`.

After looking at his physique again she told him that she would take up his offer. But first he wanted a favour from her, and that was for her to draw £60 worth of Egyptian Pounds from a cash machine so that he could get food into his kitchen, plus his 4x4 Land Rover some petrol as the tank is near empty. He explains to her that his manservant had dropped a knife on to his own foot in the kitchen this morning, who had then to be taken to a hospital for treatment which put him well behind time as regarding a meeting with a business partner. Consequently making him forget his wallet which had his bankcard and money. He assures her that the borrowed money will be given to her as soon as they arrive at his house. Stella couldn't see any problem as regarding this temporary loan, as she would be with him all the time anyway.

They made their way to his bank where a cash dispenser was in the doorway. As she was doing this transaction David put his arm on top of the machine to protect her from anybody looking to see what her pin number was, including himself who is also politely looking away. After they had bought provisions, and put the petrol into the tank they were now leaving the City, Stella was wrapping a turquoise bandana round the top of her head, where it is nice and tight just above her eyebrows, this is to stop the wind blowing sand into her long blond hair. While he is driving his range rover he felt as though he should tell her, if she hadn't already heard, that six women had gone missing over the last two years, presumably murdered.

Stella was now looking at David in an inquisitive way which he had noticed, `Surely you don't think that

I murdered them do you?` now laughing at the very thought of it, `Of course I don't, you come across to me as a big pussycat`. As they were going further out, there were fewer buildings and the roads were getting to be more bumpier as a result of turning off the main motorway. Eventually they were now turning into a side road, there was a building on the left and a building on the right and basically that was it. `Look, he is there again` said David now pointing him out. `Who is?` asks Stella `Just an old man who has nothing else to do but to sit there all day and every day in the sun` `He looks very old` queried Stella. `He is about 90 years old, he and his wife are the only neighbours I have`. They have now come to a stop, outside this as promised beautiful house which stands in its own sands, so to speak. As they are entering the house Stella turns around and sees the old man still staring from across the way, she gives him a friendly wave. When inside David takes her to a lounge and tells her he will be back in a minute, as well with the money that he borrowed from her. While she is waiting she is noticing that the house is quite beautiful as regarding the decor and furnishings.

He now comes back with the £60 Egyptian pounds for her to put in her handbag. Also he has brought with him someone who appears to be his manservant who to Stella looks quite handsome, but at the same time looking quite frightening. He is well over 6ft tall with a massive body and shoulders to match, plus a hairy body. He has a t-shirt that only comes half way down his body, with the printed words -"WE HOPE YOU ENJOY YOUR STAY"

Although he is in need of a shave, his rugged appearance makes him look altogether quite awesome. David now introduces Stella to his friend Arnaud,

Arnaud Belgard to be precise who is now awaiting instructions for what drinks to get them. `What would you like to drink Stella`? `Have you got Gin and orange with ice?` `I think that we have the Gin but no orange` said David now looking at Arnaud for confirmation, who with a straight face shakes his head from side to side, meaning no. So it would now have to be Scotch on the rocks. When Arnaud had been given permission to leave the room, Stella was now looking thru the big main window towards the beautiful desert. David had now come up behind her putting his arms around her body and now bringing it slowly into his. As she now turns round to face him, their lips have now met, where suddenly there is much vigour in their kisses. He now takes her to his bedroom, and within minutes they are both in his king –size bed totally naked, and making passionate love to each other. After now having had sexual intercourse plus an hour's sleep, Stella is now looking at the bedside clock, which tells her that it is now 3.30 pm, David is slowly waking up as well. She now leans on his body to give him a long smooch kiss and to whisper in his ear that she will have to visit the bathroom to relax in a cool shower as the temperature inside and outside the Villa must be somewhere near 40` Celsius. The luxurious en-suite is just outside the bedroom, and as she was cooling down in the cold cascade of water, she was wondering what David did for a living to afford a beautiful house like this.

After she had dried herself she went back into the bedroom to get dressed and wake her lover up, but he wasn't there, he had obviously got dressed and gone downstairs quietly. When she entered the big living room she couldn't believe her eyes, as to what she was seeing. The very man that she had spent over an hour making love to, is looking in her handbag and at the same time putting a small bundle of Egyptian Pounds into his back pocket, he also has Stella's bank card in his hand `What the fuck are you doing!` ` she screamed. `I am taking your money and bank card` `I can see that, but why?`

`Well you won't be needing it again` `Why the hell won't I?` `Because`—he suddenly paused as though something had got stuck in his throat, `Because you won't that's all` Stella is now seething mad with him. `You have taken everything that my body can give you, and now you are taking my money` Stella is still in a rage as she also tells him `What kind of scumbag are you!?` She now gives him two very hefty slaps to his face, and went for him with one of her stiletto heels which put a gash in his arm, as he tried to defend himself. He now told her in a very serious voice `Did you know that you have just put your life in serious danger as a result of your actions?` `Fuck you and go to hell!` she shouted in his face.

He was now showing Stella her bank card, informing her that he will shortly be emptying her bank account of whatever she has in it (this particular account has over £100,000 in it, although he is not aware of this at the moment) `I don't see how you can do that without my pin number` she told him. `But I already know your pin number, my dear Stella` `That is impossible for you to know what it is` `It can't be impossible if I know it surely?` For some reason Stella now has a gut feeling that he does actually know what the number is, only god knows how he got it. `Go on, tell me what the pin number is?` now looking into his face apprehensively, he now tells her "6921". `My god how could you possibly have known that?` `Quite easily my dear` She is now looking at him with nothing less than revulsion.

He now is sitting back on his favourite chair wiping the blood from his arm, at the same time looking up at Stella who is again asking how he acquired her pin number.

`Do you remember when I invited you to stay at my home, and you agreed to join me?` `Yes I do, but please don't remind me of being an idiot, and getting myself into this fucking ridiculous situation!` said Stella who has now folded her arms and is now looking up at the ceiling, and literally kicking herself. `Do you also remember when you very kindly lent me the £60 worth of Egyptian Pounds to get food and petrol from your bank card?` `Yes I do` `Well actually I didn't really need it, I had enough money of my own anyway` said a smiling David. Now with a look of total frustration, she asks him `I still want to know how you got my bank details?` `Quite simple really, if you remember I put my arm on to the back of the cash dispenser to shield you from people maybe wanting to see what numbers that you were inserting` `Yes I remember you doing that, but I also noticed as well that as I was inserting those numbers you were looking in the opposite direction, and there was no way that you could have seen my pin number being entered` `You are quite correct I didn't see you insert your pin number` `So just how did you find my pin number?` David was now showing her his wrist watch, he had a broad smile that was now spread all across his face. He now told her to examine the face of the watch that was still on his wrist.

After a close inspection she told him `I can't see anything different other than a small circle at the side of the digit 4` `Well that's it, within that small circle is a camera that can film for forty seconds, and that is how I got the information that I required, you probably may not have noticed that I wear my watch on the inside of my wrist rather than the outside`. `Well I suppose anybody with a fucking twisted mind like the one you have would know how to do such wicked things`. Now with another smile he says to her `At least I have the decency to tell you that your money will be put towards me having a very comfortable lifestyle`. She now spat in his face realising that she was in serious danger of forfeiting her life for reacting in the way that she did, all because of the now utter hatred she has for this man. David now leaves the room to speak to Arnaud. He tells him quietly that he is now going back to Alexandria to stay at a friend's house, and that tomorrow he will draw half of whatever is in Stella's bank account, and the rest the day after. He also tells Arnaud that she is his now, and that he can do whatever he wants with her. Stanton Linder has suggested to his friend to be sadistic to this particular woman who he would eventually kill (but who at least had the guts to stand up to him) he also suggested for Arnaud to firstly rape her, then spread eagle her body face down on his bed, secure her wrists and feet tightly, before lashing into her naked back. Finally with no resistance left he would finish her off by strangulation. Later around midnight her lifeless body will be thrown into some old truck and taken into the desert and dumped alongside the other six women who were robbed and shortly after murdered, whose bodies are now just bleached bones somewhere in a desert wilderness.

The time is now 4.25pm, and David has now left. Arnaud has because of the heat now opened all the windows in the house, to allow any significant breeze to enter. He entered the big living room as Stella is tightening her bandana, he tells her that there are now just the two of them in the house. She begs him to let her leave the house, so she can tell the police of this wicked man David Stanton Linder who should be behind bars. She also says `I promise that I won't tell them anything about you`. She also tells this the biggest and strongest looking man that she has ever seen in her life, that she will do anything for her release. Arnaud said to her `You will do anything is that what you just said?` `Yes anything` He now picks her up and takes her up to his bedroom and lays her across the bottom of his bed, he now strips her naked apart from her tight fitting bandana, ties her hands behind her back (because of what he has recently witnessed, she can be quite aggressive). She is now helpless and looking up at this man who is stood over her with a wicked look on his face, where his long thick black hair is now hanging over his eyebrows. She is now sure that he is about to rape and murder her.

He has now taken his jeans and briefs off showing to Stella the size of his now throbbing penis, which is so big it is making her wish she was already dead.

He has now lifted her up and put her into his bed that shows evidence that other women have shared his bed at some point. He is now laid at the side of her.

With her hands being tied behind her back, it is making her naked breasts stand out even more so. To show that she will be defiant to the end, she is making an attempt to loosen the rope around her wrists by moving from side to side, that is making her breasts wobble about, and which is getting Arnaud even more excited. After him giving her breasts a heavy maul, he is now lowering his head to hers, to hopefully spark off any sexual feelings that she may have. As his lips are pressing down on to hers, suddenly her yearning for sex has surfaced and she is wanting to give this cruel but also handsome giant of a man just as much as what she gets.

She has opened her mouth, where his tongue has taken the opportunity to bury itself in. She can now feel his muscular arms surrounding her body, which at the same time it is making it hard for her to breathe as her breasts are being squashed into his t-shirt. Looking into her face he now gets the message that she is up for it, so he released her from the rope that bound her and in no time they were now having sex as if there was no tomorrow. Her hands were now all over his body which included digging her nails into his broad back and as well his colossal penis.

Doing that aroused Arnaud to the point where he wanted intercourse with her; for her there was not an option. With her fingers running thru his long black hair, and their tongues all tied up, Stella now felt his penis slowly moving up into her body, it was the first time she had ever felt pain when having intercourse, she was naturally frightened that it could cause some damage in her stomach with it being so large. Having now reached the buffers so to speak Stella was now telling Arnaud that he was really hurting her, but he just laughed at her until he achieved the ecstasy he was wanting.

Going back to that most painful of encounters with this monster, she was now getting dressed where she now challenged him as to why he wouldn't let her go.

He now told her `If I let you go you will explain to the police what has happened, they would first arrest David and eventually me, you would get your bank card back and any other money that was taken. Which would mean that our now very comfortable lifestyle, would for a considerable time be spent in prison, does that answer your fucked up stupid question?` Stella now realizes that she is now definitely in a life threatening situation as she makes her way to the downstairs bathroom. She is being closely monitored by Arnaud as to where she goes in this big two floored house. `Don't get any ideas of climbing thru the bathroom window either, it has got immoveable bars on the windows` he tells her. After she has had a good wash, and got herself back to some sort of normality, there is apparently no towel to dry herself on.

Now stood outside the bathroom she notices that a bit further down the corridor there is a big cardboard box filled with clothes, some of which have fallen on to the floor. One of the items that she has picked up is a ladies bra, curiosity has now got the better of her as she delves further into the box. The expression that is now on her face is one of horror. As the box is just full of women's clothes. She soon came to the conclusion that these items of clothes, must have belonged to those women that were murdered. `Oh my god` she shrieked. She now makes her way into the lounge where Arnaud is doing his twice daily press ups, which is the start of a relaxing build up to when he has to get rid of Stella. She is now shouting at him `What have you gone and done, you murderous bastard!` `What are you on about you stupid cow?` `You know damn well what I am on about, it was you that murdered those six women wasn't it?`

`So what?`

`What do you mean so what !?`

She now attacks him, first slapping his face, and then severely scratching his face, where he now has four gashes down each side of his face.

Before we go any further with this story, I feel as if the time has come for me to open the Fact File on this man.

THE UNSEEN FACT FILE OF ARNAUD BELGARD

Andre Disarrays is one of many names used by Arnaud Belgard, who as a child was brought up in the slums of Paris, who rarely went to school and when he did he would get into fights. When he was a teenager he accepted with pride to be the leader of a gang who would terrorise anybody who questioned their violence. Arnaud was sent to a juvenile prison for attacking an old man who wouldn't step aside when he was walking down the street, and who was hospitalised for a month. He could never hold a job for long, as he hated people who were above him. He decided to join the French Foreign Legion under the name of Andre Disarrays. He was even feared by some members of his own regiment. He was a fitness fanatic whose body frame at the time was massive.

There was an incident when on his own, two other soldiers who were 6' footers wanted to "do him in" because they saw in him nothing but evil. They attacked him with knives, but unfortunately for them he had fighting skills that could deal with most situations. After a fight that lasted only a few minutes he had broken the neck of one of them and the back of the other. He was later convicted of the murders of these two men and given a life sentence. He was sent to a hot filthy prison somewhere in the desert, where when other prisoner's died on a quite regularly basis, they would be left there for days before being removed. After four years, new evidence came to light that the two men were hired assassins who had been paid to kill him, and that he was only defending himself which nobody believed at the time.

After his release, a few months later he was put back in prison for raping a tourist. He later escaped from the prison and went to an area way out of Alexandria, that was on the edge of the Western Desert with just two houses there, both had 2 floors. He asked the old couple in one of them if they would give him refuge so he could escape from people who were trying to kill him, which they kindly offered him. After a few months they had suddenly disappeared, but he had a letter of proof with their signatures that he could live in the house till they came back (which I think would be never). The problem now was that he needed money to live.

He made a friend in Alexandria, David Stanton Linder who would become his accomplice as well as being someone who would devise a plan that would make them both rich and comfortable. With as well the fact that Arnaud has only a low I.Q, he will do anything that David asks him. That is why Arnaud treats him with high respect. With David being so good looking, and with a body to match, he would attract beautiful single women and offer them to stay with him at his mansion in the desert. Women were like flies round a jam pot, who were looking for someone like him, to make love to.

He would tell them that he has forgotten to bring his wallet, asking them for a temporary loan until they were back in his mansion, where they would be quickly reimbursed. Most of the ladies would go to a cash machine to get the necessary amount that was required. When they got to the house he would take them into the lounge, inform Arnaud that he had brought another lady to the house. The lady would shortly be in David's bed where she would offer him usually any kind of sex he wanted, Eventually during the visit her bank card would be taken (usually without the victim's knowledge). After quickly leaving and going back to Alexandria, he would leave the woman in the hands of Arnaud to do with as he pleased.

Where she would be raped, whipped, and strangled. At night her body would be taken into the desert and dumped.

END OF FACT FILE

Arnaud has managed to wrestle Stella to the floor, and tells her that no one in his life has ever dared to do what she has done to him and expect to live. As well he tells her that before he has finished with her she will be begging him to quickly end her life. This time Stella is genuinely frightened as to what is in store for her, and she suddenly screams the loudest scream that she has ever done in her life, in the faint hope that somebody out there will have heard it.

Arnaud starts to laugh and tells her that nobody would have heard her scream, as there are only a very old couple who are in the vicinity, and who are probably deaf anyway. It goes thru her mind that he was talking of the 90 year old man who sat on his balcony every day and sometimes at night as well, if it's too hot. She is unaware that the old man **has** heard the scream from the house which is at least 50 yards away, but he has decided to go back inside and close his French windows.

We are now at the situation where Arnaud has spread eagled the naked Stella on his bed face down, with her wrists and ankles well secured. He as well tells her that before he dumps her body, he will take out her beautiful eyes and give one each to his two pet Monitor lizards (Gerard and Maurice) and watch them being swallowed within seconds, just like the other six women, some of whom suffered the same fate.

`What a really horrible bastard you are!` shouted Stella. He bends down and whispers in her ear `Sticks and Stones may break my bones……..`. He has now left the room for a short while to now remove the cardboard box that has all the clothes that were worn by those murdered women out of the back door, and to bury it in one of the sand dunes. At the same time Stella has been left to contemplate her doom. A short while later he has reappeared without his t-shirt on, but with a big bottle of water of which he is now swallowing a hefty amount of. He has also brought with him a towel and a camera plus a gruesome looking whip. Her long blond hair is now being moved out of the way, and he has found a pair of her briefs that will now fill her mouth to stop her from screaming again. Before he starts to lash into her back, he cruelly tells her that tomorrow she will join the six other girls, where already the vultures will be waiting to have a delightful feast off her beautiful body. The sun will eventually bleach her bones white, where the desert winds will cover them with sand. Just as he is about to bring the whip down heavily on her body. Suddenly the front door has been burst open. Five armed police have now entered, and in no time have Arnaud Belgard pinned to the floor and handcuffed. They release Stella from the bed and quickly wrap her in the bed sheet and take her out to a police car.

After an intense search of the house, nothing was found that could relate him to the six murdered girls, only the fact that he was about to use a brutal looking whip on a defenceless woman. So he will probably just get a couple of years in jail. Obviously they are not yet aware that this is the same man that escaped from prison nearly three years ago.

So when it all eventually comes out into the open they might as well throw away the cell key.

As they were now about to leave the premises, one of the policemen has found an envelope at the very back of a cupboard, which had been left open when Arnaud had got the whip from it. He calls the others over to have a look at the photographs that were inside the envelope. There were six pictures of naked young women with red marks around their throats, also with their hands tied behind their backs. It was quite obvious they had been strangled with bare hands. The pictures had been taken in his bedroom, which had the same furniture that was in the background of the photographs. So after two long years they now had their man, and Alexandria can now relax and get back to normal. As Stella was waiting in the police car to go back to Alexandria, she was trying to be brave over this very nasty episode in her life. It was now just beginning to sink in just how close she was to death. If she had been murdered it's almost certain nobody would ever have known what happened to her.

One thing she wanted to know from a policeman who was sat with her in the car, what made them realize that there was something nasty about to happen in that house. The policeman without speaking, was now pointing to the balcony of the house opposite, where the old man was waving, presumably to Stella with a smile that had no teeth.

It was all now beginning to come together. The old man must have heard her scream, and come to the conclusion that something terrible was about to happen in the house opposite. So he must have gone back into the room and closed the French doors so that he could phone the police. At the present moment one of the officers is coming out of the house with the gruesome looking whip, and a t-shirt he had found in the kitchen, when Stella saw it she had to laugh to herself. It was the half length t-shirt that had that slogan "HOPE YOU ENJOY YOUR STAY" printed across it. Which Arnaud had taken off a bit earlier. Anyway she put it on, and it managed to cover her boobs quite adequately, as she had already come without a bra. She asked the policeman in charge would it be alright if he took her the 50 yards to the old man's house, to thank him for almost certainly saving her life. Stella and the policeman have now got to the first floor. The wife asked them to come in. The couple's living room was quite large with an old monochrome television set. They also had an old electric fire that was hardly used, due to the hot weather that lasted most of the year. There was also a thick coating of dust on the mantel piece, due to the winds of the desert that came thru the windows. Stella went out on to the balcony where the old man was asking her to sit on his old rocking chair.

As she did she noticed that Arnaud Belgard was now being led towards the police van. Who had noticed that Stella was sarcastically waving to him, and pointing to the slogan on his old (now hers) t-shirt.

He was probably thinking that he now wished he had raped and strangled her straight away, before opening all of the windows.

The policeman asked the old man if he had seen any other girls brought to the house at any other time. He replied that he had seen other girls at various times, but had never seen them leave. Although he told him that he had noticed on some nights at around 1am, he had seen this giant of a man load his truck with what looked like rolls of carpet and taken them somewhere. `Who was the person who brought these girls here?` asked the policeman. `I think that he was English` said the old man as he turned round to Stella and said `It was the same man who brought you` Stella replied `The man who brought me, told me his name was "David Stanton Linder" and I would recognise him anywhere, not only that he has stolen my bank card, and been able to get my pin number as well`. The officer reassured her that he will not get away with it, as he is just as guilty as that animal in the van, and hopefully they will both get their just deserves.

`Just one thing is niggling me` said the policeman looking towards the old man `How is it that you rang us about this young lady and not about any of the other girls. `The simple answer to that is that when I heard that scream presumably from this young lady` now looking at Stella, I knew that there was something dreadful going to happen, but with the other girls I never heard a thing, so I wasn't sure whether they had come and left or whatever, and I certainly was not going to start snooping to find out, because if either of those men had seen me I probably wouldn't be here either`. After shaking hands with the old couple, Stella and the policeman left. As they were now going down the steps, the old man came out and looked over the banister and said `If all the windows of that house hadn't been opened because of the heat, I would never have heard the young lady scream`.

Now that David had been quickly arrested, Stella decided to stay a few more days in Alexandria, not only to get her card back and the large amount of her money that he had already taken out of the cash dispensers, but to help the police in their further investigation into the murders of the six women.

So although she knew inside that she was extremely lucky to be alive, and that both of these men will be dealt with accordingly, she was adamant that she didn't want

Cheryl or anybody else to know what had happened to her in that house of horror yesterday. So she has had to concoct a story that she was mugged by two youths, who had taken just her money, leaving her passport, and other documents still in the handbag, which she later claimed from the police station.

That was going to be her story, and she was going to stick to it. Obviously back in London Cheryl would want to know why she had stayed in Alexandria for so long. With Stella now having given her a phone call, Cheryl was now understandably satisfied with her reason for staying the few extra days. Going back to what really happened, Stella realizes that she was within a whisker of joining those other unfortunate girls, who like herself were hoodwinked into believing that there was a romantic weekend out there waiting for them, where they would be with a handsome man called David Stanton Linder where they would make love amongst the sand dunes and the millions of stars. It still sent shivers down her spine reliving the nightmare, where she had quite willingly being enticed into the insidious and devious world of Stanton Linder, as well as the subnormal mental moron Arnaud Belgard. Who obviously had not an ounce of remorse when ending the lives of those women, he just did what David told him to do.

After those extra days relaxing in the hotel she felt a lot better in herself, and ready to go back home to her best friend Cheryl. Who would have been worried enough that her pal had the misfortune to have been mugged and her money stolen (if she knew… if only she knew).

When Stella was now back in Heathrow airport she saw Cheryl making her way towards her with her arms outstretched. They had a long hug before making their way to the car and home.

The following Saturday they were now hitting the shops and coffee bars of the West End, happy and linking arms as usual.

The girls had come to an arrangement that because of the bad experience Stella had as regarding her mugging, she would now for a short while sleep in Cheryl's bedroom.

As well they could have a good natter with each other before turning on their sides and to sleep. Another week goes by and it is now time for the two girls to fly away to Bermuda for a ten day vacation. On that same morning, as Cheryl is having a shower, the postman delivers three letters two of which are the usual junk mail, the other one is addressed to Stella which looks very official and it is from the British Embassy. She feels nervous about opening it, because it might tell her that Arnaud Belgard has escaped again, and that he is now on his way to London to find her. Joking aside it would only be natural for a girl who has faced death like she did, to react in that manner. Her hands are trembling when she reads that a day before this letter was sent, Arnaud Belgard was executed by hanging, for the murders of six women.

His accomplice David Stanton Linder was on the same day found guilty of aiding and abetting in these murders, and was sentenced to 30 years hard labour. Stella was now shaking her head and thinking that David was such a handsome man who could have had literally any woman he wanted, and now because of greed he will probably die in some hot filthy jail. The families of the girls who were murdered, did receive some of the monies that was stolen from their accounts by Stanton Linder. If Stella had been another victim of his, he could have probably siphoned £100,000 from that particular account over a short period, while her body turned to dust in the hot desert. Stella could now hear Cheryl getting out of the shower, so she quickly tore the letter up and put it at the bottom of the waste bin. `What has the postman delivered today?` asks Cheryl as she comes into the lounge drying her hair with a big bath towel. `Just the same old junk mail` replied Stella as she was now fastening up one of two suitcases.

One hour later the taxi has arrived and two hours after that they are now airborne. The lady who has been given the job of running the business while they are away is a Mrs. Benson. They are now on their way to one of the millionaire playgrounds of the world where money is of no consequence. There are some instances where big mega deals are usually obtained on some golf course (of which there are plenty). Which incidentally won't apply to Stella and Cheryl who are hoping to attract some good looking men in their thirties, who have dumped their wives or at least be looking for a temporary change of sleeping partners. As they are touching down at Bermuda airport, the girls are well aware that they are now in the land of the very rich, where your manner and etiquette has to be of the highest standard, otherwise you will soon be regarded as people of no importance and not to be bothered with.

Eventually their taxi has arrived at one of the most luxurious hotels on the island. All you do is leave your luggage in reception, everything else is done for you. Most of the Reception staff are young and dressed in immaculate maroon uniforms. Stella and Cheryl have now been shown to their room which contains: a luxurious marble bath, and separate shower and Jacuzzi, one double bed with beautiful pink sheets and duvet. There also, was the breathtaking view of Hamilton Harbour. After enjoying the Jacuzzi together, they left the hotel and had a walk along the beach, watching the palm trees swaying in a warm gentle breeze. As they now looked out into the Atlantic Ocean there were massive luxury yachts ready to come in to Hamilton Harbour for the evening. They now continued their walk and were now entering Devonshire Parish where you could book a sightseeing tour of the immediate coastline and villages, which could be done tomorrow.

They arrived back at the hotel and have just 30 minutes to get ready for dinner. When they came down the spiral marble staircase, both girls looked stunning in their shimmering dresses and jewellery. Cheryl who herself was once a model for twelve years until she retired at the age of 31. She has though still managed to keep her figure in excellent shape for all of those years, she is 5'8 tall with dark brown hair. Stella's beauty seems to have won the day, as there wasn't a lady in the hotel who could match her stunning features. Men who were sat with their wives couldn't resist having a glance in her direction. Now that dinner was finished, all the guests gradually made their way into the massive lounge area. Stella and Cheryl who had found a nice plush settee, were now asking the waiter to bring them their drinks. Also looking for comfort were two young men who had now joined them.

One of the men was Tony a twenty two year old. Who had been sent to Bermuda by his father who incidentally is a self made billionaire, to investigate into there being land where they could build properties for the more exclusive client. As well his father had sent Lee Bryant 32 a widower for 3 years, who as an architect, would be able to work out just how many properties that they could legally build. The four of them were now in conversation, about: where they had come from, how long would they be stopping for, also about the various parts of the world that they had already visited, as well as other interesting stories in their lives so far. There was an early indication that Tony and Stella were building up a friendly rapport with each other. Even Cheryl was being swept off her feet by Lee who has moved up closer to her.

Both men were now visiting the small room, leaving the two girls to discuss this growing friendship that is being built up between the girls and boys.

Stella said that Tony was the kind of man that could be easy manipulated (she preferred it to be the other way round). Cheryl felt that Lee was a good looking man who she could at a push easily settle down with, (which is a u-turn on her previous thoughts that she would never marry again) . When the men returned they had brought drinks with them, Gin and orange with ice for the girls and beer for the boys. `What are you doing tomorrow girls?` asked Tony, Cheryl replied `We were thinking of going on a tour of the island and its villages?` Tony looked across at Lee and said `Can't we take them in the car? I know where there is a beautiful secluded beach` Lee has now told his friend `Yes we can but only in the afternoon, as we have to do some work in the morning, remember! now giving Tony a serious stare. `So is that a date girls?`both girls are looking at each other and they both say `It's a date`.

Later that evening the girls had forgotten to tell the management about there just being a double bed instead of two singles. Realising that it was now too late, plus the fact that they may have to change rooms and loose the beautiful view. They had no option but to sleep together for the ten nights.

The following afternoon the girls were now sat in the back of the open car as it sped to this beach that Tony had recommended. When they were going around this particular bend, the Bay just seemed to spring into view.

Both girls looked at each other excitedly after seeing a beach of such beauty. What made it better was the fact that they would have the beach to themselves. Before anything else they had to stretch their legs as they got out of the car, as it was a fair distance from Hamilton. Tony was going into the boot of the car to get out the hamper, which was another surprise for the girls. When they finally got settled on the white sands, it was noticeable that Tony and Stella were sat together on a blanket, while Cheryl and Lee were sat on a separate blanket. As they were tucking away into the sandwiches and coffee, Stella was asking Tony and Lee how they met each other. Tony said `I once got into a fight in downtown Miami, it was a one to one fight and I was walloping this guy good and proper` he starts to laugh as he now looks over to Lee, `suddenly out of the shadows comes this other clown, obviously a buddy of the man I am giving a good hiding to.

In no time at all it's now me that is now being walloped, but I honestly believe that this man, now pointing to Lee, saved my life because at one point I was now unconscious, and the fellow who I had battered was coming over apparently with a switchblade to finish me off, but Lee kicked the knife out of his hand with a Karate kick, and with a karate chop to the other guy they both ran off. That is why I am here now`. Stella and Cheryl now look over at Lee who just shrugs his shoulders and says `I just did what I had to` `I told my dad what Lee had done, and with Lee being an out of work architect he gave him a job in the Company. Lee and Cheryl decided to go for a walk on the beach holding hands.

Lee was asking Cheryl why she had never been married as there were no rings on her fingers. Cheryl told him that she **had** been married, but later found out that her husband was a bigamist, which at the time was deeply distressing, and from that moment on any future marriage was to be out of the question. Lee now stopped in his tracks, and told her that was like cutting your nose off to spite your own face, surely. ` If you come into contact with a man that you are sexually attracted to, you don't dismiss him just because you think he will be like your first husband, you should go for it, the chances of that happening again to you must be astronomical, not only that you are a beautiful lady` He now put his arm around her waist, and suddenly they were now laying in the sand kissing passionately.

When they eventually got to their feet and shaking the sand off, Cheryl felt as though she should ask Lee why he had a ring mark on the finger reserved for wedding rings. Lee knew that he would have to tell her the reason why, if he wanted their friendship to continue. They are now walking slowly back to their friends. He tells Cheryl that he and his wife had been married for two years and had been trying for a child for over a year. One morning in her own car and on her way into Miami City centre, where she worked in the offices of a shoe manufacturer, another car was travelling out of Miami at a speed of literally 100mph and being chased by police cars, it crashed thru the central reservation and ended up smashing into her car.

Lee is now taking a deep breath as he is close to tears. Cheryl is now putting her arm around Lee's waist and tells him that he doesn't need to tell her anymore, and that she can work out the rest of what happened. They have now come back to Stella and Tony, who although happy in each other's company they just somehow haven't been able to click together.

CHAPTER ELEVEN

After an hour's drive they are now back at the hotel and have arranged to meet in the big lounge after dinner. While the girls were getting ready Stella asked Cheryl if she was genuinely interested in Lee? `I must be honest` said Cheryl now looking at her best friend thru the mirror and noticing that she is topless `I really do like him, if we were together more often I think I would fall in love with him` `The only thing about that is` said Stella `if he lives in Miami and you live in London how is it going to work?` after a few moments thought, Cheryl again looking thru the mirror at her said `Come on Stella let us get real here, I have only known the Guy less than a day, we could have a big disagreement about something, and at this very early stage it could blow it all to pieces?` `Yes well that is true` agreed Stella

`Don't they always say that love finds a way?` queried Cheryl. `Well if it does I hope it finds a way for you two`.

After dinner they all meet up again. Suddenly as they were discussing something or other, Tony looked up at this gentleman who was stood at the side of him with a beer in his hand. `Hello Dad, what are you doing here? `Oh' I just thought that I would pay you a visit to see how you are coping` `We have had a few problems with the people who want to sell the land, but nothing that we can't handle` now looking at his dad rather sheepishly, which gave a good indication to his dad that things were not going quite to plan.

`Well I will talk to you later` said the gentleman . Now looking down at the two ladies he asks his son to introduce him to them. `Dad this is Cheryl Dempsey from London, and this her best friend Stella Delray also from London`. After giving the ladies a shake of the hand he is now looking round for a spare seat so he can sit with them. Tony his son finds him one.

He is now sat next to Lee who gets a hug round the shoulder from his Boss who wants to know what he thinks of Bermuda. `It is beautiful and one day I hope to retire here` now having a quick glance at Cheryl.

As the night wears on and the drinks are vanishing quicker than a U.F.O, everyone appears to be amiable with each other. Clark Duvall (Tony's dad) is now looking at his watch and is saying that it is time for bed and bids the ladies goodnight. Lee gives Cheryl a kiss on the cheek and shakes Stella's hand, `You are going a bit early aren't you?` said Cheryl. Lee with now a straight face is telling her `The thing is I don't think my boss is very happy at the way Tony is handling things as regarding this building situation, and he may get a rocket up his backside before the night is thru` `He seemed happy enough when he was sat with us` said Cheryl. `Yes Cheryl but I know him like a book, and believe me at the moment he is not a happy Bunny` `Will I see you tomorrow?` asked Cheryl, `Yes, unless I have been sacked before`. So now the two girls are sat on their own, the time is now 11.10pm, they call a waiter to get the last drinks of the day.

As they are sat there sipping their drinks, at the back of the lounge they can see Mr. Duvall having strong words with Tony and Lee, especially Tony his son. He is now pointing over to the two girls.

`I think he is saying something that isn't very nice about us` says Stella `He seemed such a nice man as well` said Cheryl. Now Mr. Duvall is coming across to the girls, and he does not look very happy. `You don't look very happy Mr. Duvall, is something wrong?`asked Cheryl with a furrowed brow. `Yes, I'm afraid something is very wrong` `How?` asked Stella. `All I can tell you is that my son has not been concentrating on the job that I gave him to do, and I think that you two Bimbo's have been the main reason` `That is a bit unfair Mr. Duvall we only made friends with them, it was them that said they had spare time, we didn't force them` `Did my son tell you that he is engaged to a girl that he has known since they went to school together?` Stella replied `No he didn't`, `Well anyway I have decided to send them back to Miami tomorrow as there is another of my projects that will be easier for them to handle, and I will handle this one myself,` he now stormed off.

Next morning at breakfast Lee and Cheryl got together to work out how they could still see each other, now that Mr. Duvall had decided to send the two boy's home where there was another project to do.

Suddenly Lee had a brilliant idea, Cheryl was keen to know what it was. `I will ask my Boss if he will let me have the ten days vacation that he owes me from earlier in the year, so that me and you can spend the ten days at my home in Miami.

There's hundreds of places to visit and things to do, what do you say?` `Sounds great but there are two problems, firstly will he let you have the time off? and secondly I would have to leave my best friend, here on her own` `Well let's go find out shall we` Lee saw Mr. Duvall sitting at a breakfast table, he explained that Cheryl was the first girl that he had fallen for since his wife was killed 3 years ago. He now wanted to take her to Miami to impress her and maybe, just maybe things could be very beneficial to him. Mr. Duvall knew what Lee had been thru since that terrible day almost 3 years ago, and had always been like a father to the lad, and had no hesitation in giving him an opportunity to being a husband again, and maybe even a father, and told him that he was crossing his fingers for him. Cheryl explained to Stella this straight out of the blue idea would enable Cheryl and Lee to continue with their whirlwind romance. She also told Stella that she didn't relish the idea of being without her best friend for the remaining holiday, but if it could bring her happiness which could include having a family surely it was worth having a go. That to Stella would be terrific news if it worked out for her friend, so she was all for it.

Down at the airport Stella was saying goodbye to her friend Cheryl, also to Tony and Lee who she told to take good care of her at all times. It was now arranged that Cheryl would return from Miami to London in ten days, and Stella would return to London roundabout the same time. Stella was one person who had got used to being alone, when she had a flat in St. John's Wood.

She had the confidence to know that she would find some man to share a bed with at some point. Otherwise it would be a vacation she would want to forget. She went back to the hotel for lunch, where she was now and again glancing up at a T.V. screen that was above her head, showing a baseball game between Los Angeles Angels and New York Yankees. Not that she knew anything about baseball anyway. Suddenly she felt a gentle hand on her shoulder. When she turned around it was Mr. Duvall smiling down at her showing his perfectly white teeth, `What on earth is a beautiful lady like you doing sat on your own?` `I'm afraid I have no option, my best friend has gone to Miami with one of your employees for a vacation` `Oh yes of course he has I had forgotten about that, and I hope things work out for them` `So do I` said Stella. They both suddenly looked up at the T.V. because the crowd were clapping and cheering something that had happened in the game.

Stella was biting into another sandwich as Mr. Duvall was himself clapping and at the same time bending down to inform Stella that Brent Osgood at the moment must be the best player in Baseball. She was now choking on her sandwich when she heard that name mentioned. Luckily Mr. Duvall was there to slap her back. `Have you lost the art of swallowing?` he casually remarked. She looked up at him as though to say `Don't be a clever asshole` `I choked because you mentioned the name Brent Osgood and that is one guy that let me down badly` Mr. Duvall has now sat down beside her looking rather bemused. `How can Brent Osgood have anything to do with you, I was told that you are from London and what I have noticed is that what you know about baseball is basically zilch?`

`Well when I have time to tell you Mr. Duvall I will, because it is a long story, trust me` `Can you start to call me "Clark" seeing as we are now on friendly terms?` `Friendly terms` said Stella with a borrowed smile, `if I remember last night you called me a Bimbo, and intimated that I should be stood on a street corner looking out for customers or something`. She was now looking into his face, and waiting for an explanation and apology of some kind. `Look I am sorry for what I said last night, I took it out on you two girls because my son, had not put enough effort into getting a proper deal as regarding the building project, so will you accept my apology?` with a now straight face she told him `I'll think about it`. Clarke was looking at what Stella was eating and he called a waiter over to order the same as his new friend had.

While he was waiting he asked Stella what were her revised plans for the rest of the vacation now that she was on her own. She told him that her plans hadn't changed and that her intentions were to find a man who she could spend some naughty nights with, which could lead to a real romance and hopefully a happy marriage. Clark is now cheekily looking at her and saying `That gives me a slight chance does it?` Stella now turns to him with a straight face and says `I don't think so, and you know the reason why, don't you?` `Because I am too old I suppose at the age of 43?`. `No that is not the reason, the simple reason is that you are a happily married man and so there is no future for me in that situation`. `What if I told you that I wasn't happily married?` `I would say that you were lying, because you don't give me the impression of being a hen pecked husband, you look like a man in full control. Though to be honest I am a bit disappointed that you are actually married`. The truth is that Clark Duvall **is** in an unhappy marriage, but to make up for that when he is on business trips or even vacations on his own, he will attract women into his bed to satisfy his desire for sex. So as he watches Stella get up from her seat to go to her room, she has turned around and tells him to enjoy his day. Although the waiter has now brought his sandwiches, he is still admiring the elegance of Stella Delray as she walks up the spiral staircase to her bedroom.

In his mind he has already decided that he would like her body wrapped around his for the remaining two nights of his stay, he really would. After having his sandwiches he was now going to sort out this problem with the building project. All during the afternoon he couldn't seem to get Stella out of his mind. To him she was the perfect woman, she was tall with a beautiful body and face, and she was very intelligent, and with a good sense of humour, plus if she had anything to say, she would say it. It was now evening and shortly the doors to the Banquet hall would open for dinner, where Clark would sit near the window.

While pouring a nice Red wine into his glass he noticed that Stella had come into the hall, and going to the same table as last night. Now because Cheryl had left, the table was occupied by another couple. As she was looking around for somewhere else, she noticed Clark trying to get her attention, he really was.

As she was about to join him he had stood up and pulled the chair out for her to sit on, `Thank you' she said `Would you like a glass of Red wine Stella?` `That would be nice` after a short pause Stella asked him if he had sorted out the problems with the building project. After taking a sip of wine and putting it back on the table he said `Yes I did, I told them that they were trying to get more money for themselves out of this project than originally agreed.

They thought that my son was still wet behind the ears, and as a result of that they would offer less. Now they would now have to deal with me instead, and now as it works out our Company will make an extra $50,000 dollars due to their greed. `You are obviously a hard person to deal with` `Well I can be a big softy as well` they were now laughing together. After the meal Clark got up first and went round to pull her chair out, `My goodness` she said, `I have never had so much attention in my life` he even had his hand on her waist to usher her out of the hall. The look on his face gave the impression that he was proud to be in her company. They made their way to a sofa in a quiet corner of the lounge. When the waiter had brought their drinks and they had settled, Stella asked Clark about this morning when he said he was not happily married did he actually mean what he said? `In a way yes, in another way no` `Would you like to be a bit more explicit?` said Stella now looking into his come to bed eyes. `Me and Janet have been married for 22 years and we have two children, Tony who you already know and Bryony who is now 20. I would say that over those twenty two years we have done more than our fair share of globetrotting.

Obviously we have had a few arguments along the way, but have always been there for each other. Taken as a whole, yes I was happy. Now as the years have passed by, she has got tired of going to Faraway destinations, and just wants to be involved in charity work, women's Guilds etc.

Even going on bus tours to look around Stately Homes with her friends for the odd week, which means that if I want to go to exotic places I have to go on my own, and I believe that we are slowly drifting apart.

`What about your sex life?` asked Stella `I manage, there is usually some lady who is looking for sex, and if I like the look of them, I can give them pleasurable satisfaction`. `You seem to be very sure of yourself Clark?` `The way I see it` said Clark `what is the point of say me and you sleeping alone in our own beds when we could be wrapped up together in one bed?` `It seems to me that you are thinking of me as being one of your next victims?` said Stella as she took a sip of her favourite short. `That never entered my head, but put it this way I wish you were` he is now smiling and looking into her face while waiting for her reaction. `Well you never know` now looking at him with a cheeky grin. His eyes suddenly came to life. `Are you serious, me and you?` Clark took this opportunity of her opening the door to him slightly, by sitting closer to her where he could have a closer look into her green /blue eyes and those beautiful moist pouting lips that were driving him crazy, they really were. What a difference he was suddenly thinking to himself, the other month at a hotel in Denver, this woman wanted to share her bed with him. She must have been in her late forties, her breasts were massive and they were stretching down to her quite slim waist, at one time when she leaned over him in bed, he ended up with one resting on each of his shoulders.

The time was now 11.15pm he and Stella were now making their way to the elevator. While it was on its way down to the ground floor, Clark looked at Stella and asked her if she was going to spend the night with him, or had she changed her mind. `No I haven't changed my mind, but I will need my nightdress and toothbrush` The elevator had now come. On its way back up it had now stopped at the 2nd floor, and as Stella was getting out she asked him what floor he was on. `It's on the top floor, Penthouse Suite 3 just ring the bell and I will let you in'. Twenty minutes later Stella was ringing his bell and he came to let her in.

He looked as though he was already for bed. He had his white silky pyjamas bottoms at a provocative angle. His chest and the rest of his seemingly fit body had plenty of black hair, for Stella to run her well manicured finger nails thru. `Would you like to use the bathroom first? asked Clark `Yes okay` While he was waiting he was combing his hair, and giving his armpits a squirt of body spray. He even looked in the long mirror sideways to congratulate himself of having no excess weight on his body. Stella now came out of the bathroom with a negligee and a pair of thongs on.

She now made her way slowly across the bedroom up to him, she now threw her arms around his neck, looked into his eyes and gave him a long lingering kiss. He has had to inform her that he will have to visit the bathroom rather quickly as a couple of his buttons have suddenly sprung off his pyjama bottoms. When he had finished his ablutions and brushing his teeth, he now came back into the bedroom. Stella was eagerly awaiting his presence between the sheets.

Above the bed was a red light that could be dimmed so you could see your partner rather than be in total darkness. Clark put the light on and brought her body into his.

His mind went back to this morning when she told him to have a nice day and he watched her walking up that spiral staircase with such elegance and grace, but now she was in his bed and the early signs were that she was hungry for sex, just like he was. She noticed again that her long hair was getting into a mess again and she told him she would have to stop till she got a white bandana from her handbag, after tying it tightly above her eyebrows she was now back in his arms. He was looking down at her and her up at him, he lowered his head towards her welcoming lips. At the same time he was relieving her of her negligee and thong, which he has thrown onto the carpet where it has now landed at the side of his pyjama bottoms which were despatched from his body by Stella just a few minutes before. It was only yesterday that Stella was sat on a beach with Clark's son.

Then after a rollicking from his father, he was sent back to Miami. That just left him and Stella, the only two left from last night's get together.

They were both now naked and he had his condom all ready, as he realized that if he made Stella pregnant it would open up a big can of worms, which in his position would be a massive embarrassment to his family and everybody else that he knew. After making their way to a satisfying climax together, they are now physically tired out and have now wrapped their bodies around each other and are now sleeping. The morning after the night before, Clark is still asleep as Stella is wide awake and doing exercises on the bedroom floor. After a while she looks at her watch and realizes that it is time for breakfast and is now going to wake up her lover. `C'mon lazy bones it's time for breakfast we can't sit around all day` Eventually he crawls out of bed and is now making his way slowly to the bathroom `Have you had a shower yet?` he asks her `I had one an hour ago` said Stella who was now finishing off with her exercises.

Twenty minutes later they were entering the Banquet hall. If another five minutes had elapsed they would have missed out. During breakfast she asked Clark if he had any business to sort out today? `Thankfully I did it all yesterday` `Does that mean you are going back to Miami today?` `What and leave you here on your own for the next eight days, .......why do you want me to go or something?` Now putting her hand on his she said `You know I don't, I just thought that you might get into trouble having days off when you should be working`.

Clark starts to laugh `So what's funny about that, I wouldn't want you to get the sack` giving him a concerned look. Still laughing, Clark tells her `I know that

I haven't told you the situation that I am in as regarding my job, but I will never get the sack` `What makes you so sure Mr. Bossy boots?` he starts to laugh again `Because I own the Company, you know, like it's all mine sort of thing` Stella was quite aware of his position anyway, she was just winding him up a bit.

She now thought to put him on the spot, just jokingly though `Does that mean if I came to live in Miami where I have no money and no job, also you knowing who I was, would you give me a chance to work for your company?` `What I would do seeing as I know you, I would make sure you were put on a priority list for you to be a cleaner or something` at the same time he was trying to keep a straight face `Is that the best you could do for me?` she said with a smile. As they were getting up from the table Clark put his arm around her shoulder and gave her a kiss on the cheek.

CHAPTER TWELVE

They decided that a good day out would be to do some Scuba diving, and have lunch at the Castaway restaurant. Even as they were walking down to the hire car, he had his arm around her waist and hers around his. They had now arrived at South shore, hired the equipment and now were on the boat that would take them both to an underwater dream world of fish such as: parrotfish, spiny lobster and snappers, there was the eerie sight of a specially built sunken wreck that they investigated, they even had time for an underwater hug. Not long after they were now back on dry land. Stella was hysterical with laughter, as Clark was being chased by a spiny lobster which was after one of his toes. As they were driving around looking out for the restaurant where they would have lunch, Stella was resting her head on his shoulder, and waiting for him to take his eye off the road and kiss her which he did twice.

They now pulled in to the Castaway Restaurant which in its elevated position gave a majestic view over the Atlantic ocean. When they had now almost finished their meal, Clark felt a tap on his shoulder, when he turned around he saw that it was Henry Chambers one of his works managers. `Hello Henry have you come to visit your summer residence?` `Yes, we just have tomorrow and then it's back to work` Clarke now asked `How long have you been over here?` `Just a fortnight` after a slight pause Clark told him` You know Henry I am beginning to think I pay you too much money` Both men start laughing and Henry is gesturing to hit Clark over the head with his fishing magazine, but thinks he had better not, as you simply cannot do things like that to a man who employs over 500 people.

Henry's wife who has been stood behind listening to the two of them, suddenly said to Clark `Aren't you going to introduce us to your friend Stella?` Clark almost went thru the floor, he looked at Stella then at Karen (Henry's wife) `How on earth did you know that she was called Stella?` Clark asked her, `When we were having lunch at the far side of the restaurant, the both of you came in and we were trying to remember where we had seen this lady before` Stella was trying her best to smile. `When I saw her smile at you, it was then when I remembered, Stella Delray the film actress`. Henry and his wife told them that they would go and get the camera from the car. Now that they were alone Stella was now looking at Clark when she said` You seem rather surprised?` `You bet your life I am surprised` replied Clark `Which way a nice surprise, or a bad surprise?` `Definitely a nice surprise` now putting his arm around her shoulder. He saw her suddenly take a deep breath and asked her what was wrong? `I just thought that you might be angry because I never told you, and that you would dump me as a result?` `That is something that I would never do, you are far too precious to me` now giving her a kiss on the cheek.

Just then Henry and his wife have come back with a camera that was hiding somewhere in the car.

So Clark was now taking a picture of Henry and Karen with Stella in the middle. Henry was also going to take a picture of Clark and Stella cheek to cheek. Henry and Karen made their apologies for leaving, but Henry told Clark that he would give him their photo into his hand later, giving Clark a nod and a wink, (obviously aware of this delicate situation where Clark was not with his wife)` After they had left and after a short pause, Clark was now shaking his head when he said `Fancy that, you being a film star` `Don't you remember yesterday when I told you about Brent Osgood and that he was a love cheat?` `Yes you did, what was the story behind that?` `I went to New York as leading lady for the film "Miracle in the rain". While I was over there he had a key already made so he could take some of his female fans to my apartment back in L/A. I know for a fact he had taken at least one dolly bird there and slept with her in my bed, as a friend of mine later showed me photographs to confirm his intrusion into my home.

When he knew I was now home he came to tell me that he had missed me, and that he had behaved while I was away, which was an outright lie.

To cut a long story short I gave him a black eye, and got security to sling him out. Clark was now laughing and told her (obviously being hypocritical) that he deserved all he got. They were now leaving the restaurant and on their way to soak up some sun on the beach. She was now rubbing the sun cream onto his back and neck `Your hands are so tender` Clark told her. `It all depends which part of the body I am working on` said Stella as she turned his head round so he could see her cheeky smile, she has now put a blob of cream on the end of his nose.

After a few kisses and cuddles he was now leaning on his elbow looking down at her and suggesting `How about a game of golf tomorrow?` `Who me?` said Stella `the last time I played golf was at Brighton when I was 13 and that was only "Crazy Golf", Susan Paxton beat me` `I do believe there is a screen actress with the same name` said Clark. `Yes I know, that's her` Clark has now sat up `You and Susan are friends?`

`We have been friends since we were about 5years old` `This is amazing my girlfriend is a movie star who knows movie stars?' With a serious face Stella interrupted him and said `I wish I was your girlfriend, but you can't have a true girlfriend if you are already married`. That statement by Stella has really got the message home to Clark that she is right, and if he wants to keep Stella he will be now under pressure to shortly come to a decision.

Which is to live a life with someone who makes him feel twenty years younger, or with his present wife who seems to have lost the plot of what life is all about, resulting in his future life being just a miserable existence, (billionaire or not). Stella can see in Clark's face that he has given a great deal of thought to this delicate situation. `What are you thinking about?` she asks Clark `I am thinking that I cannot bear the thought of you going back to London and that I will never see you again. Since the first night I met you my life has turned full circle` 'Surely you will find other young ladies to take my place `One serious question I want to ask you` said Clark `I'm ready go on` `Do you love me as much as I love you?` `Put it this way Clark I am sure I like you as much as you like me, simply because you can't love somebody after just two days it is not possible. Love has to grow, you cannot rush it` Now with a straight face Clark tells her `As regarding other ladies I am not interested. It's like my business, I knew when I was young what I wanted, and I got it, and I want you I really do`

Stella is reaching up and giving him a kiss and putting her arm around his shoulder.

He now sits up and is now leaning on his elbow looking down at Stella. With a serious face he asks her `Will you sleep with me again tonight?` `Are you sure that you want me to?` asks Stella with also a serious face `I am very sure, more than anything else in my life, I am sure`. As we all know Stella has had plenty of experience of having sex with men, most of which were casual.

With Clark this is a different kettle of fish. He either carries on relying on having sex out of a suitcase, so to speak. Or starting afresh with a woman who can give him everything he desires.

`There is a question that I must ask you` said Stella `If we do have a life together are you eventually going to feel guilty about leaving your wife? if you feel as though you are not sure, obviously we cannot make any plans, and just have to accept that we had a wild but enjoyable fling?`

His decision is of paramount importance to her, and he must be truthful, as she couldn't possibly live with a man who would later have regrets, as to whether or not he had done the right thing.

Clark has now got the message loud and clear and has just a few more days to come to a decision. As long as he remembers that she is the final piece in this convoluted jigsaw, and it's his choice if he wants to complete the jigsaw or break it up and put it back into its box. He comes up to Stella and gives her a long hug. As they are now folding the blanket and chairs up and putting them into the car, there is a silence that has descended. They are now making their way back to the hotel and Stella's head has been resting on Clark's shoulder nearly all the way. Now and again she looked up at him, where he would bend down and kiss her, and apart from that there was nothing to say. When back at the hotel they went to their own rooms to have either a shower or bath.

There was plenty to think about as they were laid on their own beds, in their own rooms looking at the ceiling, wondering what they would be feeling at this time tomorrow. Stella was also wondering how her friend Cheryl was finding what life is like over in Miami with Lee. At dinner that evening Clark and Stella were back to their normal selves laughing and joking with each other. Clark was reaching across the table and holding her hand when he asked her if she was looking forward to playing golf tomorrow. She looked him in the face and told him that yes she was looking forward to beating him. Later on in the evening Stella reminded Clark that he had invited her to his penthouse hotel room for the last drink. `Don't worry I haven't forgotten,` smiling at her over his wine glass, he now despatched the remaining wine at a stroke.

During the evening they had a few more drinks and had conversations with other guests. They eventually made their way up to his penthouse suite, where they spent an hour on the veranda. Now looking out to sea with a full moon shining down on it, that made it appear like strands of silver ribbons fluttering in a light breeze. Lights that surrounded the town and harbour made the setting very romantic. That is why he was stood behind her with one arm around her waist and the other with a glass of wine. Not long after they went to sleep and had their nightly share of eroticism.

Next morning at breakfast Stella felt as though she had to ask him if he really did have true feelings for her and not just carving another niche on an imaginary bed post that was in his head. Clark quickly put her mind at rest by saying `Like I said I love having sex with you and spending lots of time with you, if I thought otherwise I would have been back in Miami long ago, now that is for sure`. With that he put his hand on hers. After breakfast they decide that it is too hot to play golf, not only that but it entails a four mile walk, as well as pulling a golf trolley around. Besides Stella didn't know how to even address a golf ball, never mind hitting it, if as well she hit a ball into a bunker she would probably be in it all day. So Clark had another idea, that he would hire a speedboat for them both and visit the small island that was about six miles out into the Bay. When they got down to the harbour, Clark left it to Stella to pick one of the speedboats that was available. She picked the biggest one which had a lovely shade of pink. Clark had a speedboat of his own back home, so it was easy for him to manoeuvre to get the boat facing in the right direction. He was giving it full throttle and now the boat was at full speed. Stella was now given the controls for a short time which was a different kind of excitement for her. Just like the boat was leaving its wake behind as it sped across the bay, Stella's long blond hair was stretching out also. The continuous gush of air was also taking her breath away.

She kept on looking over her shoulder and smiling up at Clark with her beautiful white teeth that were gleaming in the sun. Clark had his arms around her body, but he had to keep bringing his baseball cap forward so it wouldn't blow off into the aquamarine coloured sea. After circling the island a few times (which was about half a mile in width and length) it now pulled into a makeshift quay that had been built for any would be visitors.

They picked a nice spot on the beach that was behind a rock, where they would be given the shade rather than the burning sun that was set in a steel blue sky. After tucking into their hamper as well with a bottle of Red wine to wash it down, they were now laid down on the blanket in their swimwear. They were now holding hands and talking about their possible future lives together. During their conversation Clark asked Stella `Don't you ever think of going back to Hollywood and making films again?` `I may do one day, but only if something happens where you and me are denied living together, not only that but I would have to be really encouraged to start again`. Stella has now stood up and is looking out to the distant horizon and at the serenity and beauty of the Sea, Sand and the sky.

She has now come back to reality and is now looking down at Clark, who was beginning to doze off. She picked up a couple of small pebbles and was now dropping them on to his stomach. He now opened one eye and was now getting up. She was now running away from him and he was now in hot pursuit (where she now has a sudden vision of Belgard chasing after her in the Western desert).

After a few more seconds Clark had now caught up with her and had now pulled her down into the wet sand, where she was now laid on her back with him on top of her. Almost totally out of breath they are looking into each other's eyes. He is now lowering his head to hers, she has opened her mouth for him, and moments later they are embraced in a passionate kiss. Meanwhile they have now been surrounded by a wave that has splashed into their bodies as they are now entering towards the ultimate ecstasy. When that certain thrill has come and gone, Stella is looking into the sky, she then turns around to tell Clark that she could live here for the rest of her life.

With the waves still intruding into their privacy and water still dripping from his nose and chin. He looks down at her and told her in all seriousness `We never really die, our souls will not allow us to`. Now with their arms around each other's waists, they are now making their way slowly back to the boat. Stella says to him `If and when we are really together, maybe we can come back to this island again?` `Next time we come back we will have our own boat, and If you like we will stop here for a week` said Clark. Hours later they are now sat in the restaurant of the hotel. Stella looked quite stunning in her pink gown with a shimmering necklace around her throat, as well as putting her hair up.

This was their last night together and she was getting plenty of glances from the male clientele, (well that is what Clark told her). Clark leans over and tells Stella `I know that I shouldn't say this because I am married, but I feel as though I am 10 feet tall when I am in your company' She gives him a lovely smile for his compliment. In a few hours they would be sleeping together for the last time, tonight there would be just kisses and cuddles. Their affection for each other is already now firmly established. The following morning after breakfast, they stroll down to the harbour holding hands.

They are now sat on one of the seats that ring the harbour. Looking at Stella he tells her `When I came to Bermuda last week to see how my son was managing, I never thought that I would meet someone like you, I cannot put into words just how much enjoyment you have brought into my life` There were a few tears coming down Clark's cheeks as he spoke. Stella wasn't going to escape either without shedding a few, and are now both consoling each other.

An hour later they are now in the airport lounge. Stella's plane will take off one hour after Clark's. So now Stella has been told by Clark that within 5 weeks he will be in touch with her as to what progress has been made. The time has come to say goodbye, one big hug and a kiss and he has gone. A few hours later he arrives back home to his wife and their grown up children Tony and Bryony. He has noticed that his wife: although her outlook on life hasn't changed, she seems to have lost an unacceptable amount of weight.

Clark and his children have decided that she will have to see a specialist and be checked out, as something is definitely wrong. A week later at the hospital, Clark, Tony, and Bryony are sat outside in the corridor drinking coffee as they wait for the specialist's prognosis.

Eventually the specialist comes out and beckons the family into his office. He is about to tell the family the bad news that he told Mrs. Duvall three hours ago. That she has got terminal cancer. She could possibly survive for up to 4 years. Suddenly Clark feels as though his world has suddenly fallen apart, and in just a few moments all of his dreams have now been shattered in just a few moments. Even all the money in the world will not release him from the torment of not only losing his wife, but also the slim chance of holding on to Stella's loyalty for up to four more years. He already knows what Stella's thoughts on this situation are, that she would never allow herself to be a mistress, and that he would have to make the decision of leaving his wife and getting a divorce.

But now the situation has changed, instinctively he knows that Stella would not allow him to do either of those two choices, especially now with his wife coming to the end of her life. It would have been intolerable for Stella to live with such a selfish and cruel man while his wife was elsewhere dying. Sometime later at the other side of the world, Cheryl has been met at the airport by

Stella who got in yesterday. When they got home Cheryl had some great news for Stella. `Well what is it?` asked Stella as she sits next to her friend `Me and Lee have decided to give love a chance` `You mean that you are going to live over in Miami?`

`That is exactly what I mean` `What about your business? `I will have to sell it` Cheryl is now looking at Stella realising that she might as a result lose contact with her best friend. Stella doesn't want to tell Cheryl at the moment that she may also be coming to live in Miami anyway. That is until Clark sorts out the situation with his wife, and gets that dream house for the two of them, (which as I speak is now in serious doubt). At the moment it is back to business as usual, where Stella has a few assignments to do. Cheryl has advertised the business and her house for sale, and almost straight away the business and accommodation has been under scrutiny from one or two interested parties.

Stella has had a long and emotional letter from Clark explaining that he is devastated that he and Stella will not now be able to share their lives together after all, as his wife has been struck down with terminal Cancer and will want him near to her probably most of the time.

Letting her know as well that he wouldn't expect her to put on hold a relationship which may take four years to come to a conclusion. Which now leaves Stella gutted, and to compound her misery, she may have to now look for new accommodation. A week later Cheryl's house and business has now been bought by the owners of a smaller Model Agency. Cheryl had to tell Stella that it was part of the deal that she (Stella) would still be their top model, otherwise they wouldn't buy either the business or the house. `They already know that you are one of the top models around` said Cheryl. A week later Stella now meets her new employers, brother and sister Kim and Gary Redman she is 27 and Gary is 30. Apart from the two year contract, Stella is asking them would she now have to buy a house, or could she stop in her present accommodation. Kim looks across at Gary and tells him that with four bedrooms that there would still be ample space for her anyway. Gary agrees to that request and when Cheryl moves out they will invest money to have the house modified into the way that suits the three of them. The time has now come for Cheryl to say goodbye to her parents, Stella and other friends and associates. She tells them all to visit her within the next year or else.

So now Cheryl has now departed to a sunnier climate leaving Stella without anybody that she can refer to as a true friend. At the moment she now has a bit of spare time, so she is now calling her longest and dearest friend Susan in the States. Stella can hear the phone at the other end ringing. `Hello this is Susan speaking' `Hello are you the Susan Paxton who I am looking for?` `I don't know I might be, where are you speaking from?` `London` `Oh my God! it's you at last, what on earth have you been doing Stella?` `How did you know it was me?` 'How did I know it was you, well at first I wasn't quite sure it was you, but as soon as you said London the penny dropped` `So what have you got to tell me?` asked Stella.

After quickly calming herself down she says `Well I have a baby girl who is four months old and her name is Silvi' Stella is almost shouting down the phone how she is over the moon to hear such wonderful news and that she can't wait to hold her in her arms`. `Me and Daniel wanted you to be the Godparent but we had no idea where you were. `Susan, I have been everywhere since I last saw you, and I mean everywhere` `Have you met anybody that you might settle down with?` Susan managed to squeeze in.

`I don't know about settling down, but yes there have been a few men in my life that I will tell you about when I visit you shortly`. `What is your idea of shortly?` `Just give me a few more months and I will be there` `What are you actually doing now in London?` `You might not believe me but I am a fashion model` `C'mon Stella pull the other one` `I just knew you wouldn't believe me, but it's true` `Well that has really amazed me, how on earth did you achieve that?` `Did I, or did I not go to Pollard acting Academy in Los Angeles?` `Well of course you did` `Miss Gardner apart from the acting aspect, did she teach us how to walk, and have that certain deportment and elegance?` `Yes she did` `Well there you are, so what is the problem?, I am getting the feeling that you see me as your best friend but in your mind now carrying an extra two stones of weight or something, am I correct?` `No' well yes I just thought that you might have put a bit on` `Shame on you Susan Paxton, my best friend thinking of me like that` Stella was laughing knowing that she had put her on the spot. `If you really want to know my weight, I am the same weight now as when I made "Confessions of a Lifeguard" but my boobs are a little larger`. `Well anyway I will want to know everything that has happened to you since you went back to London?` `Don't worry I will tell you, by the way how is Daniel your husband liking being a father?` `Do you know Stella he is a wonderful husband to me, we have a good sex life and hopefully there will be a couple more children on the way shortly` `Is George still your butler?` `Yes but he is thinking of retiring and going to live with his sister in

Nevada, so if you are not married by then, you might like to take George's place as our live in maid, would you like that?` Suddenly Susan can hear a laugh coming thru the phone that is almost deafening.

After a few minutes when Stella has stopped laughing she says to Susan `You cheeky bitch, is that all you think I am fit for, you would be surprised if I won an Oscar wouldn't you?` `It isn't possible for that to happen, but I would be the happiest person in the world if you did, you know that don't you?` `Of course I do` said Stella `Actually` said Susan `when I sometimes go to the studio's they still talk about you, and how good you were, they really do`. `That is nice to know, anyway I had better get off and let you put Silvi to bed, and give her a little kiss from me and tell her that aunty Stella will be coming to take her for a walk in her pram`.

With that they signed off doing a kiss over the phone. Over the next few months Stella has been involved in Fashion shows around Europe including: Rome, Barcelona, and Zurich for the newly formed "Square House Model Agency". Once again she has struck lucky that her employers have taken to her, not because she has brought in plenty of business, but she has that certain quality that top business company's desire. The week in Zurich was not only profitable on the business side, but was also memorable in another way.

Where the top executive of a top fashion house Adrien Bodner who was a very handsome man, immaculately dressed and rich, was swept away with Stella. The way she looked, her elegance, basically everything about her. He was 38, married with two teenage girls. His wife Helga for some reason had taken to heavy drinking, probably due to having depression which quite recently had a disastrous effect on their marriage.

Many a time he had to take his daughters to his parents so they wouldn't see her in the mood swings that would envelope her. Sometimes she would have to go to a hospital for a week to dry out.

CHAPTER THIRTEEN

On this particular week in Zurich, Stella with a few other models were invited to a party where they would mix with people in the fashion world. It was in one of the top hotels in Zurich. Adrien got the opportunity to talk to Stella. He told her that he was impressed in the way that she gave the clothes that she wore the best projection for the buyer to decide on his/her choice. Stella was very flattered with his appraisal and gave him a kiss on the cheek. `I hope your wife didn't mind me giving you a kiss?` `How did you know I was married?` `You have a ring on your finger, I thought that she would be with you tonight?` `No I have come on my own because she is getting treatment at the hospital` `Oh, you must be the gentleman whose wife has a drink problem?` `Where did you hear that!?` asked Adrien feeling rather dropped on. `I don't honestly know I just heard somebody stood behind me saying that Adrien's wife is in hospital again, is that your name?` `Yes` `Well I hope she soon recovers and makes your life happy again "Why do I look unhappy?` `Well to be honest, yes you do, you need someone who can make you happy` she is now looking at this very attractive man in a mischievous kind of way. With the look that she had just given him, was she meaning that she could make him really happy?` `Could you make me happy?` he was now daring to ask her. `Yes of course I can, but it would only be till the end of the week, as I will be returning to London`. You could see in his face that he was going to temporarily be unfaithful to his wife and children, because he simply wouldn't be able to resist this beautiful woman's company.

After her now being invited to spend a whole day in his house at the side of Lake Zurich, she has told one of the other models that she would be staying at a friend's house for a couple of nights, but would be still coming back for the afternoons fashion show.

She got her overnight grip with a change of clothes etc that she would need. She and Adrien now discreetly leave the hotel in his silver sports car. After a 15 minute drive they were now at his magnificent looking house which overlooked the lake, which as well had total privacy.

It was now 8.30pm they were now sat together on this most luxurious sofa having a relaxing drink with lights that had been turned low. He had taken his suit jacket off and was now with his white shirt and tie that was still in its correct place under the collar, even with a tie pin that held the knot in place. He now wanted her to lay into him where they would now be facing the same way.

He has now pressed a button on his remote control which brings nice soft music into the room. Stella has now leaned back with her head resting on his shoulder looking up at his mouth which gives him the opportunity to lower his mouth on to hers. With his arms around her and having a smooch kiss, this is what he has been missing for the last six months. She now turned around and taken the tie pin out, then removed his tie, another kiss this time when her tongue disappeared into his mouth.

After undoing the buttons on his shirt she now pulled it down his back where the collar was now hanging around his waist. Their mouths were open to each other as she ran her fingers thru his hairy chest. After her head had now been resting on his shoulder for a while, she was now looking up at him with her arm across his chest and her thumb nail digging in behind his ear. He knew now that she wanted for them both to be in bed together.

Within the hour they were now in bed, which reminded her of when Brent Osgood invited a bimbo into her apartment, and as well into her bed for sex.

Was she correct in blaming Osgood for that incident? or was the Bimbo to blame? She has no qualms, and that the blame had to rest on Osgood because he opened the door for the Bimbo when he shouldn't have done. Just like Adrien who opened the door for Stella when really he shouldn't have done either. As Stella and Adrien went on a tour of each other's body, she asked Adrien if she could borrow a headscarf from his wife's closet otherwise her hair would be a mess by the morning? As he was stood totally naked looking into the closet for a headscarf with his back facing her, she was now looking at his beautiful sexy bottom which was like one of those roman statues that are in most Museum's around the world, and she can hardly wait to dig her manicured nails into it. He eventually found a pink one, and he was now laid at the side of her as she was sat up fixing it as usual just above her eye brows. As she now laid down he was leaning on his elbow looking down at this gorgeous sexy looking woman who now is lifting her body from the bed, and now giving him the most tender smooch he has had in his life, which is driving him crazy, it really is. As she lies back down he has now followed her and now their bodies are now as one.

Everything is now poised for them to have intercourse, but not before Stella has checked his protection and dug her fingernails into those very fit buttocks of his. It wasn't till 3pm that they finally melted into each other's arms and got some sleep. Next morning at breakfast he told Stella that if he had to keep up to her demands for sex, he would be an old man by the time he was 40. Stella had been walking round the house topless and with the same style of jeans that she had on in Alexandria, cut with scissors to the top of her thighs.

She turned around and told him that if that was the case, it was a good job that she was going home on the Friday. When Stella eventually decided to put some decent attire on, Adrien asked her if she would like a trip up into the wonderful mountains of Switzerland ; which she agreed would be a good day out. A delightful boat trip down Lake Thun to Interlaken, where when they were having lunch they had a good view of the mountain Jungfraujoch, which also is the home of the North Face of the Eiger. When they arrived back at Adrien's house, he said he would make her a meal to remember while she had a lovely hot bath. When the meal had been prepared she sat down at the dining table in just a sleeveless polo neck blouse, and a tight fitting skirt.

She apologised for not looking at her best for such an occasion, but she had only brought enough clothes for a couple of days. He told her that she had no need to apologise as she would have looked terrific even if she had rags on. After the meal which Stella said was perfect in taste and arrangement, they got their pinafores on and got all the dishes and pans washed and put away together.

Adrien now took her to a section of the house where you get one of the finest views of Zurich that there is.

As well there is a small bar that has a wide choice of wines and cocktails, maybe even Gin and Orange with ice. They are sat on the Sofa together with their own type of drink in their hands (Adrien's favourite is a Cosmopolitan Cocktail). Looking out of this twenty foot wide window on to the city, Stella has now put her head on his shoulder, he is looking down at her while she is now looking up at him, they give each other a kiss. They both now want to go to bed and relive what they did last night. Stella promised him that she wouldn't wake him up during the night as it would obviously remove more of his energy.

After another satisfying night together, they spent the morning on the veranda talking about his children, and that they would be coming home on Saturday, with his wife following on Sunday. Adrien was asking Stella: `What it is like living in London? And when will she think about settling down and having children of her own? Though they are talking quite amicably, Stella can see that Adrien although being a super host and sleeping partner, there is a certain amount of guilt that he is now feeling because of his infidelity.

Even though he has always been faithful to his wife, it must be said that for the last six months, he has been starved of a woman's touch, but had never been involved with any other woman sex wise. It was only when he saw Stella at the Fashion show that he decided to stray outside his squeaky clean principles, and hoping that Stella wouldn't slap his face. On the contrary she could see that he was unhappy and offered him solace (and a bit more). As it turned out for that short time he was a happy man. She is aware that the time has come to tell him almost immediately that it is time for her to leave.

So that he can now look to the future and reinvent his life around his wife and children. Adrien appreciates Stella's concern and understanding. Suddenly you can feel that there is a euphoric movement in Adrien's body language. He is now realising that although he and Stella had a perfect relationship for those two nights, it was now time to return to reality. After getting all of her belongings together, Adrien took her back to the hotel, where she would carry on being the best model in the business. Adrien told Stella that he wouldn't be attending today because somehow it just wouldn't seem right.

He thanked her for her company and loving affection over those two days, and that he will never forget the name Stella Delray. Stella tells Adrien `Your wife is so lucky to have you as her husband. When she is cured from the depression that she has at the moment, she will realize that fact, when you will both be very happy, and hopefully for the rest of your lives, and the minuscule affair that we had will fade into insignificance`.

With that they said goodbye with a final kiss, they were waving to each other as Stella retired into the hotel and Adrien drove away. On the Friday Stella and the other models arrived back in London. She got a taxi back to her shared home with Kim and her brother Gary who had incidentally just finished for the weekend themselves. The three of them went about making a lavish meal, which was subsequently polished off in no time. They now settled down for the evening in the lounge, where not long ago Stella and Cheryl had spent many enjoyable evenings together. They were asking Stella if the Zurich trip had gone down well.

So without mentioning anything about her brief affair, she told them that as far as she knows it must have been a success as the hotel was full of customers. Gary who was now smiling said he would find out from Denis O'Keefe who was in charge of that trip on Monday at the offices of "Square House".

The weeks went by. Nothing happening that you would write home about. Kim was invited by Stella to go shopping with her in and around the Inner city of London on Saturdays, since Cheryl had gone to live in Miami. Kim was over the last few weeks finding Saturday shopping more interesting as it was one way of getting out and meeting friends, and sometimes business opportunities that came out of the blue.

Also having Stella with her made it worthwhile. On the following Monday Kim has a job lined up for her. `Where is it?` asked Stella `Paris at their annual Motor Show it's open for 14 days` `What do I have to do?` `Just sit on a car bonnet looking sexy` `Am I going on my own?` `No I will be going with you, to keep an eye on you` Stella is now laughing. `Sounds quite interesting, can't wait`.

Thursday has come and they entering this big arena of cars, trucks, basically anything with four wheels. The stand they are looking for will have "Belle" above the stand. The doors open at 10.am, so that gives Stella an hour to get her gear on. It is now time for the doors to open, everything seems to be in place. All around this big arena there are plenty of lovely girls having their pictures taken as they pose on these million dollar cars. The man who owns "Belle Motor Company" is Constantin Schadeck who has two sons and a daughter; one of his sons has come with him to sort out any problems that may occur. The photographers are asking Stella to lay on her back across the bonnet of the car with her long blond hair hanging over the side, which brings some cheering and wolf whistles into the equation.

Alain who is the eldest son of Mr. Schadeck who is 29 is finding it hard to take his eyes off Stella. With Alain having gone to Cambridge University eight years ago to study technical engineering he can speak very good English. Near the end of the first day and after speaking to Stella quite regularly, he has offered to take her out for a meal. She tells Kim about Alain's offer, who tells her to go out and enjoy herself.

This being her 5th day of six (when another model from Square House will take over for the remainder of the show). Alain now takes Stella out to a luxurious restaurant in the centre of Paris. One or two of his friends have also come to Paris for a few days of fun. They have managed to get his bedroom key and are now looking into his drawers looking for his condoms. When they eventually find them, they are now giggling to themselves like drunken yobs that they obviously are, and are now piercing one of the condoms with a pin. They put the packet back with the now damaged one at the top.

Meanwhile back at the restaurant Stella and Alain are getting to know each other so well that it is almost certain that they are going to end up sleeping together. When they return to the hotel, Stella tells Kim that she and Alain have pulled each other, so a wink of the eye is telling Kim she will see her in the morning. Now in his bedroom, they are now stripping down to just their underwear, with in between a few passionate kisses. It is noticeable that Stella is about one inch taller than Alain. Stella uses the bathroom first while Alain is combing his hair which he has plenty of.

When Alain goes into the bathroom, Stella is getting in between the sheets. As she hears that he is nearly finished in the bathroom she now lies on her stomach with her long blond hair stretching half way down her back where the top of the bed sheet is just about covering her shapely backside, which will put his sex engine (hopefully into overdrive). She is aroused herself when she sees him approaching the bed with a noticeable six pack wrapped up in a well sun tanned body, which makes his pearly white teeth stand out more so. Now having turned around, she now is laying with her head back on the pillow, looking up at this attractive man who at the moment is ticking all the boxes of what she sees as her perfect man.

With only two boxes left to tick is his performance and the size of his penis. After eyeballing his super fit body, she would be very disappointed if he hadn't enough stamina in his balls to give her full satisfaction. `Have you got your protection on yet Alain?` She asks. He pulls the bed sheet down to show her that he has. `My God!` said Stella with her mouth open in shock and saying `And how am I supposed to accommodate that?`Alain is laughing, Stella isn't. At one point Alain feels as though his body is like a piano, because her hands are wandering from one end of his body to the other, but he is confident that she will get a lovely tune out of it shortly. Nevertheless they had a night to remember.

They are now in a situation that the protection that Alain was wearing had been tampered with by his so called friends who will be regretting their actions tomorrow. When the two of them awoke next morning, it was reminiscent of a newlywed couple; feeling very relaxed in each other's company. Breakfast at the hotel saw Alain sat with his noisy friends, and Stella has met up with Kim who wanted to know how the night had gone, sleeping with that handsome man. Stella couldn't resist telling Kim how big his **thingy** was. Kim's eyes were now wide open and her mouth ready to drool over her friends assessment. `Will you be seeing him again?` asked Kim `He is taking me on a river cruise this evening`.

Hours later on that river cruise he felt as though he had to tell Stella that his drunken friends this morning had admitted to him, that they had put a hole in his condom.

Stella now visibly upset said `How could they do something so stupid? Alain is looking into her face as though he is the one to blame. `I told them that they were complete idiots, and if anything untoward happens I would break their bloody necks`, after a few moments thought he told Stella that `I just think that they may not have done what they told me, but instead just trying to frighten me`. `Well I just hope that you are right` said Stella, with a now concerned look on her face.

`After we had sex` asked Stella didn't you notice anything about the condom that could have told you that it had been damaged in some way?` `No' replied Alain because just after, I had to pay a quick visit to the john in the dark, and I straight away flushed it down the pan`. Nothing else was mentioned about this most unsavoury of incidents. After another romantic evening sleeping together they find themselves getting more and more involved with each other. Their eagerness to make love is another boost to cement their affections for each other. On her final day in Paris, Alain introduces Stella to his parents, although they obviously don't know anything about her, but at least they can see that she is a beautiful girl.

That for the moment will suffice. They suggest to their son that he should invite Stella to their Villa in Monaco in the spring. Before they parted temporarily,

Alain told her that she shouldn't worry about the possibility of her being pregnant because he would stand by her no matter what happened, and would ask her to marry him where they would settle down in Monaco and have a fantastic life together . So now back in London Stella has plenty of engagements to attend. Every other day at some point Kim asks her if there has been any text messages sent to her by Alain, and every other day she has to tell her no. Then one day Stella tells Kim that she has received a text from Alain saying that he is going to Valle di Susa in Northern Italy with some friends on a skiing vacation.

He wishes she was here too, so they could have a snowball fight, and also rub her face in the snow, he also tells her that he will see her soon. Stella is now laughing to herself. A week later as Stella and Kim are watching T.V. at home, they suddenly look at each other in horror; there has been an avalanche in the region near to the Valle di Susa and five skiers have been swept to their deaths. `Oh my God that is where your boyfriend is` said Kim, Stella can't say anything she has gone totally numb. Kim tries to take Stella's fear away by telling her that there will be hundreds of skiers in that area, and there would be a good chance that he would be safe.

As much as Stella would love to believe that, she has a gut feeling that he is one of them, as her eyes are still frozen to the TV screen. Kim has now made a strong cup of tea. Stella has no idea which hotel he was staying at. All they can do is wait until the following morning when national newspapers give more details. Luckily Stella had no appointments that day.

So hopefully she would find out if he was still alive. The fact that she hasn't had a recent text from him to assure her that he was alright was not a good sign.

The daily newspapers confirmed to her what she had already accepted: that he and three of his friends, plus two others were killed by an unstoppable surge of snow that didn't give them a chance.

Although she was stunned with the awful news, she wanted to let his parents know how sorry she was, but on reflection, how would they get any solace from someone who they hardly knew. So she let that idea slip from her mind as she lay on top of her bed, with hundreds of other thoughts flashing around inside her troubled mind. Another one of her thoughts was, would Alain have been the man that would have finally brought her happiness for the rest of her life. Now she would never know. In her life Stella has had many tragedies to live thru, just like a lot of other people, and when they happen each one is just as painful as the ones before, you can never become immune. As a few more weeks went by the anguish was slowly subsiding. Although she didn't deserve it Stella was about to realize a much more worrying chapter in her life. After a visit to the doctor, she was told that she was pregnant.

She was well past the date when she would normally have her monthlies. When she got back home she was subdued to say the least. Kim was under the impression that she was still upset about the Alain issue. She now went up to Stella putting her arm around her shoulder and asked if she was alright. When Stella turned around her eyes were full of tears, she now collapsed into Kim's arms. Within a moment they were now both sat on the settee with Kim's arm still around her shoulder,

\`What has happened for you to be like this?\` asked Kim. Stella was now going thru the whole story of what happened, and how it is now going to seriously affect her life from now on. After hearing her story Kim was in tears herself thinking of those so called friends of Alain who did such a wicked thing, whether they were drunk or not, was not an excuse. A nice cup of tea and a shoulder to cry on was what Stella needed. Kim was the one who would help her as much as she could, but it was Stella who would make the final decisions on anything that was advised.

The first thing that came into Kim's mind was would she resort to having an abortion, when she asked her friend she emphatically said **she personally** would never resort to putting an end to a human life before it had even started, and that she would never be able to live with herself if she accepted that way out. `So you are going to have the baby?` asked Kim `Yes I am, not just for my beliefs, but also for Alain where at least part of him will continue to live on.

For the next few months everything was just the same as before Stella was still the most sought after model that company's wanted. Which gave `Square House' a bigger reputation, which would create more profit. Stella and Kim were still going to the shops and coffee bars on Saturdays. Meeting friends who would never be told about the calamity surrounding Stella. Only two people knew that apart from Stella and that was Kim and Gary. Kim had noticed that Stella was on the computer quite frequently looking at houses for sale, when asked why she was interested in looking for houses.

Stella told her that `Very shortly I will be entering that stage of the pregnancy where people will begin to notice a bump in my tummy. People such as friends and neighbours, maybe even people like the postman. They would be asking each other questions knowing that I am not even married and saying to each other `I wonder who the father is etc? you know what I mean?` `I know exactly what you mean but does that mean that you are thinking of leaving us?` `Put it this way Kim if I stay here, it is not going to be fair to you and Gary listening to a baby crying during the night is it?` `Well I see what you mean, and that is very thoughtful of you looking at it from that angle` `It just simply wouldn't work said Stella. At the moment Stella is looking into Kim's face that has an ocean of sympathy knowing the predicament that her friend is in.

Kim is now asking if she has seen anywhere on the computer that she likes.

`There is a nice house for sale with 3 bedrooms, a long garden, which stands back off the road` `Where is that?` asked Kim now looking at Stella with more than a varied interest `Well according to the Internet it is a house just on the outskirts of Bagshot, which has a population of just over 5,000 residents. Where nobody knows me, or where I come from which is just what I require` Kim has now a concerned look on her face when she says `I just hope you know what you are doing, although it isn't too far away from us` `I hope that you and Gary will visit me while I am there?` `There is no problem with that, it's just you on your own that is bothering me`. `I used to live on my own when I lived in London, sometimes I enjoy my own company`.

Over the next month Stella has now bought the house, and as well had it refurbished to the style she likes. The centre of the village is about a ¼ mile away which has a: Supermarket, recreation hall, post office, library and a church. Stella is quite happy with the surroundings. Spring is just around the corner, and apart from reading the same old magazines that she had brought from London; she has learned how to grow flowers thanks to Mr. Smith (Arthur) her neighbour, who with his wife Denise live in a cottage about 20yds further up the road (he is a retired motor mechanic).He has already told Stella that if her car lets her down he will fix it for her.

Whenever she walks into the centre she knows that people are looking and wondering who she is and where she has come from. When a stranger comes to live in a village of this size, the villagers are always wary at first, as to whether they should make conversation with them or wait to see if anybody else will break the ice, they really do.

One morning Stella decided to walk down to the village as it was such a nice day. She noticed a gentleman on a push bike. He looked as though he was at retirement age, as his face was quite red with a forehead full of sweat probably as a result of trying to keep himself fit.

She asked him where the village library was. He told her to `Go down to the zebra crossing` pointing to it at the same time, carry on till you come to the first street on your right, go down there and it is about 30yds on your left.' Stella thanked him as he now sped off in the same direction as she was going. When he had reached the zebra crossing he stopped and turned around to show her that the library was down the street where he was now pointing to. She now waved to him as he now carried on down the high street, when he just suddenly disappeared round a corner.

Before she went to the library she sat on a bench which had been bought by relatives in recognition of some lady who must have spent nearly all of her life in the small town. As she looked around her she saw two older ladies with their shopping baskets walking past the butcher's window, waving to him as he was sharpening his knives. A bus pulled in to let people get on and off. The bus had Bracknell on the front. Just as she was about to go to the library, a man with a dog collar came and sat at the side of her (obviously the vicar). `Good morning` he said `Good morning` Stella replied with a smile. `Are you just a visitor to the village? he asked` `No I live here, I have only been here for a few weeks` The vicar gave her a belated welcoming smile.

`This is the first time I have seen you, where are you living? `Just down the hill as you go out of the village`

`Ah yes I know where you mean, the house that was for sale two months ago, on your right hand side` `That's right`. The vicar now tells Stella that `The couple who lived there went to live in Melbourne Australia to be near their son and his family.' although not really looking as if she is interested, she carries on the conversation by asking `How long had they lived in the village?` `I would say about 25 years` `Obviously they must have liked living here?` `Like it they loved it, in fact it was a very close decision as to whether they would stay or go`. The vicar is now looking at Stella and saying `Anyway it's time for me to go as I have a sermon to prepare for Sunday`, at the same time shrugging his shoulders, and saying `Don't forget if you want to forge some new friendships, my Church is the place to be` `Thank you I will give it a thought` with that the vicar was now making his way to the Church.

Stella thought it was about time she made a move to the library. A few months ago she would probably have sprung up from this seat like a frog from a stream, but not now she has to do it nice and easy as the lump in her stomach (now 8 months) is obviously getting larger.

CHAPTER FOURTEEN

Spending thirty minutes in the library in her present condition to find 3 murder mysteries was long enough, especially as she had to wait for her membership card as well. The librarian was one of those ladies, who you know what they were going to look like before you even see them. Usually tall and skinny with their hair done up in a bun, a silk blouse with bow, and with their glasses perched at the end of a long nose which rarely ever got used. That is unless they notice someone like Stella who is pregnant and who has no ring of any kind on her left hand. They are then put firmly back where they should be, so they can get a better view.

Getting some groceries was the last thing she was going to do that day, apart from bed a few plants in her garden. All in all she was happier now that she had found this house, and good neighbours in Arthur and Denise. As well she had a very healthy bank account, so she wouldn't need to look for a job after her baby was born.

During the week Stella had a visit from Kim and Gary, to see how she was adapting to her new life. They also told her that they were keeping their fingers crossed, that she would eventually do some more modelling for them. Which gave Stella something to look forward to.

She gave Susan a call to tell her that there would be a delay in their getting together again, but telling her also that she would get a big, big surprise when they meet. Stella was now over 8 months pregnant, and for the first time in her life she felt really alone. As she sat in her living room one night, she realized that even when her baby was a year old, it would be almost impossible to get back into modelling. Who for example would look after her child while she was going on these hour long runs, and working out at a fitness centre? There was just nobody that she knew well enough to be trusted to do it for her.

She did actually think of Arthur and Denise, the old retired couple who were her near neighbours but it wouldn't be fair to them to be regularly disturbed, also having to listen to a baby's crying. So now as a result she would put extra weight on, as the jogging and going to the fitness centre would have to be ruled out. It now looks as though all her dreams are quickly evaporating. At worst she will find another man who will give her sexual satisfaction, where in a few years from now there will be a couple of kids hanging around her apron strings as she is cooking her husband's tea, before he gets home from work.

One night when she was laid in bed trying to get some sleep, she heard a noise in her garden, as though someone had knocked one of her plant pots off the wall. She felt as though she should at least look out of the bedroom window to see if anyone was there. It was just a bit too dark to see if anyone was hanging around. As she turned to get back into bed, she noticed the light go on in the big shed at the bottom of her garden, although it only lasted a few seconds.

However next morning as she looked out again, it was as if someone had definitely been there last night, as there was a small pile of soil on the path, but the pot had found its way back on to the wall. What is going on she thought to herself. While she was having breakfast and looking into her garden, suddenly the door of the big shed opened and a man about Stella's age came out looking rather gingerly. Stella opened the back door and asked him `What are you doing in my shed?` he replied `I hope you don't mind but I slept in there last night` `But there isn't enough room to swing a cat around in there`. He smiled at Stella and said `Yes I know but I was trying to get out of the rain` Stella looked at the poor man who was wet thru. Water was dripping from his hair as he made his way slowly towards her. He was now stood at her back door.

She noticed that he was shivering` Are you going to send for the police?` he asked. `Of course I'm not`. Stella was now feeling very sorry for him. He was now making his way towards her gate, telling her that he wouldn't bother her again. `Look!` shouted Stella `come inside for a minute`. He was giving his shoes a good clean on her mat before he entered the kitchen.` Are you hungry?` she asked him, with a nervous smile he told her that he was. `Get that wet raincoat off, or you will get pneumonia, do you want to have a hot bath before I give you a good fry up?` `Are you sure?` he said giving Stella another nice smile that she thought was rather cute`

`Of course I'm sure`. After his hot bath, he shouted to her did she have a towel for him. She opened the door a few inches and threw one in. Five minutes later he came out with the bath towel wrapped around his waist, and who was now drying his black curly hair with a hand towel. Stella couldn't believe the before and after appearance of this man, he was as tall as her with a fine physique and also good looking.

`I have ironed your shirt and trousers for you` `You are the kindest person that I have met since I have been on the run `How do you mean?` asked Stella. `I have been sleeping rough in peoples garden sheds, and garages` `What did they say to you, when you were seen doing this?` `I was threatened a few times, they told me they would send for the police` `Why have you had to resort to this way of life?` Stella is now asking him with a serious look on her face, she really is. The young man has now put his shirt back on. `Are you sure that you want to hear about it?` `Of course I do, I have as much spare time as you need`. He told her that he is a script-writer for a couple of TV soaps. Who up to now had been living with his mother Irene 53. Apparently one day on his way to London from his home in Reading, he thought he would stop for a break at one of those food outlets in between. As he was sat at the bar having a drink while his order was being made up, a man came in and sat down at the side of him, he was a total stranger, soon they were discussing the football match that had just been on the car radio, which they had been listening to in their own separate cars. It seems that this man was ranting and raving that Liverpool had hit the upright and crossbar four times and had been well on top, but had lost 2-1 to their neighbours Everton.

This man surely must have already planned to rob this food outlet earlier in the day because he now produced a gun from his jacket, along with a bag that he was now telling the cashier to fill with money from the till.

The young man (Chris Tennyson) was unable to move because the man had obviously lost his marbles, and any sudden movement by him could have been the last thing he ever did. What made it worse was that he was stood next to Chris all the time. When the cashier had given him the money, the manager came out to tell the man to give himself up, as the police were now outside. In Chris's own words `I couldn't believe it, the idiot shot at the manager, he really did. I actually saw the bullet enter his arm, it was like one of those American gangster movies, you know what I mean. As the two police officers came in, he turned the gun on them, but before he could fire they had no alternative but to shoot him dead. I had never moved an inch I swear during the whole incident. The cashier told the cops that I was in cahoots with this madman. She assumed that because me and this man were sat in conversation that I was part of this attempted robbery`.

Before I had time to explain that I didn't even know this guy, there I was now sat in a police car with my hands behind my back and in cuffs. When down at the station I was thrown into a cell. The following day I was given the "third degree" but they didn't want to believe my version of what happened, they really didn't. One of the detectives told me that I would probably get ten years in prison, for being an accessory to an attempted robbery and attempted murder`. Stella looked quite shocked that somebody could be given such a sentence for something they had nothing to do with.

`Eventually I was released on police bail`, my Mum knew that I would never do anything so stupid like what I was accused of, she has been wonderful to me since my dad was killed in a freak accident when I was six years old, anyway that is a different story`. Stella interrupts him to ask if he would like tea or coffee?` `Coffee if that is okay` `By the way shouldn't we introduce ourselves, my name is Stella Delray`, the look on Chris's face tells you that he has heard that name before, `That name rings a bell, there is someone, who has been in showbiz magazines or suchlike`, after a few moments he says to her `It will come to me eventually, anyway my name is Chris Tennyson' now they both shake hands.

As Chris is now taking a sip of coffee, he carries on telling Stella about the awful predicament that he has found himself in. `Being told that I could be behind bars for 10 years frightened the crap out of me, it really did` `So what did you do?` `On the morning I was supposed to attend court, I didn't turn up simple as that. There was no way that I was going to go down for something that was none of my making. If the police hadn't gone into that Fast Food outlet with that "shoot first ask questions later" attitude I wouldn't be sat in your kitchen a fugitive, instead I would be a free man` `What did your mother think of you jumping bail?` `She was more bothered about me being on the run from the law` `So you haven't seen your mother for over a week?` `That's right, if I went back home the police would have me back in cuffs quicker than you can say "Alcatraz" `What are you doing about money?` Stella asked `I am down to my last few pounds, I left the car at home because I realized they would soon have picked me up, so I was now rushing around the house to fill my duffle bag before the police would arrive, but stupid me forgot my bank card` `Can't your mum send you the card thru the post?` `Of course she could, but I have no permanent address that she can send it to`.

Stella is now wondering if she can help him some more by offering him a roof over his head till his card comes. Not only that but it would be nice to have a good looking man around the house, who is about the same age as well.

Chris has now drank his coffee and intimated that he will bother her no more with his problems and move on. Stella now tells him that it is only right that she should offer him accommodation until his bank card arrives. `It is very kind of you to offer but how can I, you look as though you are about to give birth to a child, and I don't think that your husband will allow a stranger accommodation, especially in this situation` `I'm not married or have a partner` Chris is suddenly looking aghast at her. `How can a woman so beautiful be having a child but with no husband?` He now puts his duffle bag back on the floor, and sits down just looking up at Stella waiting for an explanation to this out of the blue puzzle.

Stella who is now embarrassed tells him it is a long story, and if he wants to eventually hear it he will have to change his mind and stay. Chris is now smiling as he agrees to stay. Stella tells him to make himself at home as she will now get one of the bedrooms ready for him. While she is doing that she tells him to ring his mum up to send the bank card to this address. While she is putting clean bed sheets on she can hear him talking to his mother. After a few minutes he is at the bottom of the stairs calling up to her, that she will send it today.

`Come upstairs and see your bedroom` as he enters he says `That is beautiful,you really are very kind` `Well it's a lot better than my garden hut isn't it?` Chris is now looking at her and saying `You aren't kidding`. They are now back downstairs and Stella asks him if he would like something else to eat. `I'm alright at the moment thank you, but I feel as though I am bothering you` `Think nothing of it, I'm sure you would do the same for me if it had been the other way round` `All I know, is that when my card comes I will repay you, plus I will take you out for a nice meal somewhere that is quiet` `I will look forward to that` said Stella. In the days that followed, the two of them were almost like a married couple, she cooked all the meals and he did the washing up.

She put the washing out while he vacuumed the carpets. She made the beds while he did her gardening. Stella watched TV while Chris went on to her computer to do some scripts for television soaps. The time may be getting near to when she might be going into labour. Chris didn't have to wait long before his mum sent the bank card thru the post.

He would now be able to pay his way, rather than feel like a beggar. Stella wouldn't accept any money from him under any circumstances. As the police already knew his registration he wouldn't dare use his car, that is why he left it in Reading. Stella told him to use her car. So he drove down to the town centre of Bagshot to get some new clothes, and some shopping for Stella for the weekend. He was going to take Stella out for a meal that he had promised her, but she had a feeling that this could be the weekend she would give birth.

If ever she needed someone at her side it was now, and Chris was going to stay with her until its arrival. It was 10 pm when she felt the pain, plus she was beginning to sweat a lot. He told her that he was going to take her to hospital in her car, he got her comfortable and was at the hospital within 10 minutes. You would have thought that he was the father of the baby the way that he was walking up and down the corridor. It wasn't long before he could hear a new born baby being born, was it either Stella's or somebody else's. A nurse came out and asked him if he was Mr. Delray.

He was so excited for Stella that he at first said `Yes, I mean no, er yes well sort of I suppose' the nurse looked at him as though she didn't quite know who he was himself, but told him anyway that Mrs. Delray had a baby boy, who weighed 7lb 9 ounces. `You can go in and see them both if you want to` `Only if she wants me to` said Chris, the nurse went back in but soon came out to tell him that Stella did want him to go in. As Chris went in she was smiling at him, she had the baby in her arms. As he was looking at the baby, he asked her if she had chosen any names yet. `I think I will name him Alain, it's a French name as his father was French` `That is a good name` Chris gave Stella a kiss on the cheek for being brave. `When can she go home? Chris asked the nurse `There seem to be no complications, so if you come tomorrow afternoon that should be alright`.

He told Stella that tomorrow he would come for her at 4pm.

The following day Stella was now back home with baby Alain and her new friend Chris. Stella was very much hoping that Chris would say that he would stop for a while, rather than say he would now have to go. As it turned out there was no way he was going to leave her on her own until she was back into her stride.

He was now going to make a meal for himself and Stella. Chris even got the baby's bath ready to pour the warm water into, and in doing so amazed Stella that he tested the warmth of the water with his elbow `Where did you learn about making sure that the water wasn't too hot by using your elbow?` `It's just something that I remember seeing, probably on TV`. Apart from when the midwife came, Chris was always there for her. After a month had gone by Stella was now back into her stride, not only that Chris was still there. Both of them were now very close to each other, in fact if you didn't already know you would assume that baby Alain was his child. Stella told Chris of the anger she felt when the doctor told her that she was going to be a mother a lot earlier in life than she had anticipated, but now she is the mother of a beautiful baby boy, the anger has now disappeared and is now allowing her to enter a situation in her life that she is now fully prepared for.

She had the baby because she personally didn't believe that abortion was the correct way to get out of the mess that she was in. Chris was very sympathetic to her predicament.

Chris kept in touch with his mum, although it would be foolhardy to visit her, as there would be neighbours that would tell the police, and he would be arrested and put back in prison. So it was arranged that his mum would come and see him at Stella's house.

CHAPTER FIFTEEN

So Chris arranged to meet his mum outside the railway station in Bagshot. He would be waiting in Stella's silver Ford car. On that day Stella was a bit nervous about meeting his mum, as like most mothers they are very protective towards their children. With Stella now being a one parent family, Irene his mother would probably want to know what happened to the father of the child, or why she was living alone.

However on the way back to the house Chris explained to his mother what happened to her life, and how they were now the best of friends. Also the fact that she had given him help when he most needed it. As they were now coming up the path, Stella already had the kettle boiling. As soon as Chris introduced them to each other, Irene couldn't have been nicer if she tried. She wanted to hold baby Alain even though there were none of her genes in its body.

Irene was content that her son was reasonably happy in the desperate circumstances he was at the moment embroiled in. When they were sat in the lounge with coffee and biscuits, there was still the dilemma of Chris jumping bail and being hunted by the police. If and when caught he would probably have the book thrown at him. Eventually during that afternoon, Chris and his mother came to the conclusion that he should now, although reluctantly hand himself over to the police. As hopefully the truth would come out sooner or later, that he simply didn't know the man in the Food Outlet at any time in his life. And that the young girl cashier had made a sudden and wrongful miscalculation, on something that had basically happened in a flash. Stella was upset that he may never return, but Chris after giving her a kiss on the cheek promised her that he would definitely come back at some point.

After saying their goodbyes Chris and his mum arranged for a taxi to take them to the police station, where he was again arrested. When Irene got back home, she gave Stella a call to tell her that he had now been transferred to London, and she was now going to hire a top lawyer to represent her son and to clear his name. Stella tells her that she will keep her fingers crossed until she hears he is free.

A month later to the day Irene has given Stella a call telling her that Chris had been released and cleared of a crime that he had never committed, or even been a part of. Stella was now asking Irene if he was going to come and visit her at any time soon. Irene told her that his uncle Adam after hearing of his favourite nephews plight, told him over the phone to pack his suitcase and to get his backside over there for as long as he wants to stay for. Stella was curious to know where **over there** was. Irene told her that his uncle Adam had a half share in a hotel in Praia which is on the island of Santiago in the Cape Verde islands. That is where Chris would be based. `What would happen as regarding his script writing for the TV soaps?` was what Stella now asked Irene. `Apparently before he left, he came to an arrangement that he would regularly send them back to London as he would now have plenty of time to catch up on his work, which was all down to that wrong accusation and of being held in custody` There was nothing else that Irene could tell Stella, but promised her that when he comes back she will tell him immediately to get in touch. Stella in a way was happy that Chris had been rewarded for all the torment that he had been put thru in the last month or so.

So now for the foreseeable future she is back to where she originally was. The days quickly turn into weeks, then months, and before you know another year has now gone by, and now Alain is amazingly not far off being two years old, but at the moment nothing is happening in Stella's life. Only that she is frustrated that she is putting on more weight. Also that she is not in a position to do much about it. She would like to do a three mile jog every other day, and also regularly go to a Fitness centre, but can't because of the baby. As regarding Chris there has still been no communication. So she has now assumed that he probably doesn't want to have a relationship with a girl, who has had a child by another man. Which in a way is quite understandable.

Stella at the moment was feeling trapped in a situation that was completely reverse to the life she had in L/A. What kept her chin up was the fact that she could see the light at the end of this unfortunate tunnel. She was confident her modelling career would be reborn, by moving back to London. However at the moment there is a fly in the ointment. His name was Ethan Byrne who lived in the vicinity aged 48, who apparently had a bad name in the community for being lazy; jobless, scruffy; as well as being a habitual drinker. He had found out that this gorgeous woman was living on her own. As soon as he saw her, he wanted her into his life as soon as possible. After some enquiries he found out that she was as well a single parent.

THE FACT FILE OF ETHAN BYRNE

At the moment it would be ridiculous to even imagine any woman wanting to show the slightest bit of interest in this man who has simply nothing going for him. When young he had rippling muscles with a well toned body. And to his credit he managed to keep his body in good shape. Unfortunately that was then and not now. Now his general demeanour has sunk to a degrading low level within the last three years, he has been rightly referred to as "The Scavenger" by people who wouldn't now give him the time of day. Up to the point when he had been told that his sporting life (Rugby Union)was over, he had been very popular with the ladies, a six footer with a good fit body and who had given sexual satisfaction aplenty. But the general feeling is that in his playing days, his head and body had taken more than its fair share of a battering, plus occasionally the odd concussion.

For example he cannot now sustain an intelligent conversation for long, it's as if half of his brain isn't quite up to speed, though it obviously doesn't stop him from noticing a pretty girl when he sees one. When as a younger man he could charm many a woman into his bed with his enticing vocabulary and his handsome looks.

All that, I'm sorry to say has now deserted him; having an obscene looking beer gut doesn't help either. Another spanner in his works is that he spent some months in prison after trying to get teenage girls to have sex with him, as a result he was regularly beaten up by the inmates. He was later transferred to a mental institution to try and get him thinking like normal again. The Governor released him back into the community hoping he had made the correct decision, but for some psychological reason he has now become allergic to work, and wanting to be involved in only pornographic sex activities.

His eldest daughter who is reasonably sympathetic to his mental disability, still keeps in touch with him, but the other members of his family don't want to know this now lazy, mental moron anymore.

END OF FACT FILE

So two years after being thrown out of his home by his wife, his obsession was now to think of a way that would get this beautiful woman to make passionate love to him, and who hopefully would eventually want to be the bearer of his children. It must be pointed out that Stella is totally unaware of this man's unpopularity in the town, or of his mental problems. One day as he was walking past her house (accidentally on purpose I might add) he noticed that she was trying to move some old heavy fencing to the front gate for disposal.

With it being a hot day he as well noticed that she was wearing only a white sleeveless cropped t-shirt, which made her breast nipples stand out quite prominently, with as well the same style of cutaway jeans that she wore in Alexandria two years ago. This was now his chance to acquaint himself with this gorgeous female who seems to have everything that a hungry for sex man lusts for. He now goes to help her, and to tell her that she shouldn't be exerting herself moving about heavy fencing and such like. After sweating like a pig for the last half hour; the job has been done. As he was making his way towards her kitchen door, Stella was impishly clapping this perfect stranger's effort to help making the garden reasonably tidy. She was now welcoming him into her kitchen.

Letting him get a foothold into her house could and probably would in the long term be a bad mistake; though in the short term due to a growing nymphomania problem which for some unknown reason had entered her life, which was not long after Alain was born (which could be the significant cause?) It could be quite advantageous in her attempt to finally bring sex back into her life, but the last man she needed was of the Ethan Byrne calibre. He is the kind of man who won't do work without reward, that reward hopefully is having a long passionate affair with Stella. After being invited in to her house, he is now sat on a bar stool in her kitchen with a well earned can of beer. He was listening to this beautiful woman explaining to him how she was hoping to make her garden nicer.

She had already noticed that he is quite a bit older than her, but to his credit being tall, and still muscular. A noticeable downturn though is his now fading good looks, his down to the shoulders greasy matted hair protruding beer gut; nevertheless he could be the answer to the sexual starvation she has had to endure. As he gets up from his stool to trash the empty beer can, Stella has come up behind him to thank him again for moving the fencing. When he turns around he is more than surprised to see her looking straight into his eyes with a look that he not seen from another woman for quite a few years; a look that says `I desperately need and want you,` both of her hands are now moving up past his sweat filled t-shirt to rest behind his neck. Still looking into each other's eyes, she reaches up to plant her beautiful mouth on to his for a longer than normal smooch kiss. In his mind this now proved that she was desperate to be more than just a friend, and that he feels sure that when the time arrives she will be eager to accept the depraved sexual acts that he has already assembled in his mind for her in her bedroom.

At the moment he decides to play it cool by moving towards the kitchen door and asking was there anything else she needed doing around the house, which was not the kind of response she had expected. The first thing that entered her head was that she now wanted this rough and ready man to be around the house regularly. She said to him that `There could be a few jobs next week if you want to come?` `Let me know` he told her with a sly grin`(on this occasion: not as daft as he looks).

During that following week where Ethan is now becoming a regular visitor and Stella is steadily warming to him. She has been close enough up to him to know that he could do with a hot bath with plenty of soap.

At the same time she knows that she could easily push him to the limits of fulfilling her sexual desires. Doing the odd jobs in her house and garden would be the key that would shortly lead him to her bedroom. Her body language tells us that she is quite willing to lower herself down to his degrading level to achieve sexual satisfaction with this degenerate . In the countless months that she has been in this small town, there has never been an opportunity to meet some normal man to have a romantic fling with.

The temptation of whether to accept this man into her life was (even from the first day) going to be overwhelming in Ethan's favour. As a result, any future ideas of getting her life back on track is now on a knife edge, which could now be the beginning of her moving towards a life of degradation. Chris Tennyson who looked upon Stella as a good friend hasn't got in touch for nearly two years. Normally she has regular tearful memories of Alain (father of her young son) who very probably would by now have been her husband, and living in Monaco. Coming back to reality Ethan has made a good impression in the following week doing odd jobs around the house and garden, which included a new sturdy fence.

In that same following week, after moving some heavy unwanted stones from her garden, she asked him if he would like to come round later for a meal and a relaxing evening, as well finding out more about each other. Obviously there was no chance of him refusing, after all he had bent his back (unusual for him) to make her garden look nice. So with him being so helpful to her (for a very obvious reason) she thought it was the least she could do.

Something came back into her mind from when she and Susan had come back from a vacation in southern Spain when they were in their teens, where she had handsome young men with tanned muscular bodies drooling over and wanting her affections. Though later confessing to some other friends that just for a change she wouldn't say no to having an affair with some older and more experienced man who was rough in appearance as well as being rough in other ways (could this be just the guy?)

That night as they were sat together on the settee, him with plenty of canned beer, and Stella with a Gin and orange or two. He was telling her that being a single parent was not ideal, and that there should be a man at her side (presumably meaning himself no doubt). `It would make things easier for you` he was quick to add before gulping down another can of beer, and wiping his mouth with the back of his hand. Stella told him, that she wouldn't rule him out, now looking into his eyes, and giving him the signals that she was willing to be more than just a friend by also giving him a friendly kiss on his scruffy unshaven cheek.

He certainly wasn't going to tell her that he had been thrown out of his house by his wife, for never attempting to find a job, and as well spending all day in the Bars and bookies losing money that was intended for his wife and family. Instead he told Stella that his wife was two –timing him and that he just packed his bags and left (which turned out to be the first in a long line of his lies), another kept secret that was never revealed was that he had been caught trying to seduce young girls into having sex with him.

Which resulted in him being put away from society for a while, where he was continually beaten up and given a hard time by most of the inmates. Looking rather sympathetic after believing his pack of lies, Stella now puts her head on his shoulder (she actually felt rather sorry for him, and wanted to give him some help as it looks as though he may have been betrayed by his wife). To him it was almost a certainty that he would soon be sleeping with her. Even though he wasn't quite Compos Mentis he could see that she was seemingly quite eager to find a man who would help her thru the night to more than just disarray the bed sheets. Amazingly he had never once enquired what the circumstances were that led up to this beautiful woman living alone with her young son (Maybe his brain antenna has its limitations to reach out quite so far for that kind of information to be revealed?).

Later on in the evening she asked him if he would like a night cap, `I would love to have one` he said. While they are sat on the settee drinking hot chocolate there was a sudden flash of lightning, Ethan looked out of the window, he told her that there was a river now running down the road. Obviously she couldn't let him go home in those conditions, and told him he could stay the night.

Once again there was no way that he would refuse such an offer. Unable to control a sudden surge of Nymphomania, she sees Ethan as the man who can at this moment in time can give her sexual satisfaction. After locking the doors they went upstairs together. Stella showed Ethan to his bedroom. He has now undressed down to his (seen better days) t-shirt and briefs, he realizes that he needs to relieve himself, after all the cans of beer he has downed in the last few hours. He had to walk past Stella's bedroom to get to the bathroom, he noticed that her door was almost closed. While in the bathroom he doesn't bother to wash his hands or face, but instead uses a mouth wash that would put at least a fresh taste back into his mouth. The use of some deodorant, that was half hidden in the bathroom cabinet, would be used on his much neglected unhygienic body.

He is now walking past Stella's bedroom, only this time her door is now more than halfway open. `Why has she now left her bedroom door open so wide?` he thought to himself. As he casually looked into her bedroom, she was sat up in bed in her hanging off the shoulder negligee. Reckoning not to have noticed him stood there, she now turned on to her side to switch the bedside lamp off, which purposely revealed her beautiful shaped hips, that glistens with a quite recently applied amount of baby oil which along with the skimpy looking thong will hopefully excite him enough to accept her teasing challenge. Now that the bedroom was in semi-darkness she turned around supposedly being quite surprised to see him just stood there in the doorway with just his briefs, plus the sleeveless t-shirt that was well short in trying to cover all of his beer gut.

Making a quick apology for making her jump he now goes back to his bedroom. This was definitely not what she had intended to happen. With the Nymphomania now literally spilling over, and her being so desperate to have sex, she had wanted this older, rough looking man to be in her bed, where she was more than ready to make passionate love to him all thru the night if need be, working her way towards something she had long been starved of: Intercourse. Instead she is now looking glumly to the other side of the bedroom, where the mirror on the closet is reflecting a now forlorn and so disappointed looking female, who also has the feeling of being somewhat scorned.

With her mass of long blond curly hair stretching halfway down her back, whose moist pouting mouth had as well been anticipating the probability of him seeking oral sex, where they both would get the maximum amount of pleasure by extracting from each other's body much more than just the normal sexual satisfaction.

At the moment she is at a loss trying to work out why he didn't seem to have any interest in what he has just seen on offer, which is certainly one big let down to her, especially as she was looking so stunningly seductive after giving herself the extra care and attention when putting her makeup on. She at the moment is now so frustrated that she has turned around to the pillows and is bashing into them before she decides to lay her head down, and sadly call it a day. With her eyes now beginning to close, she suddenly hears her bedroom door squeaking (which to her is usually quite annoying but not tonight for an obvious reason). She now sits up in bed and sees Ethan stood there, just like he was ten minutes ago.

Realising now that he had-had a change of mind, (whose teasing who here?) there was now the strong possibility of a heavy night of sex after all. Stella has now produced a brown crumpled up headscarf from a bedside drawer that she swiftly ties tightly around the top of her head which will safeguard her long blond hair getting messed up.

Now laying back on her pillows, it wasn't long before Ethan was stood over her at the side of her bed, where she was now looking up into his dark lustful eyes. He now shows her a sample of his intended aggression, by speedily removing the negligee from her body to the bedroom floor, which reveals a very healthy pair of firm protruding breasts.

After that rather aggressive introduction she was now anticipating a very stormy night, that will produce plenty of sexual satisfaction from him during those moonlight hours. But before that, wanting to give him the false impression that she was very frightened of this intrusion, and that his obvious intention was surely to rape her. Stella now purposely makes a rather slow and feeble attempt to get out of the bed at the other side but he easily pulls her back. Now with her wrists pinned by his hands against the pillows he now lowers his head down to hers, where suddenly all the fight and pretence to protect her body from this unprovoked attack has simply disappeared.

Now laid at the side of her with his arms surrounding her body in a vice like grip, he is amazed that so soon after supposedly trying to escape from his clutches, she seems firstly to be very passionate with her open mouth kisses. Not wanting to waste time after her quickly removing his grubby briefs, her fingers are now gently (with almost loving care) fondling his elongated testicles with an occasional squeeze, (along with a wicked smile) that brings a pained expression to his face.

It now seems obvious, even to Ethan's impoverished brain, that up to that point Stella had been trying to hide the fact that she was just as keen if not more so to have sex. So with the walls of her nonexistent resistance now razed to the ground, he has gained full control of her body. At one point she can feel his prickly stubble as he is biting into her throat, where her head is so arched back she is almost facing the headboard, at the same time she is running all of her fingers thru his long greasy matted hair. With him now removing her thong in just a matter of seconds, it gave her the feeling that this man was not going to take any prisoners in his quest to give her the satisfaction he now knows she is begging for.

With her lying on her back she is now giving him the opportunity for him to be quite physical as well with her large firm naked breasts, where she has purposely pushed her chest forward to the point where they are now close up to his face, where he had no hesitation in filling his ravenous looking mouth with those large pink protruding nipples.

With her sexual pleasure building up she is suddenly wanting to increase the pace, so she is now wrapping her long fingers quite firmly around his long, thick; throbbing, and heavily veined penis. After a sustained physical effort by her, it is now fully extended, almost straight away this well worn part of his anatomy has now firmly been wedged into Stella's now wide open mouth. Her facial expression is saying that she is now so sexually aroused that her intention is to drain as much sperm from his unhygienic body as she can.

Not surprisingly the blow job at this moment is literally sending his mind blissfully into orbit, especially as she is purposely and repeatedly running her razor sharp tongue over the tip and around the sides of his now red hot, and fully outstretched penis.

Minutes later after now being overwhelmed by Stella's continual sexual demands, he is unable to control a sudden gush of semen from his body, which moments later is spilling out from both corners of her mouth. With this buffoon still standing his ground, she is suddenly in danger of choking. Eventually his slow thinking brain and stubbornness now relent, and he is now removing his penis quickly from her still wide open mouth, where it has now left strands of sperm stretching from the tip of his penis down to her mouth.

Apparently because she was in sudden danger, Stella made a quick decision to swallow most of it in one sudden gulp. (or was it maybe the inclusion of stale beer that could have made it much more palatable?). Much later into the night Stella woke up and felt as though she wanted more from her now taken for granted new boyfriend, who was still sleeping. So she put the bedside lamp on, leaned over and put her mouth on to his for a long smooch kiss.

He had now sufficiently woken up to see her looking down into his still sleepy eyes, which indicated to him that she was now more than eager to have intercourse with him. Ethan is telling Stella that he wants to sleep until tomorrow `I just feel so tired` now closing his eyes again. Stella has now leant over him and is saying` I want you to fuck me now, not tomorrow, it's too long to wait. She has now threatened him, saying that she will squeeze his testicles so hard it will turn them into mush, which will end his sex life there and then, and she wasn't even smiling. Hopefully for Ethan the few hours of sleep will probably have built up his strength enough to give Stella her continuous sexual pleasures.

It is not as well ideal that her partner is 20 years her senior, but unfortunately at this moment in time he is the only man in her life that can give her the sexual satisfaction required. The reality is that if these two do start a relationship it will be based on sex only, due to the simple fact that when she is in the grip of sudden lust, she needs this locally despised and hated social outcast (who she hardly knows) to think of nothing else but being rough with her in bed, Ethan with his shallow way of thinking may see the possibility of seeing this beautiful woman as his new partner in life, with who knows, children to follow? For her to tell him the truth that because of the slovenly way in which he projects himself, she could never allow herself to be seen in public with him, which could lead him to giving her a heavy beating and then walking out on her. That happening would again leave her on her own, with no Ethan to warm her bed, plus the deprived thrill of him giving her a good shagging, that is why she keeps schtum.

But at the present moment she can feel his long; warm, thick and fully extended penis now moving around in her body. She luckily had remembered about her protection. She wasn't ready yet to have any more children, that is until she finds the right man (still hanging on to the idea of Chris returning). So with her body now underneath his and her fingers spread eagled on his naked buttocks, they are soon moving in unison at a fast and furious pace. With both of them both putting maximum effort into achieving their own individual ecstasy, Ethan's sleeveless t-shirt has now moved up his body, and is at the moment flapping around his neck.

Still working towards a climax, Stella beginning to lose her breath, has whispered to Ethan that she wants him to penetrate even further up into her body. That immediately tells him that every forceful thrust he administers from now on will enhance her affectionate feelings toward him. A feeling of ecstasy is imminent and her fingernails are now digging into his back, where there is an abundance of thick black hair. Her beautiful eyes are opening and closing like some faulty traffic lights. Suddenly for a few seconds both of their bodies have now gone rigid. There is a sudden gasp from her, which is now telling him that she is now (as well as him) enjoying the ecstasy of being fully satisfied.

He did actually tell Stella before they had intercourse, that anytime in the future it would be safe for her to have sex up to just a few days before the birth of a child. He should know, he has already got four children to his first wife who decided long ago that he was a: good for nothing; filthy looking sex pervert. Could it be that there will be a long sexual relationship between the two of them?

Another visit to the bathroom was inevitable for him, due to his excessive consumption of beer. As he was looking in the bathroom mirror at himself; full on, even sideways; he wasn't very happy what he saw: an ugly amount of hair on his back and chest that led up and over his obtrusive beer gut towards his double chin that had lots of unsightly prickly stubble, plus the long greasy matted hair that straggled down to his shoulders. It was only the other week he promised himself that he would make himself a bit more presentable, and to get a worthwhile job. The very fact that this young gorgeous woman, Stella, who is classed as one of the most beautiful models in Europe, and who has mingled with some of the most handsome and eligible men, has suddenly offered her curvaceous body to this: down at heel; uneducated and it must also be said, worthless degenerate Ethan Byrne, is surely unbelievable.

It could be a really bad sign of things to come, as Ethan now falsely assumes that he has now won the battle of winning her love and affections, as well letting her know that from now on she belongs to him, and that he would kill any other man who tried to take her from him. A smile now crosses Stella's face as she is now assuming that such a remark from her new lover is just sheer bravado, and nothing else. After such a momentous night, she is all smiles as she tells him that she wants him now regularly in her bed, as she likes his, aggressive sexual behaviour.

Although at the same time she already has misgivings regarding having a full blown sexual relationship with a man who's already obtrusive looking body nowhere near reaches an acceptable level of hygiene. He has already told her that if she wants another child, he would gladly oblige, plus offering to be father to Alain. Ethan's wife who is obese and also with a few teeth missing in all of the most inconvenient places (quite unsightly to say the least), told her friends it was the best thing she ever did, getting that creep out of her life.

Also that his new woman (Stella) should see a psychiatrist, lowering herself down to such a degrading level. Ethan was at the moment living in squalor, in some filthy lodgings a few streets away.

Can all this possibly be happening to this, the same beautiful woman who not too long ago was signing a contract to be a movie star in Hollywood where men would turn their heads to look at this gorgeous woman who was destined to be a showbiz celebrity? That is the way it was heading until a spate of bad luck ruined all of her dreams, and now there is the distinct possibility of things like “auto suggestion” where she could shortly forget about all of her ambitions and instead slowly enter into a life of filth and squalor. That is if she doesn’t quickly wake up from an impending nightmare in which she would surely soon be engulfed in. Before going to sleep, she has to admit to herself that he is not someone that other women would find even remotely attractive, (yes but they are probably not dogged by nymphomania !). Although I think with him having lots of other lovers in his younger life it has given him valuable experience which at this moment is leaving a broad smile of immense satisfaction on Stella’s face.

Nevertheless she had now to be firm with Ethan, telling him that from now on, when they had used up their sexual energies on each other, he would have to retreat to one of the other bedrooms (once again hygiene problems). Next morning they are now having breakfast together when Stella asks `Ethan, when was the last time you had a job?` `Two years ago’ `That seems to me a long time to be without work?` `I was unfairly sacked` replied Ethan. `What was the reason?` asked Stella now taking two slices of toast out of the toaster. `It was the manager he didn’t like me, he said I was a lazy good for nothing waster` `Why should he say that?` Stella now showing a sudden frown. `It’s all because he caught me sleeping behind some boxes, when I should have been unloading a wagon`.

`Oh well, what did you expect?` `Yes but I had already told him I had been up half of the fucking night spewing my guts up` Stella is now looking at him with a really disgusting stare, she really is. `I think you drink too much beer`. Now trying to wind him up, `There is no doubt that you are going to have to get a job, otherwise I will find another boyfriend, someone who will be the breadwinner for me and my child` (which would only be fair if she did let him move in with her). If she let him know that she was a rich woman, it would ruin the sexual relationship that she had forged with this man, who she very much needs to control her you know what. With Nymphomania still well in control of her mind, she has already in the last few weeks willingly performed every known sexual act on this man's unhygienic and repulsive naked body.

Now his not too distant plan is to make her pregnant with his child, so he can move from his squalid tenement hovel, and into her well kept home on a permanent basis, where (he) I would assume live happily ever after . Ethan has falsely assured Stella that his first priority is to definitely find a job, (yes and pigs might fly). A week or so later there was an incident that could have created a catastrophe as regarding Stella being able to keep her sanity. When on a rare visit to see her father in his filthy habitat, Laura (Ethan's daughter) had noticed a photo of her dad with his arms around a beautiful and lot younger woman in someone's bedroom (and it certainly wasn't his bedroom). Laura herself was sexually attractive, having long jet black hair, as well as being a regular page 3 pin-up girl in countless papers and magazines.

Now she was stood in front of her dad demanding to know who this young woman was. `Where did you find this photo?' Ethan was now asking his daughter. She replied `I was just dusting a few of the books on your shelf, and it just dropped out' `She is a young lady I am friendly with' he told her. Laura came back with `She must be very friendly, just wearing a thong, also without a bra and her arms up and around the back of your head` Not being able to look at his daughter in the eye thru being embarrassed he now mutters `OK she is very friendly'. `Can I ask what the handcuffs are used for?` asked Laura `They are hers not mine, she told me that when she is in a certain mood she wants me to strip her naked, put the cuffs on behind her back; stuff her panties into her mouth, before I give her a good shagging` Looking at the girl in the photo and then looking up at her dad, she now gives him her true thoughts. `I just don't get it, I would like to know how a beautiful young woman like her could find anything remotely interesting in an old, revolting, penniless man like yourself?` `Yes but I helped her get her garden nice and tidy, and as well put her new fencing up' he was quick to say. `How long have the both of you been together?` `At the moment it's about a month' he informs her.

`Does she know that your living conditions are utterly disgusting?` `No she doesn't, all she wants is to make love to me, and me to her', still looking at the photograph, Laura replies `It is quite obvious she is sex mad, but even so I would very much like to meet her'. Suddenly her father tells her 'I think that would be a bad idea, and you know why that would be a bad idea don't you?' now looking at his daughter with a very serious stare. `Why just because I am a Lesbian?' `Stop right there!' he bellowed `that is the main reason why I don't want you to meet her, not only that but she obviously is not that way inclined, you can tell that by the way she continually begs me for sex' `Even so I would still like to meet her' replied Laura.

There followed no reply from her dad. After spending an hour in his homemade hovel and making very little improvement to his living conditions, she was now putting her coat on to go home. Suddenly her dad told her `I have had a change of mind, if you really want to meet my girlfriend I will arrange it' `That's the spirit dad', now giving him a kiss on his cheek. Within two days the two girls have met, who going by their body language etc, seem to have hit it off.

Ethan forgot to inform his daughter that Stella had a young son, `What a beautiful boy you have Stella' now picking him up and giving him a cuddle. Ethan in the background isn't quite sure of his daughter's intention, he knows his daughter is a Lesbian and that she has had countless affairs with other women. After arranging to see Stella later tonight, Ethan and Laura have left her house.

In the car Ethan is suddenly shaken by Laura's admission that she would like to bed Stella. `I knew it, I just damn well knew it, I wish I had never introduced you to her' `I'm sorry dad but I can't help the way I feel can I?' Ethan is now telling her `If you do manage to bed her as you say, she simply won't be interested, it's only me she wants and certainly not someone like you'. After a few moments thought Laura now tells her dad `Give me the chance and I will prove you wrong believe me`. With his daughter almost pleading with him, he now gives in, but wants to know how Laura will achieve her goal. Still in the car she explains her intentions to her now much agitated father `You will have to tell Stella that you have to visit a friend in Hospital, let's say in….. Derby which will mean you stopping overnight. Earlier you will have suggested to Stella that I could keep her company if she wanted me to' `What if she doesn't require your company?` replied her dad. `Well in that case it is simply a lost cause, although I am sure she will not be so rude as to refuse the friendly offer'.

Two days later the plan was put into operation, Ethan was supposedly now on his way to Derby, when he was actually at the Bar of a cheap hotel in Bagshot, where he would stay the night. Stella was now welcoming Laura into her living room, and straight away she is looking for Stella's young son Alain. `I have put him to bed now' she tells Laura` `Oh never mind hopefully there will be other times' she said with a borrowed smile. Settling down on the settee both girls were wearing casual clothing.

With Laura being a page three pinup, her breasts were very prominent, although Stella wasn't too far behind. Stella asks Laura what she would like to drink, she asks for a Whiskey and Soda, while Stella has her usual Gin and Orange. When the drinks are brought over to the coffee table by Stella, Laura asks her for a napkin. Stella now retreats to the kitchen to get the napkin but also to check on the hot meal that she has made for the two of them later on.

This has now given Laura enough time to put a rogue (not on prescription) tablet into her drink, one that she has used on other women to get her evil way.

After an hour Laura noticed that the way Stella was now beginning to talk, was to be expected. Where the chitchat between the two women had been up to now normal, Stella was now starting to talk dirty, which included women having sex with other women. Now before tonight she had never in her whole life ever made any mention or opinions whatsoever to that particular alternative where women have sex with women. This is just what Laura had expected to happen, where before much longer Stella would start to feel the hot's for Laura who incidentally would play it cool and let her host do the initial running. To hurry the situation on a bit Laura now looking at her watch has intimated that time was pressing and that it was time maybe for her to be going home. And as sure as night follows day Stella said `Can't you stay the night? besides I have a meal that is almost ready` Now looking at Laura who was ready to use her much used reply `Are you sure about this?` `Of course I'm sure' said Stella, who was now going up close to her new friend, and putting both hands on her waist. What happened next was pivotal to the night's proceedings > they were now stood as one with at first their lips pressing firmly together, which quickly led to their tongues being wrapped around each others. Shortly after enjoying their hot meal and a rest, they now made their way to the same bedroom that she makes love to Ethan. After stripping each other naked and now laid in between the sheets, Laura was going to make sure that after all of her previous experiences she would get all the pleasures from Stella that she wanted. Which included each girl using their fingers and tongues to explore every inch of each other's body.

Eventually sleep took over, and both girls were sleeping with their arms around each other's body. Laura must have an alarm clock integrated into her head, because in these circumstances 5.am means time to go home. If she stays and Stella wakes up to Laura being at her side, it could be very embarrassing to both parties. So Stella when waking up later and being alone, had no recollections of the previous night, only having an unusual (for her) thumping headache, which at this moment was enough to be going on with.

Much later in the day, all she remembers was Ethan's daughter coming to keep her company while Ethan was visiting a friend in Hospital, but after that absolutely nothing. Ethan came the following evening to make up for his absence the night before. He did ask if Laura had paid her a visit while he was in Derby, and yes, apparently everything had worked out OK, which left Ethan with a furrowed brow and deep in thought.

It seems to be ages ago since Stella made a promise to herself, that she would never be seen in public with Ethan Byrne, especially with him looking far too old to be classed as her boyfriend, as well as his appearance always being so untidy. After now being lovers for over a month, Ethan's mother is so excited that her son has at last found a girlfriend. She wants her son 50 to view a small terraced house in the same street, with the intention that he and his small newly acquired family would be closer to her. Ethan wanted very much to take Stella and her son to visit his mother for the day anyway, as it was her 70th birthday.Stella quite amazingly agreed to go, using London transport instead of her own car.

Apparantly the district they were visiting was like a gangland, with muggers, thieves and drug barons around every corner.After viewing the house, Stella politely turned it down.

On their way home,it was a big surprise to see Stella linking arms with her new lover, especially after her above abrasive comments. Could it be that she has become closer to her boyfriend, especially when he gives her all the sex she needs. Is she now accepting Ethan's way of life, not realising that if she did, her life would almost certainly spiral downwards into a world of filth and squalor.Another question is: has she now turned her back on Hollywood because she has grown closer to Ethan, If so,then there would be surely no resumption of her aspirations for a return to Hollywood,although inside she still feels quite confident for a possible successful return. At the moment she is stood in an old draughty bus shelter, in one of the poor districts of London,huddled up to this apology for a man, who was carrying Alain on his other arm, whose down at heel shoes were beginning to split, that revealed holes in his socks.

When back at Stella's home, it appears that the postman has delivered letters that belong to her neighbours Arthur and Denise Smith's letter box. She tells Ethan that she will nip around and give them their letters. That nip around lasted about twenty minutes, due to being trapped into listening to all the local gossip. Meanwhile Ethan has his chance to scold Alain about him pouring a cup of tea down the drain that was made at his mother's house by his mother. Alain being a bit scared of Ethan said `I just didn't like it, it was too strong, and the cup was dirty`. This has infuriated Ethan so much that he has ordered him to go to his bedroom, as he now will get no supper. `I want my mummy, so I can have my goodnight kiss`without saying a word Ethan lifts him up and takes him to the boy's bedroom, he then tells the boy to get into the bed and stay there as he now locks the door. When Stella came back she asks Ethan`Where is my boy?` He told me he wanted to go to bed` now looking at Ethan rather suspiciously, she says`He never goes to bed without a kiss from me, besides he hasn't had his supper yet` Beginning to wish he had not done what he did, because he knows that his girlfriend will get nasty if she finds out what really happened. Ethan is making it worse for himself by saying `I think he should be alright by now` Stella now stands right up to his face `What the fuck do you mean

"by now" have you done something to my child ?` She now runs up the stairs to his bedroom, straight away she can see that the mite had been crying, as he had those giveaway red rimmed eyes. But because he was now sleeping, she bent down and kissed his cheek. She went back down the stairs and stood in front of Ethan, firstly she slapped his face hard, then punching his face. She would really in normal circumstances tell him to get out of her house and do not ever come back, but as we already know, she needs him to give her the sexual satisfaction that she requires regularly. But in future and while the relationship is still intact, Ethan will be monitored for any more upset towards her son.

CHAPTER SIXTEEN

After another week goes by, Stella has now been pushing Ethan into seeking work, instead of being lazy. Ethan is not happy with this continual niggling from Stella to find work, and is telling her to back off, or he will have to dump her (which coming from him is a laugh and a half). What more does this ungrateful idiot want? At the moment he has a beautiful girlfriend who showers him with affection, and as much sex as he wants, where even having his children isn't totally out of the question, which would almost certainly rule out any return to her film career (which he knows nothing about).

So an angry Ethan decides to stay away for the following week supposedly to teach her a lesson. He is already telling his drinking mates a wicked lie, that she is already begging him to come home, as she can't live without him. If his sordid intentions did come to fruition, it might just tip the scales in his effort to take complete control of her life, more than likely she would slowly descend into a world where morality and its values disintegrate: a world that would be increasingly hard to escape from.

There is no Knight in shining armour that will rescue her from entering this, one of life's darkest alley's.

One particular night just after sorting out their differences, they were partaking in some crude sexual act together, when they could hear what they thought was someone knocking on the bedroom door. It was Alain saying `Are you in there Mummy, I'm thirsty and I can't sleep?' Now realising the seriousness of the situation Stella immediately got up, quickly put her up to the backside robe on and opened the door and got hold of his hand and took him to the kitchen and got him some orange juice from the fridge. After drinking it his mum asked `Has your thirst gone now Alain?` `Yes I'm alright now Mummy, can I go back to bed now?` A few minutes later Stella is now sat in the living room with her head in her hands and is now visibly shaking.

It was the thought that if her son had opened the door just a few minutes earlier and walked in, he would have just witnessed his mother laid naked across the bottom of her bed, with Uncle Ethan also naked astride her, removing his wrinkled, elongated balls from her open mouth.

It was that possibility of her son seeing her involved in something that looked truly abhorrent that was making her feel quite sick and disgusted with herself. A few minutes later Ethan comes into the room asking `Are you coming back to bed to finish off or not?` Next morning Stella told Ethan that after what happened last night she would not for the foreseeable future have anymore sex, and that for the first time in her life she felt so dirty and ashamed for participating in such disgusting sex acts with him, and it had to come to a stop right now.

Obviously he wasn't very pleased with his crude sexual acts being swept aside. Although inwardly he knew that eventually she would forget about what she had just said, because it will be her Nymphomania problem that will push her back towards depravity. The next time he will put a lock on the bedroom door to stop that infuriating little brat of hers from entering, (obviously for some reason he has a dislike towards her son). You can call it what you want, but I think it was a definite `Wake Up Call` for her to now seriously contemplate her future. This kind of life was a million miles away from when she was becoming a beautiful well known actress in America, where everything was just about as good as it gets. Unfortunately it has turned out to be completely the opposite.

Now in the following few days thank God common sense seems to have prevailed, where she now thankfully has had a quick change of thought towards this worthless sex pervert in the making, who quite recently had started to treat her as just an outlet for his grubby sexual fantasies. There was up to quite recently the problem of trying to get him off his lazy backside and to find himself employment, instead of him drinking and gambling his life away.

She at one time thought that she could change him and bring him back into the normal world where a significant change in attitude, such as: Smart clothes; clean shaven, a clean and well fit body and above all a good steady job. Unfortunately it was never going to happen, it turned out to be a lost cause simply because he was too far immersed into the life of being a no-hoper, where he would never change.

At this moment Stella is now gradually for the want of a better word getting really pissed off with his lazy, uncaring attitude towards life. He had the audacity to be laughing when he told one of his beer guzzling friends at the Bar, one of their private secrets, that his girlfriend Stella is completely sex mad. Where most nights before having intercourse she starts off by rubbing her naked body up against his, she then puts her arm across his chest, slowly moving her hands up and around the back of his head, then lowers her moist pouty lips on to his, where her tongue then stretches deep into his mouth.

His friend told him he should be very grateful, because his wife took all her teeth out before she got into bed. Ethan now had a worrying feeling that his association with Stella maybe coming to an end, and was asking Laura what he should do. She told him that she would visit him later today to sort it out.

As soon as she came thru the door, she brought with her a broad smile. She told her dad that she had as good as raped Stella the other week, no problem. Since he had phoned her she now had thought of an idea to get Stella off the planet, period. `I told you that she would eventually dump you because you are too fucking old, too unhygienic; and too lazy for her, didn't I?` `Yes you did, so what is your plan?' asked Ethan, who at the moment is a bag of nerves. `There are only two possible ways out of this mess, you must in some way trick her into marrying you,' now looking at him with a very serious look. `It may be a bit too late for that' he replied with a borrowed smile. `The only other way' she now tells him `you must make her pregnant, at the same time temporarily change your couldn't care less attitude towards life and to her.

Go out and get a job, I know it will hurt but at least it will make out as though you are ready to be a doting father, and I think she will be happy and willing to see you at the side of her at the Altar. `You mentioned something about getting rid of her permanently didn't you?' asked her dad. `Yes I did, and that still stands' replied Laura.

`Laura you are getting me all fucking mixed up, I can't keep up to the way you are thinking`. `Look dad it's quite simple, when you have been married for a month I will give you 5 rogue tablets for you to put in her drink, it's the same unsafe pill that I gave her last time OK, so those extra four tablets that you give her whenever, they would from what I was told give the recipient an hour before having a fatal heart attack'. Ethan was quick to realize `Yes but that would mean that I have to go to fucking prison, wouldn't it?` `If you administered any normal prescribed tablets with the same intention, well yes you would face a long prison sentence, but these tablets are very different, one hundred per cent undetectable, plus they are very expensive and not at all easy to obtain, but they would definitely protect the villain that committed such a hideous crime`.

`But I still do not understand why Stella should be murdered?' `Dad, do you really want to know why I want her murdered?' `Obviously I do' `I think you will be interested in what I am going to tell you okay, she dies: you being her husband now inherit her house, as well as custody of her child, I would imagine that any money she has banked, plus as well any Life insurance she may have taken out, would be yours, so how does that grab you?' Now looking quite excited at the prospect Ethan replies `Do you know I had never thought of that, and shamefully I have to admit I like the idea,… but hold on a minute what do you get out of all this?' he was curious to know `All I want is for you to give me Alain her child and nothing else' now looking over at her dad with one or two tears that are now quite evident. `I always wanted a child, especially a boy, and this is my only chance of that dream ever coming true, as time goes by he will forget about his real mother and love me instead'.

As Laura was leaving his hovel she told him that if Stella decides to marry him he would have to get a divorce from Laura's mother first, otherwise he would have to definitely spend time in Prison.

Ever heard the old saying `Old habits die hard?` this certainly was the case with Ethan, because having been told by his daughter to get his act together for a very obvious reason, he instead decides he cannot go ahead with the horrible idea of killing Stella. He believes he can get her to love him again, so he can return back to his normal dead beat life. One day when Stella had to go into the town she saw Ethan coming out of a book-makers, he was now crossing the street and going in to a Bar. He hadn't seen her.

That night when he came round to spend the night with her, she asked him if he had got a job yet. He told her that he had spent all day looking for a job, but there were no vacancies anywhere. Now looking at him in a way that looks could kill, `You are such a fucking liar Ethan!, and I agree what that manager told you two years ago, you are a lazy good for nothing creep, you have no intention of getting a job, you come here almost every night and I give you food, plus love and affection but you are just using me` `I swear I spent all day looking for work! ` he now said adamantly. `How is it then I saw you coming out of the bookmakers, where you then walked straight into a Bar?` `That must have been my double, it wasn't me` `It was you alright, I recognised the Arsenal F.C. t-shirt you had on, plus your fat gut that stood out a mile` `But` `But nothing, I will give you just another week to find a job, otherwise there can never be a future for us`. There is no doubt looking at Ethan's face that she now means business.

Probably the most annoying thing about Ethan Byrne is that he doesn't seem to appreciate or even realize just how well off he is (in the love stakes I mean).

Firstly he has a wife who basically looks like one of those neighbours from hell, and quite understandably because he is devious, lazy; scruffy and a sex fiend, and she doesn't want him anywhere near her. Amazingly he is lucky enough to find a beautiful single woman (now his girlfriend) who would I am sure not too long ago, stand up for him by saying that she did enjoy having normal and regular sex with him.

Two evenings later Ethan came to Stella's house for dinner, after spending all day at the Bar and the bookmakers. They had finished their meal about an hour ago at 9 pm when there was news of a serious gas leak somewhere in the street. So it was now a case of quickly finding overnight accommodation elsewhere for Stella and Alain. The very worst thing that Ethan could have done was to invite Stella and her son to stay at his bedsit for the night, but unfortunately (for him that is) that's just what he did (basically he has now shot himself in the foot, big time as they say).

This will be the first time that she has seen where he lives (four days of the week). Straightaway she is not at all impressed with the grubby looking washing that is hanging over people's balconies: An upturned supermarket trolley; and a few broken windows, where she can see electric bulbs shining that had no shades. Someone was playing a Bob Marley record so the whole street could hear, even though it was now 10.30pm.

The staircase up to his (shall we be kind and say his room with a view) abode which is full of graffiti, which I think would take a full day at least to read, it really would.

Stella is now shaking her head in disbelief as she enters his hovel. She is in for an even bigger shock when she sees that his windows are dirty; the curtains are filthy and torn with gaping holes, as most of the hooks are missing. In the small kitchenette area, there are a pile of dirty dishes and pans all piled up.

Ethan notices that Stella is looking down at the dirty carpet, so now pathetically he gets a brush out of the pantry which is void of bristles, (like his fucking brain which appears to be void of cells). This bedsit is a complete and utter joke. The wallpaper must have been up for at least thirty years, plus there is a pile of dirty clothes just thrown into a corner. With it being a bedsit, the bed is actually in the living room, where the sheets and pillows are not exactly looking hygienic, (oh my god!). Straightaway it now means that any idea of him wanting sex has now been quickly ruled out by Stella. Although she doesn't like the idea of staying overnight in this hovel at all, miraculously he persuades her to.

She has put Alain into a small box room for the night. Ethan's intelligence is so much out of sync that he thinks because he has given Stella and her child accommodation for the night, that she will now rule out the threat of their sexual affair ending. My advice to Ethan is in future: `Never take anything for granted mate`! The following morning (about 6.am) Stella is awakened by somebody presumably living in the adjacent flat that has his or her radio on; it's so loud she can hear almost every word being said. As she lay there unable to get any further sleep, she is looking around again at this so called dwelling which is telling her that she must never ever visit this hovel again.

From the bed she can still see that the pile of dirty dishes and pans that are still there, so are the pile of presumably smelly beer stained shirts etc in the corner.

She now looks to the side of her, there is this very much dishevelled man sleeping, who after yesterday's supposedly kind gesture has unwittingly now introduced her into a world of complete and utter squalor. How she ever managed to sleep in his grimy looking bed, in this old filthy dilapidated lodging house she just doesn't know. Surely it isn't possible for a woman of her stature to sink any lower into the dregs of life? Unfortunately what she sees thru her eyes is fact and not fiction.

If Burford Maunder could see the level that she has sunk to, he would turn in his grave, he really would. As well I shudder to think what her best friend Susan would say about this preposterous situation that her friend has got herself involved in. Now if we suddenly look at the expression on Stella's face, it tells us that the inner strength that has laid dormant for far too long is now needed to bring an end to this being slowly sucked into a quicksand of total degradation, and is now about to erupt. Which in reality means that there is about to be a sudden and dramatic change in her immediate life.

There is one thing now for certain, she has now reached the point where her association with Ethan Byrne will very shortly reach its conclusion, period. She has now paid a visit to the tiny bathroom, this time in day light, she is looking up at the empty light socket on the ceiling, when last night all it needed was a bulb. Looking at the bath it hasn't recently been used, as there is a line of scum that is caked around the sides, probably from way back when.

She knew there would be no toothbrush without even looking. Later that morning Stella has told Ethan in no uncertain terms that he and his lodgings are an absolute disgrace. `How on earth can you live in such squalor? `Well it is at the moment, but I have a good idea` `An idea, such as what, place a bomb in it? ` says Stella, and this time she wasn't even smiling. `No` said Ethan `if you sell your house, **we** will have enough money to get this flat all done up, and still have plenty in the bank`. At the moment Stella's brain is doing a somersault with this stupid and ridiculous idea. `Are you expecting me and Alain to live with you in this bed-sit together?` `Yeah that's the idea'

`By the way` said Stella `what do you mean when you say `**we**' will have enough money?` `Well I was thinking of asking my wife for a divorce, if then me and you get married we could open a joint account, what do you think? ` `I won't tell you what I think at the moment `said Stella, who was now fuming. `There was something else that I also wanted to mention` said Ethan. `What now !` asked Stella, who is quickly losing patience with this now all of a sudden worthless, no hoper, and repulsive looking imbecile.

`I wanted to mention that it could be a good idea if we put Alain up for adoption, .......what I mean is, he is not my child is he? I want this to be our home, for our children, not him`. At this point Stella is finding it so infuriating just listening to this low life, who is coming out with very hurtful remarks indeed. She has decided for the moment that she is going to go along with, and more or less agree with anything that he is saying, just to see how much further he will lower himself in her estimations, (if that is possible) before she herself comes out with a tirade of furious and aggressive criticism towards him. `So what are you suggesting?` Stella is now asking `Like I say I think you should put him up for adoption, there must be a couple somewhere that would give him a home?` `Are you saying that you don't like my son?` `The question I am asking is, is he my son? – No!, do I want him in our home? – No! looking to the future I just want you and me together and living with our own kids` `Okay fair enough, so what do we do now?` asked Stella concealing for the moment her hatred for him. `Well actually there is a man upstairs, who lives alone who said he is very much interested in the adopting process especially as the boy is about three years old` `Oh I see`, said Stella `(if looks could kill, he would now be dead) `so you have already got the wheels in motion, before even discussing it with me have you?` `Well I had an idea that you would agree that us being together is much more important` `So if we give Alain to the man upstairs, thru adoption` said Stella, `do you think he would let me see him now and again, seeing as me and you would be just down the hall?` `Well I see no problem with that, because to me the man is a gentle-man who comes across as being kind and friendly `Is he in now, because I would like to see what he is like first?` asked Stella. `I will just nip upstairs and see if he is in`. Within two minutes he has brought the man down.

Straightaway Stella has noticed that the man is about forty years old, who also looks a dishevelled character, with a ring pierced into the side of his nose, plus a ragged pair of jeans that drag on the floor, also with trainers that are dirty and coming apart. `There you are Bernard` said Ethan who is now picking Alain up and sitting him on Bernard's knee as though he is already his father.

`Are you working Bernard?` asked Stella `No, not at the moment, but as long as I have this little lad as my son I will be happy` `Have you got a spare bed ready, just in case for Alain?` `No I won't need one he will be sleeping with me` suddenly Stella felt a cold shiver run down her spine. Stella could tell by the evil way that he was looking at her son, this man wanted to be more than just a father to him. Stella (at the moment feeling rather sick) told the man that he would get to know soon if he will be his father. Bernard was now leaving to go back upstairs being followed by Ethan into the hallway. Bernard has quickly turned around and has now lifted Ethan off the floor and up against the wall by the scruff of his shirt, now with his face close up to Ethan, he is now warning him `If I happen to get custody of the young lad, I don't want you or your girlfriend to start thinking that you will be able to see him, because I won't allow it OK? I also want you to know that what goes on in my flat is my business and not for anybody else. If the lad doesn't behave himself then me now being his father, he will know what to expect` Ethan had earlier decided not to tell Stella what a cruel bastard this man was, otherwise she would certainly not have gone along with Ethan's already stupid unacceptable idea of adoption for this man. If Ethan has his wish come true, the thinking is that Alain would be better off dead.

Bernard now let's go of Ethan's shirt, then watching him crumble to the floor before he makes his way upstairs. Back inside after straightening his shirt collar, Ethan now told Stella `There you are, this time next week, hopefully he will be out of our lives for good` smiling and rubbing his hands at the very thought. Stella is almost going ballistic. Knowing now that Ethan's nature isn't of the aggressive type, which is because his brain hasn't and never will evolve into one of a proper grown man. Now because of his cruel remarks guided towards her son in the last hour, she now slaps his face twice and hard. There is one thing for certain Ethan

Byrne will soon be out of her life forever; at the very moment she opens the door and leaves. Now she is putting on her coat.

With his face still stinging, he now ruefully asks her where she is going `I am going home!` `What so soon?` `The quicker I get out of this fucking shithouse the better, how you had the nerve to bring me to a place like this, just proves to me that you have no conception or understanding of the human being whatsoever.` `It's not all that bad is it?`

`It won't be to you will it!? you live here most of the time, I mean how long have those curtains been like that, and the dishes and those filthy smelly clothes?` `Well I was hoping that when you saw the state of the flat you would clean it up for me, you being a woman who likes to keep her own house so very tidy' `Well you cheeky bastard!, and while I would be cleaning up your flat where would you be?` `I would be helping you` `Oh no you wouldn't you fucking creep, you would be down at that Bar guzzling beer` Ethan is now looking on to the filthy carpet knowing that she was speaking the truth.

`Are you getting annoyed because your son will soon be living with Bernard?'

Stella with a borrowed smile answered `I can assure you that he is not going to Bernard or anybody else for that matter, he is staying with me, his biological mother, and as for you, keep away from me and my house, or the police will be involved`. As she was going out of the door, with Alain at her side, she turned around and said `What as well put that fucking bee in your bonnet that I would sell my house, do yours up, and give you access to my money, where you would eventually lose all of it gambling and drinking?` `I just thought it was a good idea` `Well you would do wouldn't you, you lousy filthy creep, that manager and your wife were both right, you are the pits, you really are`. Minutes later Stella is now in her car driving home with Alain at her side, who is looking up at her wondering what is going on. When they come to traffic lights, she bends down where she now puts her arm around him and gives him a loving kiss.

I would imagine that you are now thinking whatever happened to the idea that Laura had planned to get Stella off the Planet?

Well a few weeks before the above bust up, Ethan arranged to meet his daughter to inform her that his conscience couldn't possibly allow him to do such a wicked crime like she had suggested.

Instead he would do his best to get back on the right side of her, just like it was at the beginning of their sexual relationship. Now because her dad had disobeyed her wishes, this would be the last time she would ever see him, so before leaving she was now with added venom telling him he was just a useless; dirty, obscene old fart.

Amazingly just a couple of weeks have now gone by when Stella gets a very unexpected phone call from Irene (Chris's mother). She was giving Stella the good news that Chris would soon be on his way home from Cape Verdi after spending over two years living in the hotel that his uncle has a half share in. `He told me to pass on the message that he in about a month will be visiting you and Alain`. `I can't wait to see him` said Stella. When Stella puts the phone down, she is looking out of the window thinking to herself `If only I knew that he hadn't forgotten about me, I would never have started up the relationship with that worthless creep Ethan` The unsavoury truth is that she did. She is now making a nice cup of tea for herself.

As she is now sat down, a million thoughts are getting clogged up in her mind. By the time she has finished the tea, she has come to a decision what her next steps will be. The computer has now been turned on. While it is warming up she is working out a plan of action, hoping this time life will be a bit kinder to her, and that she gets the result that she requires. Bagshot is a nice enough village but somehow it hasn't been the place where she ever felt at home, especially when she couldn't get out to make new friends. The information that she was looking for on the computer is now being revealed to her. A house in London, (St. John's Wood to be exact) a place she knows like the back of her hand.

London had always been like a magnet to her and if she had any future at all it would have to start there. The thought of staying in Bagshot worried her as it could have resulted in a possible confrontation between Ethan and Chris that could have been dangerous. As well Ethan could start shouting his mouth off, telling Chris and the neighbours that she was nothing more than the village bike. Almost certainly Chris would want to know what Stella had got up to while he was living on the west coast of Africa. After finding out he would be soon out of here. To be fair to Stella, she thought that Chris had forgotten what he had promised, and that was to come back. Somehow it wouldn't be right for her to query his extra long vacation.

Buying the house in London would be no problem to Stella. She had already made herself into a wealthy woman, with the films she made, plus her being a top model as well. Having money behind you gives a person independence which is fine, trying to realize a particular dream is very much different. Although at the moment she has spun off the track of life so to speak, the "I can and I will" determination has now returned with a vengeance.

The house that she wants is vacant which now means she can move in fairly quickly, obviously after being modified to her liking and decor. She now drives to London with young Alain in the back seat chair hoping to secure the house after an inspection.

It is a 4 bedroom house with an oval drive in a decent sized front garden, with a small garden at the rear.

She has been assured that the house after the modifications and decor, will be ready in 3 weeks which suits Stella perfectly.

Before she goes home she calls in at Square House Model agency to see her good friends Kim and Gary, who are very pleased to see her and her young child. As Kim is holding Alain she tells Stella that with her not being available, their profits have been reduced by a quarter. `Though we are not complaining are we?` said Kim now looking over at Gary. `Oh no, instead of making 2 million a year ago, we are still on course for achieving one and a half million this year which is still good` Stella tells them that she has just bought a house in St. John's Wood.

Kim and Gary are now looking at each other in bewilderment. `How on earth could you afford to buy a house in such an exclusive area, even the money that we paid you couldn't possibly cover that surely?`

`No you are right it couldn't, but that is another story' `Why have you suddenly wanted to leave Bagshot?` asked Kim `The village wasn't right for me, because after Alain was born, I couldn't get out of the house to meet new friends, and to work myself up to proper fitness.

Instead this meathead who is 20 years older than me, introduced himself knowing that I was on my own, he offered to do odd jobs for me. So me being me I couldn't refuse being friendly to him. Eventually he got into my knickers, and we had sex'. `So where is he now? `asked Gary `I don't know and I don't care, it's because of him, the main reason I wanted out` Kim is now giving her a hug, telling her that `It will be nice to have you back in London`, although Kim had to be truthful by telling her that if she wanted to come back into modelling with them, she would have to lose some of the weight that has gathered on her body. `I know` said Stella `to be honest I feel embarrassed to be stood in front of you like this, but as Arnold Schwarzenegger said "I'll be back and I mean it"! `That is what we want to hear` said Kim. So after getting a little kiss on his cheek Stella and Alain were now on their way back to Bagshot.

Having to wait another three weeks, wasn't doing her nerves any good, because of phone calls from Ethan, saying that if she didn't start to see him again, he would set her house on fire.

A quick call to the police soon put a stop to that. Eventually the waiting was now over, she had already the previous week arranged for the removal van from London to move everything to her new address today, as she had confirmation at the same time that her new house was now ready to move into.

She also told her neighbours, Denise and Arthur Smith that if **that** man asks who the removers were, they had to tell him that they never saw a van. They told her that they were sorry to see her go, but she did right to get away from that horrible man.

`He has been a layabout ever since we came here and that is 10years ago, and don't worry we won't tell him anything`.

Stella had also given instructions to `Cresswell's` to have the "For Sale" sign put up tomorrow after she had left, also for them not to give **that** man her forwarding address. Two hours later everything was now in her new house, and she felt quite excited about a new start.

She now gave Irene a call to tell her that she has moved to a new address in London. She could hear Irene scribbling down the address and phone number on a pad that was obviously at the side of the phone somewhere in Reading. `He will be ever so pleased that you have moved to London, as he has friends there`. You could not be blamed for thinking that Stella has somehow jumped out of the frying pan and into the fire as she will still be on her own, and still not being able to trust anybody enough to mind her child so that she can go jogging and join a fitness club. So how will she ever make friends if she can't go jogging or mix socially in the evenings?

These were the questions that had been a headache to her even when in Bagshot. Like all problems, there usually is somewhere a solution to them. She has a train of thought that there is one person (possibly two) that she knows who could be her knight/s in shining armour, who would eradicate the problem at a stroke, that is if things go to plan. It is all in the balance.

If we move on it is now a week to the day since she moved in, she at last gets a phone call from Chris Tennyson. `Hello Chris` said Stella `how wonderful to hear your voice again` `Very nice to hear yours as well` `Are you coming to visit me and Alain?` `Of course I am, It's just that I am checking that you are in before I come` `How long will you be so I know when to put the kettle on?` `Make it 15 minutes okay`. Being just a few minutes late, she could now hear his car tyres crunching into the gravel on the drive, she was watching from the living room window waiting for his reaction to her new home.

The look on his face suggested that he may have come to the wrong house. When she opened the door to him he was quick to ask `By what magic is this?` as he made his way into the hall wiping his feet as he was looking around. Stella told him to sit down while she poured the tea. Eventually he asked her `Can you tell me how a one parent family could possibly afford a four bedroom house in the middle of London?` `One day I will tell you, but not now` still being very curious to know, he now asks her `What is your mortgage a month?` `I haven't got a mortgage I have bought it cash` Looking at her now totally shocked he said `You are obviously joking` `No it's perfectly true` said Stella `So you must have had a quick sale on the other house?` `No that goes up for sale tomorrow` now scratching his head he says `Therefore you must have won on the lottery or something?` Stella told him to stop guessing as he will never find out until she tells him later. `Now you are here, I hope that you are going to stop over a few nights` asked Stella as she rests her arm on his shoulder. `Yes I would love to` `C'mon I will show you round the house (she made sure that Alain was still asleep in his bed). Chris was walking behind her as they climbed the stairs. She turns around to him, `I hope you are not looking at my backside with all the weight on?` he now replies `I most certainly am not, and anyway I don't care whether you are fat or slim, you will always be my friend'

`Is that all I will be?` she was thinking to herself. She now shows him the bedrooms, two of which have ¾ beds with a chair and a closet, the third one has a double bed with en-suite, a bigger closet, and chair. `Very nice` said Chris `this looks quite adequate for me`. She now has got hold of his hand and is now leading him into the Master bedroom `What about this one?` looking into his eyes with a smile, waiting for a reaction.

`What a beautiful bedroom` he now makes his way to the full size window that faces onto a small park across the way. She follows and stands behind him with her arms around his slim but muscular body `Do you like the view?` asks Stella `Yes it's nice and quiet, and I can see me taking Alain for walk around there a few times` said Chris. `Anytime you want to you can` Stella has now put her head on his shoulder. Stella decides to make sandwiches for lunch leaving dinner till tonight. During the afternoon they get Alain all wrapped up nice and warm in his push chair (after all it is still only early May). They are now taking him around the small park that has a pond (about the same size as a highway roundabout). Stella has brought some bread for the ducks.

When they eventually sit on a park bench there are a few things to discuss. `Are you still writing scripts for T.V. soap's?` Stella asks Chris `Oh yes, although I was well behind before I went to stay in Cape Verde, I have now caught up again, no thanks to that Fast Food outlet fiasco over two years ago, why do you ask?` she now replied `It's just that I have an idea, where we could help each other`. `Sounds good, go on` `Why don't you base yourself here in my house instead of Reading?` Chris is listening intently with a straight face, she carries on `In that small room next to the kitchen, you can have your Computer and all your paperwork at the side of you' `That is a good idea, but how does that help you?'

`Quite simple really, while you do your writing, you can also keep an eye on Alain, it will give me the chance of getting myself fit again, just like I used to be`.

`That's fine by me` said Chris. Stella also remembered to mention that there would have to be a few times when she visited a Fitness Centre as well. `That's still okay, as me and Alain will I am sure look after each other'. Within the next fortnight Chris had now moved in. Everything is going to plan apart from Stella not being able to entice Chris into her bed where she would probably devour him, she really would. He is a handsome young man 28 and he has been brought up in the conventional way. The love of his life is his mother who he adores, just as much as she adores him. People might see him as just a mummy's boy, but that is not true, he has the freedom to do whatever he wants to do. She remains in the background of his life, and only steps forward if he needs advice.

For example it was his decision to move in with Stella, to help her get herself fit so she could resume her career as a model. That was because Stella had helped him when he was desperate. As it was, Irene was already full of appreciation for what Stella did for her son. Chris was her only child and at the moment there is nothing on the horizon that has suggested that she will ever have a grandchild. Though when she saw baby Alain for the first and only time,(about two years ago) she responded to him like a moth to a flame, forever wanting to hold him.

She now had the opportunity to take him in his push chair for a short walk, stopping now and again to make sure his blanket was up to his chin. Coming back to Stella she has to realize that trying to rush Chris into a sex relationship where shoving her tongue down his throat would suddenly change his attitude to one like Ethan Byrne. That too aggressive approach simply wouldn't work in this situation, obviously at the moment it seems that he is not yet ready for anything but a steady friendly relationship.

She will have to be a lot more patient, and hopefully he will eventually seize the opportunity that has been staring him in the face all this time. So at the moment Stella is not being able to enjoy a sexual relationship that she and Ethan Byrne at one time had together. If she ever did get back into her adopted modelling profession, she promised herself that she would never accept anybody, or even look at a man who resembled Ethan Byrne. One of the more serious problems that brought about the sudden end to that relationship was his growing resentment of her child (probably because he was jealous that Alain would get more attention than him) plus the way he was leading her steadily towards a life of Squalor where his bedsit wasn't fit for even a pig to live in, which she was quite aware of anyway. So if I may reiterate, Stella and Chris live together and anybody (apart from you and me) would assume that they were a young married couple: shopping at the supermarket; having walks in the park each time with Alain, they also watch TV together; and enjoy to a degree the same music. There is an equal amount of time that they share each other's company.

CHAPTER SEVENTEEN

The friendship and respect for each other is definitely there, but the one thing that is missing is Chris and Stella being in the same bed making love. Stella has now slimmed down to the figure that she had when she was top model which is down to all the jogging she has been doing over the last two months, as well as two visits a week to the fitness centre. Where on the latest visit she had caught the attention of the centre manager David who is a well muscled 6ft giant, who has noticed that she has no rings on her fingers.

They get talking and seem to be enjoying each other's company, laughing and joking with each other. He asks her for a date, she on this occasion amazingly says **no.** She now makes her way to her car where she sits for a short while in some sort of trance, still wondering why she had said **no**..................What happens next is quite amazing as you will soon find out.

Within the next few minutes she has now gone back into the Fitness Centre and tells him that she has changed her mind and now agrees to meet him later the same night. He escorts her back to her car and suddenly their lips have met. When she arrives home she feels a slight guilt as she gives Chris a kiss on the cheek. `Have you put Alain to bed?` She asks Chris `Yes an hour ago` She goes upstairs to see her little boy who is fast asleep, who she notices is now beginning to look very much like his father. As she is looking down at him a few tears are running down her cheek, because all of a sudden she doesn't now know what direction in life she is going in.

The man downstairs is the man she wants to spend the rest of her life with, but she wants him now, not when he decides it is time to wake up to reality, which could be in 6 months or even a year, or maybe even never. Being fully aware that she has been cursed with being a nymphomaniac and that at certain times she is desperately in need of sex. That is why she has arranged to meet this man who will give her what she needs. So she tells Chris a white lie that she met one of her old school friends while jogging today, and had arranged a night out. `That's okay` said Chris `you have a good time`.

Stella went upstairs to get ready for her date. When she arrived at David's house, the windows were open as it was a rather humid kind of evening. She knocked on his door, when he opened it, he looked quite awesome with sporting slacks on with white trainers.

With him having jet black hair and no hairs on his body he looked quite sexy. That night Stella had her turquoise bandana wrapped around her head which matched her eye shadow. As well with her boobs now back to their normal size. She wore a white sleeveless top that hung loosely around her body, and as it was a warm sticky evening she was braless. When he closed the door they were soon in each other's arms, followed by a long smooch kiss. As they sat down on the settee for a few more embraces, David's father was coming in thru the front door. A quite physical looking man who had a flat stomach plus all of his teeth, not bad for a man of 75.

Stella was introduced to Reg who would then go up the stairs to watch TV. in his bedroom. Stella had for some reason thought that this was David's house. `Oh no this is the family home, my mother died 3 years ago. Me and my brother regularly visit my dad, just to make sure that he is alright` just then the phone rang it was his brother who's car had burst a tyre and he didn't have a spare. David explained that he was with a beautiful girl and that it wouldn't be right if he just left her twiddling her thumbs for an hour. Stella not being selfish tells David to take him a spare wheel, she will wait. `Are you sure?`

`Of course I am sure` So David has now gone, leaving Stella and his dad together in the house. After ten minutes Reg came down with just his shorts on, `He won't be coming back tonight you know that don't you?` said Reg `He said he would be back within the hour` Stella assured him `No he won't`. `Why?` `He has done this before, he entices beautiful girls like you to my house, he assumes that because I am very fit for my age, and that I should still be able to have a good sex life` `Do you think that your son is right to assume that?`

Without answering Reg is now putting his arms around Stella's waist and as he gets closer he can now feel her nipples wobbling about on his bare rather sunken chest. `You haven't got a bra on!` Reg was quick to tell her. `It is too warm for a bra` she answered. He is about 2 inches taller than her. They are now looking into each other's eyes, his face is heavily lined, and his neck is sadly sagging, but he has a good shock of grey hair. They both make a move together and now they are locked together, his arms now holding her tightly round her waist and her arms are now around his neck and suddenly their lips are together. He now picks her up and carries her up the stairs to his bedroom, where they are now stripping each other naked, (not that there is much left to strip).

As they are laid in bed he tells Stella that her turquoise coloured bandana round the top of her head makes her look very sexy. As a thank you she is now leaning over his body to bury her tongue into his mouth, at the same time her hand is playing chutes and ladders with his penis. All this is driving him crazy, it really is. Whether his heart can stand up to all this attention is open to conjecture.

My feeling is that he may have dipped his hand into the pool, hoping for a goldfish, but has ended up instead with a man eating shark.

Worse is yet to come for the poor old devil, as she now wants intercourse with him. Not wanting to look a spoil sport he agrees, and after another gruelling ten minutes, he actually does manage to come thru it alive!

As they are both laid together and recovering from their exertions, suddenly Stella is in a state of panic, she never checked to see if Reg had got protection on. When she asked him he told her no he hadn't. `Oh my God!` she screamed. `What am I going to do!? what is Chris going to say and do when he finds out? what will his mother think of me?` Stella knows that Irene thinks the world of baby Alain, which would I imagine ruin their little friendship, all because of her stupidity not to check not only that, but if she is now pregnant (which seems likely as they both climaxed at the same time). It also means that all the training and getting fit would have been a complete waste of time.

Where her and Alain would be deserted by her friends and associates, thus being left alone in the house, with a baby on the way. She is sat up in bed with her head in her hands. When suddenly Reg who is laid at the side of her starts laughing and it is getting louder by the second, she turns around to see what is so funny. Reg is now suddenly looking more like 95 than 75, with his mouth open she can see that he now has no teeth in his head, but he just keeps on laughing.

She is not sure what is happening to her, she is now climbing out of the bed, but slips and bangs her head on the corner of the closet. All of a sudden her eyes have opened, where she is now sat behind the wheel of her car, which is still in the same parking place at the Fitness Centre parking lot. She notices, and then straightens her rear view mirror which had been knocked sideways, now revealing a cut on her forehead.

After spending a few moments with her eyes now shut, she again looks out thru the windscreen to see people going about their daily routines, like they were a few minutes ago. `What a fucking relief that is` she thought to herself.

Although her heart beat is still going at fifty to the dozen, she now realizes that it was a wakeup call to seek treatment that will remove this devil from her mind. The last thing she needs is now to have nymphomaniac nightmares whenever she goes to sleep or in a trance. She has now arrived back home and it is teatime, Chris has managed to make the tea as well as keeping his eye on Alain, and also doing his script writing.

Stella gives him a kiss on his cheek, also with an arm around his shoulder. Next day she made an appointment with her doctor, who now arranged for her to see a psychiatrist in a week's time. It was now time to visit Kim and Gary at Square House to see if they needed her.

`You bet your life we do` said Kim pulling out the forms for her to sign a new agreement. And as she was a special friend, Kim told her that if in the future anything dramatic happened in her life she would be able to cancel her agreement at any time.

If we zoom into the following week, she is now meeting a top Harley street psychiatrist who is asking Stella lots of questions. After an hour's consultation, she told Stella that she would either cure or at least subdue her Nymphomania to a much lower level within two months, but with her going private, there will be a big amount to pay. That wouldn't be a problem, as getting rid of her affliction would be like music to Stella's ears.

The first modelling work given to her from her friends Kim and Gary at Square House, was in Birmingham at a fashion show. She was again feeling confident within herself, it was as if she had never been away.

The next day she got good praise from the organisers which found its way down to Kim and Gary in London, who now asked her to come and see them as they had some good news for her. Stella gave them a call instead. Gary told her that a top British company wanted Square House's top model to project their merchandise on T.V. in America. Gary asked Stella if she is up for it? `Of course I would love to do it, when do you want me to go?` `When they let me know I will give you a few days to prepare yourself`. Stella couldn't wait to tell Chris that she was going to New York to make the T.V. commercial for five days.

Chris is very happy for her and that it would be no problem for him to look after Alain while she was away. Stella had an idea `Why don't you ask your mum to come and stay for a few days, where she could get more involved with Alain` `I will do that, it is a good idea` A week later Kim told Stella that the British company had now worked out a deal for her to go to New York to make the commercial for T.V. Five days later she has now flown in, and is now in a taxi heading to her favourite hotel (which she stayed in on her last visit). When the Porter was taking her two suitcases in, he remembered her, `Miss Delray` he said `how are you doing, have you come to make another film?` Stella turned around to him and recognised that it was `Chu` (Chu wasn't his real first name, it was Adetokunbo) or something.

So everyone instead calls him after his Modern Jazz hero `Chu Berry` `I have come to make a Commercial on American T.V` `You are a good actress, people who I know think you are as well` 'That is very kind of you and your friends to say that` When he finally got her suitcases to her bedroom, which was after she had signed in, Stella now gave him a good tip (she always did).

As he was about to leave her room he turned around with now a serious face and advised her to forget Commercials and get back into films as soon as possible. When she was laid in bed that night, she was going back in her mind, to when she and Susan first came to Los Angeles about four years ago. When dear old Burford Maunder gave them the golden opportunity to get into movies, plus all the hundreds of friends that she made in those four years. It was a run of bad luck and grief that had put her career on hold for the last few of years. At the time Burford advised her to have a complete break until she felt confident within herself.

I think that Burford would have been disappointed, that she up to this point had not resurrected her acting career.

Next morning after breakfast she receives a phone call that a taxi will pick her up in ten minutes. As she is waiting in the hotel lounge reading a magazine, a man with a yellow cap comes in and calls `Stella Delray?` The taxi is now going thru Manhattan where the skyscrapers are like giant monoliths. Stella always had a soft spot for the "Big Apple" not because she made "Miracle in the Rain" there, but probably because it is so vibrant and full of life, where you can pick up on that certain buzz of excitement that is always around you. If you want to escape from all that for a short rest, Central Park is the instant remedy.

She as well always remembers John Lennon saying that `New York was the centre of the Universe`. Now she has arrived at "Nimbus" T.V. studio's in Manhattan-Seaport. She is welcomed by the director of advertising Samantha Telford who takes her on a tour of the T.V. station. Showing her how the system works as regarding cameras and all the other things that go into making a commercial, (which basically is no difference from making a film anyway) but Stella is playing dumb as she knows everything that Samantha is telling her. It isn't everybody that knows that Stella Delray is or was a screen actress, and it certainly is not up to Stella to tell her that she is or was.

It will take three days to rehearse and shoot the commercial. On the third day Stella is going thru the lines in the peace and quiet of one of the offices.

She can hear someone come in and start one of the other computers up, obviously seeking some information or something. As she continues to rehearse her lines, she hears this man's voice say `Stella!` When she looks up, straight away she says `Peter Clay!` They are now both hugging each other. `Where on earth have you been for the last three years?` Peter demands to know. `Well since I left "Metropolis" I went back home to London` `Yes I did hear that, but where have you been since?` `Have you got about four hours spare so I can tell you?`

`At the moment no, but I still want to know, hey you look even more beautiful now than you did three years ago` `That's nice of you to say' replied Stella. She carries on `Can I say that you have turned into a very good looking man yourself, your face has filled out more, you must have put on a stone in weight, which I would say is down to your muscles` `Yes, I do a bit of Karate when I have any spare time,........ now how would you like me to take you out tonight for a meal at a top New York restaurant?"I would like that very much` answered Stella with her usual smile that opened out those perfect sparkling white teeth. `What is the name of the hotel where you are staying so I can pick you up?`

`It's the "Four Seasons Hotel" on 57th St.` `I will be there at 8pm okay?` `Yes that is fine` said Stella. At 8.05pm Peter and Stella were now on their way to "Windy Gates" restaurant on Broadway.

At 10.05 pm after apparently a beautiful 5 course meal they are now talking about almost everything that has had some significance in their lives. Stella tells him about all the people she has met plus the situations that has happened and how she has dealt with them, apart from two people: Arnaud Belgard, nobody that has any connection with her will ever be told of that terrible day, and of course Ethan Byrne where she feels disgusted with herself for being a willing partner in a sordid sexual relationship with that lazy dishevelled man.

As regarding Peter he has over the last few years worked his way from being a camera technician to a producer and now director of films. His achievements as it stands at the moment are verging on fair to not so fair. His private life is that he was born in the same year as Stella but is six months younger.

He was engaged to a girl who was a typist at the studios in Los Angeles but she turned out to be a gold digger who got her claws into a lot older man who was rich, who in turn dumped his wife for her. Since then he has concentrated on making films. Going on vacations with his brother Oliver (favourite vacation destination Alaska), plus having an interest in karate, and baseball, any remaining time was keeping an eye out for his parents who live in Carmel (California). So now they know what makes each other tick.

As the waiter brought them their favourite drinks, Peter seemed quite excited when he told Stella that he had a Movie in mind that was either going to make or break him. That is why he was in New York because Nimbus T.V. had all the information about the characters in the story and a much more detailed account of what actually happened all those centuries ago. He told Stella `If this Movie is a success it will ensure my future in the film industry` `What if it fails?` queried Stella, Peter is now going from one side of his throat to the other with his finger. Stella now goes up to him and gives him a kiss on his cheek and tells him `I have a feeling you will be a success` `There is just one other thing?` said Peter `What is that?` `Whether it was a coincidence or not I do not know, but when I saw you this morning I was convinced in just a few seconds that you were the girl that I had been searching for since I got the idea for making this film three months ago` `Me?` said Stella `Yes you` `But it is well over two years since I last made a film?` `That makes no difference, if you were an actress two years ago, you still are in my reckoning`. `Yes I suppose you are right, but what would be the part you wanted me to play?` `Well I am determined to make an Epic film of "Joan Of Arc" and guess what, you would be the central figure`.

She is looking at Peter in a way that, he is giving her good news, but she is now going to let him know the bad news, of which she is now informing him `If I remember from my school days Joan of Arc had darker hair, it was also short, plus the fact that she was only 19 years old when she died at the stake` now looking at Peter with a serious look. `Yes you are right with your interpretation of her, but there are such things as scissors and hair colouring available, and a girl of 27 can easily with makeup be made to look 19' `Are you sure about this Peter?` `I am very sure believe me` now putting his arm around her shoulders. `That is one of the two reasons why I want you to come back and live in Los Angeles again` `What is the other reason?` `Quite simple really, I have become rather attracted to you because of your friendly attitude and your beauty, basically I like everything about you` He is now facing her with his hands stretched forward onto her shoulders saying `Even if we do not hit it off together I still think that you should kick –start your career back at "Metropolis" studio's as soon as possible`. They are making their way to the coat rail where Peter is helping her to put her coat on.

They say goodnight to the waiter as they leave and enter the cold night air (it is the first week in December). As they are now making their way to 57th St. Stella is leaning her head on Peter's shoulder, a man that she had always looked to as a close friend (apart from once when they had a mini row over a certain Brent Osgood). They have now arrived at the hotel where he tells her that he will see her again tomorrow morning at the T.V. studio before he flies back to L/A. They have a goodnight kiss, she now gets out of the car and disappears thru the entrance of the hotel, but not before waving to Peter whose hand she can see waving thru the rear window of his speeding off car.

The following morning at the studio's, Stella had just finished making the commercial, when Peter came to tell her that he now had all the information that was required, and would now be able to press along with his last ditch effort to make his dream come true. He and Stella were now having a coffee in the restaurant which was on the tenth floor, which overlooked Brooklyn Bridge and the Statue of Liberty. Peter now asked her `Since we talked last night, have you given any thought about the possibility of you moving back to Los Angeles to restart your career in films?`

`Well, I hardly got any sleep last night as I was tossing and turning, thinking about it` she is now smiling and looking into the very apprehensive looking face of Peter. `Well what did you come up with?`

`Yes I will come to L/A and start my acting career again, and if you think that I will make a good Joan of Arc for your film, I will do my best to make it successful` They are now locked in an embrace that eventually ends with a kiss which means that Stella Delray is now "A Star who is Reborn" They sit down again to work out a strategy from now till when the start of the film. They have decided it will take about five months to: find the location; the clothes to be made, all the film extras to be found; and a hundred other things to be outlined including special effects. Stella is explaining to Peter that she does modelling for a good friend, who would not stand in her way to be in the film.

`That is okay` said Peter `As long as you arrange that you will have sorted things out over there, and ready to start when I decide to commence with this production` now looking at her in all seriousness `I will do that no problem` said Stella. With that Peter is looking at his watch and telling Stella that his flight to Los Angeles will be in two and a half hours.

After swapping telephone numbers he is now making his way towards the elevator with his briefcase, he turns around and calls to her that he watched her making the T.V. commercial and that he was quite impressed. As she had seen much of New York when she was the leading lady in "Miracle in the Rain", she decided that with the cold weather closing in, home was now beckoning.

She was back in London the next day. After a week at home with Chris and Alain, it was back to normal modelling duties the week after.

Which included her first visit to Blanche White the psychiatrist where for the next eight weeks she will have Psychodynamic psychotherapy to hopefully rid her of this torment she possesses, or at least bring it down to an acceptable level. Christmas has now arrived and Chris has volunteered to be Father Christmas for Alain, who is being helped to open his presents by Stella and Chris. Stella is remembering not long ago when Ethan Byrne was more than willing to give her baby son to a forty year old single man, who was a down at heel stranger who would surely have used him for his own perverted pleasures in that tumbledown tenement. She shudders at the very thought.

Coming back to Christmas, Irene was also there to join in the fun as well, bringing a nice present for Alain. Stella and Irene have a growing rapport for each other, where now Stella calls her "Mum". The New year quickly follows, and Stella has now regained her reputation as one of the top models in Europe. During the New Year family gathering, Alain is looking round for his nana (Irene) and suddenly she has come thru the front door. As she is taking her coat off, he is holding his arms out for her to pick him up, as she does Stella tells him to give his nana a kiss on the cheek, which he does.

Irene to Stella is like the mother that she lost when she was 5 years old; always being there and ready to help and give advice when needed. When Chris is not going with Stella and Alain over to the park to feed the ducks, he is getting stuck into the occupation that he loves, scriptwriting.

One afternoon when Stella wasn't at home there was a phone call from Los Angeles. It was Peter Clay that was on the other end with some good news for Stella. At first Chris thought the gentleman had phoned the wrong number. When Peter explained that this call was to give Stella the good news that everything that they had discussed in New York was nearing completion and that the green light would soon be shining to go. Chris is more than curious to know what Stella has got herself involved in. On the other hand Peter is curious to know who he is talking to. `I am Chris who is a friend of Stella` `Right, she is not your girlfriend?` `No not exactly, well I mean not in the sexual department` `I have already assumed that you are not working?` `Actually I am but why do you ask?` `Well over here in L/A the time is 8am, so in London the time is 4pm` `Dead on` said Chris `So` said Peter if you are in Stella's house now, it means that maybe you are either unemployed or working from home?` `You would make a very good Sherlock Holmes` said Chris. He could hear Peter laughing. `So which one is it?` `I am working from home, I am a scriptwriter for a couple of

T.V. soaps` `Hey that is interesting, why not send me some of your work, you never know what may come from it, Stella should have my address somewhere`

`That is very kind of you and I will do that` said Chris.

`Don't forget to tell her the good news, she may want to ring me anyway`. When Stella came home at 5.30pm, Chris had made some dish that he knows she loves for dinner.

While they were having their meal with a nice Red wine, Chris mentioned that someone called Peter Clay had phoned from America to tell her that some project that she had discussed with him in New York was almost ready to go. Stella has a big smile on her face as she takes her first sip of wine. Chris is now understandably curious to know what they had been discussing in New York. She puts her hand on his with her usual smile that reassures him that there is nothing untoward.

CHAPTER EIGHTEEN

After their meal they leave the dishes for the time being and relax on to the settee. Stella is now going to tell him everything about her life before they met. About her lifelong friend Susan who she shared an apartment with in Los Angeles, when they would be then given the chance to appear in a film that would be made in the city. Which led to a host of films that they both made. Then there was that wonderful man Burford Maunder who made it all possible for them. She told him also of the tragedies that had suddenly come into her life, where she lost the best and closest friend she ever had, Kelly.

She told him also of the woman that she saved from drowning in London and lots of other things including now, where she is a successful model. Though she never mentioned to him any of the sexual relationships she has had. Or the cruellest man she ever met in her life (Arnaud Belgard). As Stella has now told him the gist of everything, she is now looking over at Chris whose mouth is open in total amazement, and he is now shaking his head when he tells her `I was just thinking to myself, I don't think that there is anything for you to ever come back for, you seem to have done it all` `Not yet I haven't` as she now gets up to take away the dishes into the kitchen with a serious look on her face.

Chris is now clearing the condiments and the half bottle of wine back to where they belong. He is now stood behind her with his hands on her shoulders saying `Why what else have you got lined up for yourself?` `Well I will tell you what I have got lined up`. Now turning round to him with a look of sheer determination that he had never seen from her before. `When me and Susan were about 14 years old we had visions of us being film stars when we were grown up, and as I have just told you we achieved that landmark` Chris is now stood at the side of her, his backside resting on the kitchen sink with his arms folded and his legs crossed, listening intently to what she had been saying.

`Where does the American come into all this?` asks Chris `Peter was a camera technician when we were at "Metropolis" he actually was a big fan of mine, he really was`. Chris manages a smile, still at times shaking his head. Stella sees him doing this and says `It's no good shaking your head, what I am telling you is true!` `Sorreee!` said Chris now backing off, with his arms now raised, in a kind of surrender and looking rather startled after her sudden outburst. `I am only letting you know just how amazing I think your life seems to have been up to now`. She carried on `When I met him in New York last month, he told me that he was now a Movie Director but with only a modest amount of success up to that point`.

They had now washed and dried the dishes, and were now making their way back into the lounge area. Chris was walking behind Stella as she continued to tell him that Peter was going into a situation where it would move him well up the list of being a top director, or alternatively he would just be another flop. `So where do you come into this then?` asked Chris `Peter wants me to be the central character in an Epic film about "Joan Of Arc" so what do you think?` after a few moments of consideration, he tells her `I think it's a great idea, but somehow you simply don't come across to me as a Joan of Arc?` `How do you know, were you around in those days?` said Stella with a straight face. `Put it this way I think your face would probably be ideal for the part, but the long hair and the colour of it wouldn't suit. `That is just what I said to Peter in New York, but he said that a pair of scissors and a change of colour would do the trick` `Well yes I suppose it would`.

They are now a bit more relaxed now. Chris says to Stella `I can just see it now outside a big movie theatre on Broadway' `What can you see?` `I see your name Stella Delray in lights'. Chris has now suddenly realized that the Stella Delray that he knows, is the same Stella Delray he had read about in a magazine just weeks before they first met on that wet morning over three years ago' and Chris soon reminds her of it. `Yes that was me alright` said a smiling Stella.

`Yes I have already worked that out... silly`

`I was just making sure that you knew it was me that's all` said Stella

`It has just dawned on me as well, that is probably why you could afford a house like this in London`

`That is right, said Stella `I have always looked after my money`.

A few days later she again visited her Psychiatrist to carry on the treatment. I don't know what went on behind those doors, but the look on the Psychiatrists face seem to indicate that she is satisfied with her patient's progress. Now that summer was getting a bit nearer, there would be plenty of occasions when they could go for picnics in the countryside and seaside with Alain.

The idea of having a vacation abroad was never, mentioned between the two of them. Simply because a vacation like that has to have a splash of romance brought into play, and at the moment there was nothing forthcoming. Irene came to visit, which was quite regular to say that she lived in Reading. One day Stella and Irene were sat together in the lounge, with Alain sat on Irene's knee. Although Stella didn't want to open any old wounds, she was curious to know what had happened to her husband. After putting Alain on to the floor, Irene settled back on the settee. `Well it was on a cold winter's night, Chris was six years old the day before, and Richard had bought him a toy Fire engine for his birthday. He had already told his dad that he was going to be a fireman when he was old enough` Stella is now smiling. `His dad always took him upstairs to bed and told him stories which got him to sleep in no time.

Try as he might Richard couldn't seem to get him interested in sport or the like. He was more interested in reading, he would tell you everything that you wanted to know about William Shakespeare as he was his one and only Idol.

He was good at history but he didn't want to read about famous battles, where multitudes of people lost their lives, or of people who were murderers. Anyway the night in question, there was a lot of snow about which made getting home very difficult. There were no mobile phones in those days, so getting in touch was almost impossible.

Richard was a man that always made sure that he had: blankets, a flask and chocolate for any emergency in bad weather, oh not forgetting a shovel. What happened according to eyewitnesses who were close to the scene, was that as he was moving slowly in heavy traffic down the motorway. He noticed a driver had skidded into a snow drift, who was now trying to push his car out into the stream of traffic. Richard always the good Samaritan pulled up behind him and went into his boot to get his shovel out. Shortly after the two men had got most of the snow out of the way, and were both now waiting to get their breath back, suddenly a juggernaut had skidded sideways and smashed into the back of the car where they were both stood. The result was that both Richard and the other man were killed instantly`. `That must have left you devastated?` said Stella `I had to have a year off work, my nerves were in tatters.

What I can't get to grips with is why should anybody who is helping somebody who is in trouble, have to pay with their lives, it just doesn't seem fair` Stella has now come and sat beside Irene who is shedding a few tears. `I wish I had never asked you now`. `It doesn't matter about that because I think about it nearly every day that comes along anyway, it will always be there I'm afraid`. Now moving on, when Stella goes to the fitness centre she is still propositioned by the attractive 6ft muscle man.

She still declines his offer as she is still waiting for Chris to explode into the wonderful world of having sex. The following Tuesday it is the final day of her treatment to eliminate Nymphomania from her brain. It was the final test to prove that she was now free of it, Blanche had now brought out six photographs of men who were naked, who all had fit bodies, plus they all had good looks. So the question was now, which of these men would she prefer to have sex with.

If Stella told her that she liked just one (or maybe two at a push) of the six, it would mean that she should now be normal in relation to being attracted to men.

If on the other hand Stella told her that she would like sex with all of them (hopefully not one after the other) stretching maybe down to four, it would mean that there was still more work to do. Which would mean that she would still be attracted to basically anything in trousers.

Stella actually selected just one photograph of the six, which made Blanche a happy woman now knowing that Stella could now be freed from her private curse.

Before she left the psychiatrists, and feeling like a new woman, she had a question for Blanche, to see if she could help her with another particular problem that she had. Blanche was more than willing to help her if she could with the extra problem. Stella explained the story of Chris from the first day that she met him, up to the present. Where they lived in the same house, but in different bedrooms, also that they were the same age, and that she was hoping that they would have had sex by now.

But nothing had materialised from their platonic friendship. After a few minutes Blanche is almost certain that she knows the reason why. Stella is very attentive for her opinion. `First of all I think you are a beautiful young lady, and you should have been snapped up by now.

There would appear to be something wrong with a man who doesn't get a sexual urge looking at a woman who is as attractive as you, however there is another side to the coin. If after nearly a year where he has had countless opportunities to make some sexual approach to you and doesn't, then in my opinion that means one thing`

`Are you thinking what I am just beginning to think?` said Stella

`Yes I'm afraid so, he is "gay" which means that your platonic friendship will either have to remain that way, or he should be asked to leave and find another address` `I must have been stupid not to realize that he was like that` said Stella `He is such a nice looking man as well` `If you want to give him a true test, all you have to do is to make an excuse to go into his bedroom as he is about to get into bed. Put something on that reveals most of your body, if he looks away or pretends that he didn't see you come in; or even puts his robe quickly over your shoulders, then there is your answer`.

On her way home, after deep thought she has come to the conclusion that as she will soon be going to Los Angeles in a month or so, where she and Alain will be living for a few months. The best thing is for there to be that good friendship they have for each other to remain. Deep down Stella knows that it was her and her alone that wanted a sexual relationship with him from day one, (maybe because she was a bit over sexed) and just because he didn't or couldn't deliver, doesn't mean that he has done anything wrong.

The bottom line is that she did him a great favour by giving him a home when he needed help. On the other hand he helped her by looking after her son as if it was his own, so she could get fit and reclaim her modelling career.

One night she had the opportunity to do what Blanche had told her to do, and that was to enter his bedroom with hardly anything on. When that situation arose Chris was actually laid in bed reading a book when she came in to ask him if he had locked the front door. He immediately put his head under the sheets before telling her in a muffled voice that he had.

Another month goes by, and in the meantime she has come to terms with the obvious fact that she and Chris could now never be an item. A few times in the past she had suffered frustration as to why he didn't just grab hold of her and take her to his bedroom and make her a happy woman; now she knows why. One Monday when she has a day off she gets a call from Peter Clay who is very pleased to have at last made contact with her. `Are you ready for lift off Stella?` asked Peter `You bet I am, have you now got everything ready?` `Yes we will be up and running in a month, that is why I am giving you enough time to get yourself prepared for the film of your life.

`I can't wait I really can't, now you are sure that I will fit the part` `My dear Stella I have invested a lot of money into this production, and my future in movies is now simply shit or bust, if you will pardon the expression, and if I had any doubt in my mind that you were not the one, I would have told you months ago, trust me` `That has made feel a lot better now.` `Good, now who was that guy I was talking to the other week, he told me that you were just a friend of his is that right?` `Yes that is all he is' Stella is now doing a sigh, with also a look of frustration.

`He said he was going to send me some of his work, didn't he tell you?` `Well no he didn't` `He told me that he was a scriptwriter for T.V. shows and by the tone of his voice he seemed to be quite proud of what he had written` `Well if you want I will bring some of his work to L/A for you to look at`. `That will be great, do you want me to book a hotel for you to stay in or have you arranged to stay at your friend Susan's house in Santa Barbara?' `No I haven't yet arranged for me to stay at Susan's, but I will today at some point`

`So I will expect to see you at Metropolis Studio's at 9am on the 20th of April`. Straight after that conversation with Peter, Stella is now calling Susan `Hello Susan speaking'

`It's me` Suddenly there was laughter `I know who me is` said Susan `I thought you might` `Everything is alright isn't it, you are not in any trouble are you?` `No, far from it actually I feel very happy for a change` `Why what has happened?` `I am coming over to Los Angeles to make a film` `You are what!!…. you can't be serious?` `No I am deadly serious, and I was wondering if you had any room at yours for a month?` `Of course we have, when are you coming?` `The middle of April if that is okay?` `No problem, but this is like a bolt out of the blue, it really is, not long ago I was thinking that you would never return to L/A never mind making a film here`. It's Stella's turn to start laughing now. `Never say never Susan` `This has really knocked the wind out of my sails` said Susan. Stella replied `When I see you I will tell you all about what has happened` Susan still wanted to know what the big surprise was that Stella had told her about the other month. `I can assure you that if you think that me coming back to make a film is a big surprise, just you wait and see, you had better get those smelling salts out and ready`

`My God! I just can't wait to know what it is? `I almost forgot to ask you, how is your married life progressing?` asked Stella `I couldn't wish to be happier, Daniel has been my rock. As you already know, we have a daughter Silvi but believe it or not there is yet another one on the way in 6 months time, anyway like you I will tell you all about it when you are here`.

During the next fortnight Stella has told Kim and Gary that she won't be available for about 3 months, as she has been invited to the Los Angeles home of Susan Paxton. Gary asked Stella how she had come to know that beautiful actress?

`You have heard of her then?` said Stella `Of course I have, she won the Oscar for best supporting actress the other year` `Well I have known her all of my life, we went to school together` `You kept that quiet didn't you?` said Gary who is now looking over his glasses at Kim who is dumbstruck just as much as what Gary is. `So do you mix with any of the other stars when you are over there?` asked Kim `But of course, I have been seen in the company of Wayne Flannery` Kim has suddenly exploded. `Every night I go to my bedroom I am hoping that he is sat up in bed waiting for me, I really do` Stella is now laughing when she says `When I am over there I probably will be talking to him, so if you like I will tell him that you are interested eh?` `You bitch!` said Kim to her friend. A couple of days later Irene comes to visit, and as usual she and Stella give each other a big hug. Stella tells her that she is going to America for about 2 months to visit a friend. You can tell by the expression on Irene's face that she is disappointed to be without her and Alain's company for so long. Stella tells her that while she is away or even at any other time, she can stay for as long as she wants. Later on she tells Chris that his mother has decided to stay here for a few weeks to look after him, rather than keep going backwards and forwards to Reading. `That's fine by me` said Chris. He asks Stella if she will give Peter Clay some of his scriptwriting work, as he promised he would look at them.

We will now fast forward to departure day. Chris has taken Stella and Alain to the airport, and has given them both a peck on the cheek before leaving. The journey always seems longer when you are travelling alone. Alain keeps looking up at his mother with the same brown eyes that his father had. Now with plenty of time to kill, she is going back in time where she would have strangled those idiots who stuck those pins into that condom that changed her life completely. As a result of that incident she could have sunk quite easily into a life of depravity, which would be the exact opposite of where she wanted to be, where she may also never have been able to escape from. Put it this way she was very close. Now with the pendulum swinging for her, she has a child that she loves, and has got everything to look forward to, still at the age of 27.

They have finally arrived in Los Angeles. Unfortunately she won't have the same attention that she had in New York a few years ago, when all her luggage was attended to, where people turned their heads to get a look at this new rising star, as well as asking for her autograph. She hires a taxi to take her to Santa Barbara where Susan lives.

When they arrived, she asked the driver just to wait till the lady comes out of the house. A minute later Stella could see Susan making her way out of the house. She told Alain to bob down while she herself got out of the taxi. Both women now hugged each other, `So where is this big surprise?` asked Susan. The driver had got out of the car and opened the rear door, and now Alain was now just stood there. Stella was now looking at Susan whose mouth was wide open where nothing verbal was coming out (which means she was speechless to say the least). Now as Alain is walking slowly towards them, his mum asks him to say hello to Aunty Susan. He says `hello` and quickly disappears behind his mummy's skirt. Susan now goes up to him and is now bending down having a word with him.

He is very shy and is still holding his mother's hand. Eventually he is slowly being a bit braver, and when Susan asks him if he likes ice cream, he is now nodding his head letting her know that he does. The taxi driver has put the luggage on the doorstep and had now gone. Alain is walking to the house holding his mummy and Aunty Susan's hands who are at either side of him.

They are now in the house and Susan is getting some ice cream for Alain and her own daughter Silvi. Gradually After a few days Alain got rid of all that shyness, and soon became very attached to his Aunty Susan. He would now regularly sit on her knee. Susan had given Stella a very nice bedroom for her and Alain. Susan's husband Daniel who had worked his way up to be financial Director within the company was obviously a loving family man.

Stella could see that, the way he would come home and start to play games with both Silvi and Alain.

He would also go up behind Susan and put his arms around her and kiss the back of her neck. This was just the kind of situation that Stella herself now wanted in life.

On quite a few nights when the kids were in bed, the three of them would talk about various times in their lives. Looking back, since that certain day when they were spotted by their dear friend Burford Maunder, life for both girls has had its traumas. Susan would agree that she has come off the better than her friend Stella. With a fair amount of luck Susan had managed to put her life quickly back on track. For example, at this moment in time she could have been sharing a life with somebody, who could never have given her children, without her probably not realising the problem till it was too late. James Walsh the new liaison officer at the studios was the man with the magic wand, who led her out of the woods on that occasion. The other time was when she was plucked out of a raging river, by a complete stranger, who later became her husband, who then not only gave her a beautiful daughter, but also with one on the way. As regarding love and affection for each other, it couldn't be better. In Stella's case, when her great friend Kelly died, there was no one with a magic wand to help her out of that particular crisis. In fact it got worse when Burford passed away.

In a way coming back to London seemed to be like jumping out of the frying pan, and into the fire. That is until she was offered the job as a model, something she had never considered, even before coming back to London. After being blessed with height, a beautiful face and body, plus as well having been taught the elegance of walking and deportment in L/A, this should have been her first objective when she left America. She is now again being acclaimed as one of Europe's top models. She is as well remembering visiting all the big Cities of Europe when enjoying her new found fame.

On these visits she sometimes found romance (although only temporary) with some of the richest men in Europe. Her glamorous lifestyle however came to a grinding halt, when she was saddled with a pregnancy thru no fault of her own. To follow was a very regretful sexual relationship with the lazy, filthy and dishevelled degenerate Ethan Byrne. If he had ever discovered the large amount of money in her Bank account and been allowed access whenever he ran out of money, it would have been quickly squandered on beer and gambling, eventually she would have been left penniless, and her glamorous looks and figure would soon have deserted her. Her partner would eventually look upon her as something like dog dirt on his shoe, where she would have no alternative than to be accustomed to living in what would be her probable permanent squalid surroundings. Before that probability could happen, as already mentioned in the story, the penny had suddenly dropped that she was not going to descend any deeper into the cesspit of life more than she already had, and that the only way out was going to be up.

That is why we are now looking forward to a sudden upsurge in fortunes that is well overdue.

She is now rehearsing for the biggest challenge of her acting life. As promised Peter Clay gave her a call to arrange a meeting for the following Friday. On that day Stella has driven down to the studios in one of Susan's cars, with her son, now three year old Alain. Peter is there to welcome her, along with quite a gathering of old and new friends, where a couple of office girls had even brought their autograph books for her to sign. As she was doing so a voice came from the back of the packed corridor `Welcome back Stella, we have really missed you` at first it didn't register who it was who was calling to her, but a few moments later it did, without any doubt in her mind that was Burford Maunder's voice. She now quickly made her way to the back, apologising as she shoved her way thru, but there was nobody there. Thinking she had made a mistake, she started to make her way back, but had now noticed at the end of the corridor the elevator door was closing with seemingly a tall elegant grey haired gentleman with his back turned, going to the floor above.

After running up the stairs to the next floor (which was also the top floor) she was now shaking her head in disbelief that there was no one there, only two men and a lady who seemed to be heavily engrossed in probably some future project.

She enquired if a tall gentleman had just got out of the elevator, they told her that it had been broken down since yesterday afternoon. Stella asked herself if she was imagining things. But even thru the rest of her life she remained adamant that she had heard him call her just before he disappeared into the elevator. She never mentioned to Peter (who's office was coincidentally Burford's before he died) of this apparition she had just seen of her great friend Burford. She didn't want him to think she had gone a bit crazy. As she sits down on his settee, he explains to her that he and the team at the Studio have done all the spade work and planning for this epic film. With Peter being courteous he asks her if she still has the same drink that she got accustomed to when Burford was here? `Yes` Stella replied `Don't tell me` said Peter `Was it Gin and Orange with ice?` Stella was surprised that he could remember such a triviality. `It was Burford who told me the other year, that was your favourite short'. Stella for the moment is reflecting on Burford, and she is telling Peter what a wonderful man he was.

`He once told me` said Peter `that when you left the studios to go to London, he really missed you being around the place, but he also told me that one day you would come back, and bring that special talent back to the screen` Stella is now reaching for a tissue from her handbag to wipe some tears away, now confirming her belief that that was almost certainly him that called her name.

Meanwhile Alain is getting a bit restless, just sat on a chair next to his mummy. Peter calls one of the staff on the phone to ask if they would take Alain down to Studio C, where they are filming some fantasy films for the kids. One of the office girls from upstairs comes down to take him. Now Peter and Stella can now discuss the plans for the film, with how he wants her to dominate the screen, and captivate the audience. He also explains that the indoor scenes would be filmed first in the studio complex in L/A. Also that most of the outdoor scenes would be filmed in the countryside around Ohio, which has a similar landscape as that of France.

Peter tells Stella that there would be a week's break in between locations, which would now leave another month to finish in Ohio. Peter can see that Stella is definitely up for it. So he now gives her the good news that Monday would be the start of everything. When Alain is brought back to his mummy, he tells her that he had just been talking to "Freddie the frog". `Have you made friends with Freddie? asked his mummy `Yes, I have asked him to come for tea at our house` `Well it's not really our house is it Alain? it's aunty Susan's house, but I don't think she will mind him coming`.

Stella is now looking at Peter who has a broad smile on his face, maybe realising what he is missing, not yet married. When Stella got back home to Susan's, she explained the situation, that as from Monday, there would be four weeks of filming at the studios Metropolis. `Which means that is the good news, as I will be home every night. The bad news is that I don't have anybody during the day to look after Alain` `Of course you have' said Susan `Who? `asked Stella `You are looking at her you Charlie… me!'. Stella is now going up to her best friend and is smothering her with kisses. `I just knew that you would do it for me, I really did`

`What are friends for?` replied Susan `Not only that I am beginning to love the little angel` Stella is now very pleased, because that was a problem out of the way.

There was some hilarity on the first day of production. Stella had gone to the studios, as usual looking a million dollars, with her long blond hair being one of the main features of her appearance. On her return home, and getting out of her car, from the window Susan and Alain wondered who this strange lady was getting out of the car.

On her entry into the entrance hall she was met by a barrage of laughter from Susan, although Alain couldn't see the funny side, and for a short while he was now hiding behind Aunty Susan's skirt, that is until he was sure it was his mummy. Although she had been told weeks before that to get the image of her character, she would have to have her hair well and truly cropped to what is now referred to as a "bowl cut". Not only that but being a natural blond all of her life, her hair was now the same colour as Susan's.

When Susan's husband came home, she was waiting for some comment from him about Stella's new hair style and colour. He told her that he and most of the studio personnel had witnessed the transformation, and thought it suited her and that she really did look like the character "Joan".

After the following four weeks of rehearsing and filming at the studios, Stella had to admit to Susan that those four weeks, were the most strenuous of her working life. Even though she had been told by various people connected to the film, including Peter Clay, that she was already putting together a tremendous performance. As well that she should be proud of herself.

What gave her an added boost, was that when she came home at night, there would be Susan and Alain stood at the window waving to her as she made her way up the garden path. Alain now accepted Susan as someone who gave him love, especially when his mummy wasn't there.

When filming in L/A had finished, there was now a week off. There would however be a problem the week following when the filming would be moved to Ohio. It was the general feeling that it wouldn't be fair to Alain to be without his mummy for a month.

Susan had an idea, why not send for Irene (Chris Tennyson's mother) to come over to the States to look after Alain. As she remembers Stella telling her that Alain looked upon her as her nana, and that his eyes always lit up whenever he saw her. As far as Stella was concerned that was a great idea. One that she quickly fastened onto, and after a phone call back to London (where she was staying with her son Chris), Irene said she would love to come and look after Alain, while his mummy would be busy filming. So Stella's agent sorted out the plane ticket and departure time for her. Susan had told Stella that it would be alright for Irene to stay with them when she arrived. On the Saturday a taxi had now arrived at Susan's house. Stella and Alain went to the door to see who was coming (Stella obviously knew who it was). When the taxi door opened and Irene got out, Stella was waiting to see what Alain's reaction would be. His eyes have now lit up because he knows that it is his nana, and he is now running to meet her. She bends down to put her arms around him.

She gives him a kiss, while the driver is taking the luggage out of the taxi. Irene and Alain are now making their way up the garden path to the house, with Alain happily skipping. Stella had already told Susan about the circumstances of how Irene came into her life. Also that she is probably just like the mother that she never had the chance to really get to know.

So for the next few days it was just like one big happy family. Most of the people in Stella's life that meant anything to her, were assembled under one roof, and that was important to her. Monday morning has now arrived, and it is time for Stella, Alain and Irene to go to the airport. Where they would meet Peter and everybody else concerned with the making of "Joan of Arc" all of which nearly filled the plane. On the arrival at Columbus International Airport everyone had been given their own Itinerary of where they were staying, and when they would be required in the making of the film.

Stella, Irene and Alain had been allocated a house in a nice area of Schiller Park, which had a security team patrolling the complex. So this will be their new home for the next month. All the luggage has now been put away, and they are now relaxing with a warm drink. Two cars have now pulled up outside their house. On looking out of the window Stella notices Peter with another man coming up to the door.

On entering Peter gives both ladies a hug. Stella is now looking at Peter waiting for him to give her some indication, as to what happens now. He tells her that the car outside is for her to come down to the Studios in Columbus, and for any other trip they want to make. The other gentleman tells them of where places are, such as shopping areas, and of other places of interest including a complex for the youngsters.

Before they leave Peter faces Stella, with his hands straight forward on her shoulders, to reassure her that she is doing a brilliant job recreating the legendary figure of "Joan". She thanks him for his kind words. Now that all the information had been absorbed, and where Peter has now left. Stella is now looking at her watch and decides that it is time to go to the big supermarket which is two miles away, according to the map that was given to her. On their return, all the food has been put away plus Alain is now sleeping upstairs, they can now settle down for the evening. Up to now Stella and Irene haven't had much time to have a proper conversation. Irene tells Stella `I was so glad when you rang me up last week` `Why?` replied Stella `It's because of Chris really` Stella is looking quite shocked that Irene seems to be quite upset by something that Chris has done or got involved in. `What has happened where he has made you so unhappy?`

`Well when you invited me to come to your house in London and stay with Chris, I was looking forward to looking after him, like I always have done` `Yes,well that was the original intention` said Stella. Irene now told her `Everything was going along fine, but one day after I had been shopping I came back into the house, and although he wasn't around I could hear him upstairs` `So what did you do?` `I just carried on in the kitchen preparing our evening meal, when all of a sudden a young man came running into the kitchen, obviously not knowing that I was there` `Was it a friend of his that had come to visit?`. Now looking at Stella feeling embarrassed she said

`By looking at him I realized that he was definitely more than just a friend` `How do you mean?` `To put it bluntly Stella he was totally naked` `What!` said Stella `Yes he had come from Chris's bedroom for some orange juice from the fridge` `So what did you do?` queried Stella `Nothing, I was just stood there rigid with a long thick red carrot in my hand, that I was just about to chop up, and after a few seconds I threw it in the sink, as it suddenly resembled something that was conjunctive to the present situation, it really was` Stella is trying not to laugh. `Did you go upstairs and challenge Chris as to what was going on?` `No I didn't, I didn't want to embarrass him, but everything that I had hoped for had suddenly been shattered` `Such as?` asked Stella `When I first met you, after Chris had told me that you had helped him, that was when I was hoping that you and him would become an item` `Well that is what I was aiming towards as well`, said Stella, she continued `Before Alain was born and even after, he had been just like a husband and father, but he just didn't seem to be interested in starting a romance whatsoever.

All he wanted was to be a good friend, and at the time I felt a bit let down` said Stella `In a way `said Irene, `I feel as though it is me that has let you down, with him being gay` Stella went up to Irene who now was very teary and put her arm around her, and told her `It's not your fault that he is gay, and there is nothing that anybody can do to reverse that` a question from Irene was `When we are back in London, will you want me to keep away from you and Alain?` `Mum (instead of Irene) that is exactly the opposite of what I want, you are a big part of my life now, in fact this situation has brought me closer to you`. They are now giving each other a big hug. From that moment on nothing was ever mentioned again to Chris, or about what his vocation in life might be.

CHAPTER NINETEEN

The next four weeks turned out to be more rigorous than the first four weeks, because of there being more action in the outdoor scenes. But now it was finally over, and everybody could now go home. Again Peter reiterated that the main character "Joan" had been superbly portrayed by Stella, and as well as patting himself on the back for choosing her to play the part. He as well told everybody on the set that he had high expectations for the film to be an outstanding success. Thanking all the other actors and actresses who contributed to it.

Before going back to London, Stella gives Susan a call to thank her for all the wonderful hospitality, that she and Daniel had given her and her family while staying at their beautiful home, and hopefully in the near future they could all get together again. Susan told her that they were welcome anytime, and that she hopes that the film "Joan of Arc" will be a box office hit, and that she is very much looking forward to seeing it. Another phone call, this time to London to tell Chris to make sure the fridge is full of food for when they get home; as she didn't want to go to a busy supermarket so soon after opening her front door.

When they did finally arrive home and sank into the settee, Stella asked Irene if she would like to stay for a few days to be with her and Alain, she said she would love to. At that point Chris came into the lounge to welcome them back, giving his mother a hug and a kiss on the cheek, elevating Alain up to the ceiling, and giving a kiss on the cheek also to Stella. Later when Stella and Chris were alone he asked if she had given Mr. Clay the samples of his work. `Yes I did` `Did he actually say anything about them?` `He told me to tell you that he had a quick look at them, and at first glance they looked promising, but because he had to be totally focused on the film, he would have a proper look after the film was finished` `That seems fair enough to me, there's no rush anyway` said Chris.

Stella never mentioned anything about one of his friends running round the house naked, whom his mother had seen. She has already accepted that he wasn't quite the man that she hoped he would be when they had first met. She was wanting to tell him, that as far as she was concerned, it was perfectly okay that he was gay, but quickly realized that kind of admission would be better coming from the man himself.

Chris had just remembered that there had been some mail for her while she had been away. Shortly after he was giving her a box full. `My God what are all these?` asked Stella as she put them on the kitchen table. At this moment Irene was taking Alain for a walk, so Stella decided to work her way thru this mini-mountain of mail, where 75% of it was junk mail and a few bills. Suddenly there is a letter with a Miami post mark. Straightaway she was thinking that it was a letter from Cheryl to let her know what was happening in her life. When she opened it the letter wasn't from Cheryl, it was from Clark Duvall. She looked on the envelope to find out the date it was sent. It was three weeks ago. After quickly opening it, the letter read.

> Dear Stella
>
> Hope you are well and still single, and that you are still as beautiful as you were when we said goodbye to each other over three years ago. The reason I am writing to you, is because I think you should know that my wife died a year ago. If you are still a single girl and you want to pick up where we left off, all you have to do is send me a letter, or you can phone, and we will work it out from there.
>
> Love Clark xx

Whenever Stella looks back and remembers that wonderful time that she had in Bermuda with Clark, she gets a bit emotional, because there had been a good chance for them to have a great life together. Unfortunately due to unforeseen circumstances it was going to be a non starter. Although she hadn't been hoping for Clark's wife to be in a situation where her life would come to a close. She knows probably more than anybody, that whenever tragedies occur the bottom line is that life will always carry on, no matter what.

So the door was now open for them to resume an affair which at one time was on the rocks. Where now the only conceivable problem to that happening would be for Clark not to accept a child that Stella had by someone else, who tragically never lived to see his son growing up. If that is the outcome then her search would have to continue elsewhere. She is now phoning the number, After a moment or two, she gets thru to a lady, who says `Duvall Construction Ltd. How can I help you?` Stella answers `Is Mr. Clark Duvall available please?`

`Who is it that is calling?` `Miss Stella Delray from London` `I'm now putting you thru` suddenly there is a voice, `Stella is that really you?` `It most certainly is`, now showing those perfect teeth, as she was smiling. `I got your letter given to me today` `Well I sent it a month ago, I don't know why it has taken so long to reach you?`

`It's because I have been in America making a film`

`You have? Oh I am so happy that you have changed your mind, and returned to acting`

`I also would like to say how genuinely sorry I am that your wife passed away`

`Actually Stella, it was a blessing in the end, as she did suffer so much pain, and I now feel so contented that she is now in eternal peace`.

`How is my friend Cheryl going on down there?` asked Stella `Oh, Lee's wife, she had a baby girl about a month ago whom she named `Grace`

`That is wonderful news!`

`So anyway when am I going to see you again?` asked Clark, `Well I am thinking within a month, if that is OK`

`That would be wonderful if you could`. During the remainder of that phone call, they arranged that she would also be able to visit Cheryl as well.

During the following month, Stella has gone back to Square House to do some more modelling work for her friends Kim and Gary. Chris is working from home writing scripts, while Irene visits them regularly from Reading. July has now arrived and Stella gives Clark a call just to tell him that she will arrive at Miami airport tomorrow at around midday. Stella, Chris and Irene have come to an agreement that it would be better that Alain doesn't go with his mother this time.

As it would be awkward turning up with her child, when she would be trying to rebuild a special relationship. So now Irene would be staying the whole time that Stella is away. After saying goodbye to Alain and his now (temporary) adopted mum Irene, Stella is now being taken to the airport by Chris. After a hug and a peck on her cheek, Stella will soon be in the clouds. At the Florida airport waiting for her arrival is Clark. Suddenly he sees this beautiful lady walking towards him with that same elegant walk, and the same slimness.

They both complimented each other on how well they looked. Clark wanted to know what had happened to her long blond hair, as it was now a different colour and much shorter . Stella told him that she had it cut short because she had the part of Joan in the film that she had just finished filming "Joan of Arc". `Oh yes I remember you telling me now` As they were now making their way to his house, he told her that his children had gone to visit their own individual friends, so that it would give them more privacy and space.

Clark had now shown Stella around the house, which included the bedroom that she wouldn't be sleeping in, plus his bedroom that she would be sleeping in. When they settled down for the evening in his beautiful lounge, Clark said to her that he had waited a year after his wife had died, in respect. Stella told him `You did right, it would have been bad manners to do anything else` `I just was hoping that in the meantime you hadn't found a Mr. Right` looking at this beautiful woman, who was now resting her head on his shoulder. She was now looking into his face when she told him `I did actually find a Mr. Right about two years ago` Clark with a surprised look on his face said `You did, what happened?` `Well after I got your letter saying that we wouldn't be able to do the things that we had planned. It created a situation where firstly I was sorry to be told that your wife was terminally ill, and secondly, sorry that our dreams were never going to materialise.

So with my modelling job getting me to all the big cities in Europe I came into contact with the son of a leading French manufacturer of luxury cars, at the French Motor show` `What was the name of the manufacturer?` asked Clark `Belle` replied Stella `Yes I have heard that name` said Clark. She has now told him the full story of what happened, right up to the point that she had a child, due to the stupidity of Alain's so called friends. Clark is very understanding and sympathetic to the situation.

`People advised me to have an abortion, but one of my main principles in life is that I would never have an abortion, to me it is so inhuman` `So where is your son now?` asks Clark. `Back in London and being looked after by a rather special lady called Irene. One of the reasons why I have come to see you is to find out if there would be a problem with you accepting him into our relationship?` `No there would be no problem, because I have two children also, who will I hope accept you being my partner` Stella now went into her handbag and brought out some photos of Alain with Susan at her Los Angeles mansion. `I must admit` says Clark `I can see a part of you in him, and I know that I would accept him into my house anyway, especially if he has a nature like his mother`.

Now that Clark has seemingly taken to the mite, she gives him a kiss on the cheek. Clark has two servants in the house, one does the cleaning of the house, as well as being the Butler. The other does the cooking and the laundry. Plus there is a gardener who comes once a week to give the garden much bloom. At 7 pm the two servants finish for the day, and retire to a nice chalet at the rear of the house which they share. Clark and Stella spend a nice relaxed five days (and nights) together. Clark mentions to Stella that he is quite happy to carry on living here, she agrees that the house was in a lovely area, and as far as she was concerned there would be no problem with that at all.

Half way thru her stay Clark gave Cheryl a call to tell her that he needed to see her about something (he didn't really, it was just a pretence). She told him to come over this afternoon. When he and Stella arrived at her house, Stella stayed in the car while he went in to the house to bring Cheryl to the door.

When they were making their way to the entrance, Clark was telling Cheryl that it was some lady wanting to know what London was like. On opening the door, Cheryl suddenly opens her mouth in disbelief as she sees her friend Stella leaning back on the car, with her arms folded, smiling at her with the usual smile that shows those dazzling white teeth. In no time at all they are hugging each other, `I thought that you were never going to come?` Cheryl told her. `I was always going to come, it was just a case of when` replied Stella.

They were now making their way into the house, with Clark walking behind. The house was quite large, with exquisite furnishings plus five bedrooms, and a good view of the Atlantic Ocean. Inside Stella was introduced to Cheryl's first child Grace, who was being cradled by their part time maid Annette a black lady who probably was in her fifties. Annette now gave the baby to Stella, who gave the baby a kiss on the forehead.

Cheryl asked Annette if she would like to get the silver tray and serve tea and biscuits for her guests.

Stella asked Cheryl if Lee was still working for Clark, looking also at Clark who was now sat at the side of her. Before Cheryl could answer that question, Clark intervened by telling her `Lee is doing tremendously well at the company and is gradually working his way up, Stella is now looking at Cheryl, who is beaming with pride after his remarks.

Cheryl is curious to know how the Modelling business that she sold over a year ago is progressing. Stella tells her that `It is actually doing very well, and now goes under the name of `Square House' and the brother and sister who own it are just as nice to me as what you were`. On hearing that Cheryl comes across to her still best friend and gives her a kiss and a hug, while Clark sits back on the settee with a broad smile. Eventually Clark has to remind Cheryl that as it is a year ago since his wife died, and it was time for him to look for a suitable partner, who would love each other and also share in all the good things that life can offer . Cheryl has now quickly got the message, and her mouth is opening in total amazement. `I don't believe it!` she said `You two, together?` `You seem to be surprised? ` said Clark now with a smile back on his face. `Well to be honest I am, because if I remember correctly`, said Cheryl `the last time that we three were together, which was in a hotel in Hamilton you told me and Stella that we were just a couple of bimbo's looking for a good time` `Yes, and I did apologise to Stella the next day`, who is now getting hold of her hand at the same time looking into her blue green eyes.

Clark was now informing Cheryl that with Stella at that time being alone on the island, it was only right that (if she would forgive him for the previous night's outburst) he would make her vacation as enjoyable as he could. `It is one vacation I will never forget` said Stella putting her head now on his shoulder. `So in that time you both got well acquainted with each other?` said Cheryl `Very much so said Stella now smiling at Clark. `That is why I never mentioned anything to you when we met back at the airport in London, because you surely wouldn't believe that me and Clark could ever become great friends.

Cheryl couldn't say anything other than `You are Probably right` now having a smiling glance at Clark, who returned her smile. `So what happens now?` queried Cheryl looking over at Clark `What happens now is that we are going to live together as partners, that will quash any suggestion that Stella would automatically inherit my fortune on my death, or even if things went pear shaped with our relationship.

My fortune would be shared between my already grown up children, and any children that me and Stella had between us`. Looking slightly mystified, Cheryl now asks Clark 'Just as a matter of interest, if like what you said, the relationship did go pear shaped, or whatever, wouldn't Stella be allowed anything?` Clark now looking at Stella says to her `Haven't you told Cheryl about your acting career yet?` Cheryl responded to that remark very quickly, `Acting career! what acting career? `you never mentioned anything to me about acting` now looking at Stella with a dumbfounded stare, `I was going to tell you when I came to live with you, but I didn't want to relive that upsetting part of my life, I really didn't`. `Why is it such a long story?` `Very long, but I will tell you that while I was in Los Angeles, I did actually make a lot of money` being a film star. `Are you now telling me that you really were a proper movie star?` `Yes I was, and a leading lady in a couple of the films` `Well all I can say` said Cheryl `is that something pretty dreadful must have happened to you, for you to come back to London and giving up on a career like that` `It did` `Exactly what?` asked Cheryl.

Stella is now looking towards Clark for some solace, but who is just as much in the dark, as to why Stella did actually want to desert Los Angeles and go back to London. Suddenly she finds the strength to tell them that `In a nutshell, I had a flat mate in L/A, her name was Kelly Baxter and we forged a friendship together that would have lasted forever.

We toured Europe for a month, our friendship was so strong that if we were apart from each other making different films, it would hurt, it really would. People thought that we were twins, we were the same height, she as well had blond hair, and that I was just one year older. She was such a good actress, that it was a certainty that she was going to go right to the top. She was given top billing in a film being made in Kenya, and she desperately wanted me to be with her, so I went with her.

On this particular day, they were doing a shoot, just outside Mombasa, about five miles from base. She called in at a supermarket for some cool drinks for her and the crew, but while she was being served robbers burst in and demanded money from the tills, but they were followed in by the police. All of a sudden there was a shoot out, and my best friend in the whole world was shot by one of the robbers. I was holding her hand when she died in hospital. `Cheryl at the moment has tears streaming down her face unable to speak, and anyone could see that Clark had also been also affected with the story. After wiping the tears away Cheryl asked Stella if that was why she finished making films after that tragedy.

Stella replied `Yes it was, that it is well over three years ago since I felt as though everything was going wrong, and that I needed to get away. But quite recently I was offered the leading role in the film epic "Joan of Arc" by my old friend from Hollywood Peter Clay, and although it was hard work I really enjoyed making it` Clark is full of admiration for the lady he now loves. Cheryl is amazed that the girl that she employed over three years ago, who actually earned her company big profits, was as well a Hollywood film star.

After staying for tea, it was time to leave. Cheryl and Stella are now giving each other a big hug. She tells Stella that she can't wait till the time when they will be neighbours again (which would be about five miles apart). On their way back to Clark's mansion, he asked why she hadn't told Cheryl about Alain her son? `I was going to but I thought to myself that I had already given her more than enough information for one day "Yes I think you were right`.

On the day before Stella was going to return to London, they once again planned out their future together. It now meant that Stella and her young son would in a month's time start a new life in Miami, hopefully with the blessing of Clark's grown up children Tony and Bryony. Where they will all live together as a family. On her arrival back at Heathrow, Chris was there to welcome her, and to reunite her with her son Alain, who had spotted her in amongst a thousand or so people.

On their way home Stella sees a noticeable change in Chris, he seems to be happy and relaxed, certainly more than usual. She now asks him `Has something happened, you seem to be quite happy with yourself` `Stella I have some great news to tell you` `Go on then tell me` now looking into his smiling face. `Well I got a phone call from Peter Clay, telling me that my script-writing work is very encouraging, and they have invited me to Los Angeles to do a script for a "soap", and if it is up to their standards, they will give me a contract`. `That is wonderful news Chris` she now leans over and gives him a kiss on his cheek.

As the car now pulls up outside the house, Irene has made her way to the front door to welcome Stella. As they are giving each other a hug, Chris is getting the luggage out of the boot. Now inside the house Irene suggests a nice cup of tea before they have their evening meal, which has been prepared by Irene. As they are now settled Stella asks her "mum" Irene what she thinks of the invitation that Chris has been offered, that may result in him living in California. `I think it is wonderful, I really do` `If he were successful, would you go over there and live with him?` `Yes I would, if he wanted me to` Chris overhears his mum as he walks into the dining room.

`Of course I do mum, you already know that surely` `But that would leave you and Alain alone in this big house, wouldn't it?` said Irene. `Actually mum it wouldn't, because me and Alain will be starting a new life in Miami, with a man who I met on vacation in Bermuda about three years ago, and we now have the chance to start again` Irene looks visibly upset that she may never see them both again.

`I know what you are thinking mum, and you needn't worry because I will arrange with Clark that you can visit us twice a year, a month at a time, how does that suit you?` Irene's face has suddenly done a "U" turn, and is now giving Stella another big hug, and tells her that she is so kind to think of her in that way. `So when are you going to California to take up the offer?` Stella asks

Chris `I have arranged to go on Saturday, so I can start on Monday` Stella now turns around to Irene `Are you stopping with us mum till he comes back?` `Oh yes most definitely` answered Irene with a smile. After quickly working things out, she now tells Irene and Chris that tomorrow she will put this house up for sale, and when it is eventually sold she will give them each £50,000 towards a new start in America, which as well with the selling of their own house in Reading, (that's if he gets the job) that would be an even better start.

They can't believe how generous she has been to them. She tells them `You both came into my life at a time when I needed some inspiration to kick start my life again.

At the time I was heading towards a life of degradation, but with your help I feel as though I am now back on track`. After nearly a month has passed by, Chris has returned home with a two year contract under his belt, and is now sorting out him and his mother's move to Los Angeles. A Russian business man has now bought the house in St John's Wood. Next week Stella and Alain will be saying goodbye to London, and heading to warmer climes, in a way she is sorry to leave London as it has always been a big part of her life.

Like anything else in life there have been good times and also bad times. Before she goes she will now honour her decision to give the Tennyson's the two cheques she promised.

So now with their house up for sale in Reading, Irene and her son have just been seen off at the airport by Stella and Alain. Chris has given Stella his address and phone number to contact them in a month's time when the mayhem of moving settles down. So in the remaining few days Stella has visited Kim and Gary, who were very teary at the thought of losing the best friend and model they ever had.

Stella insisted that if they want to visit her and Clark, all they have to do is to ring the number that she has just written on Kim's pad, and "Hey Presto" their vacation would be sealed. She also visited Susan's mum and dad, who still lived in the same house from when she and Susan were infants.

Mrs Paxton picks Alain up and tells Stella `What a lovely looking little boy you have` giving him a kiss on his cheek. After a few hugs, she asks Catherine (Mrs. Paxton) when is she next going to visit Susan, who now has to look round to her husband asking him when they were going. `Oh, in about four month's time, September I think? ` `Well I might see you then` said Stella. With that they were now leaving, `Oh I forgot to ask, where is Craig?` `He is at work?` `How old is he now?` `He will be twenty this year` `There's me thinking that he is still at school, doesn't time pass` `So what is his job?` Keith (Mr. Paxton) tells her `He is now a landscape gardener, I think he sees himself as another "Capability Brown" or something`. If we now move the clock on a couple of days. It is now Tuesday and Stella and her son are now on their way to Miami. On arrival at Miami airport, as expected Clark is there to welcome them.

Clark is now bending down to Alain and says `Now little fellow what is your name?` `Alain` who is now pointing to a plane, to tell this total stranger, that was the plane that they were on. Now, after exchanging kisses Stella and Clark went to the car lot where his limousine was waiting, with his butler being his now and again chauffeur.

When they arrived at Clark's mansion, he had a surprise for her. Meeting his son Tony (who she already knew) and daughter Bryony, who would be just eight years younger than Stella.

During the last few weeks Clark must have told Bryony everything he knew about the lady who would be his new partner in life. It must have all been good because Stella got a pleasant feeling that Bryony was happy that her father had found love again.

Stella was hoping that Tony and Bryony would also accept Alain into their family as well, which was just as important to her. As Stella began to settle in quite nicely, Clark took her to visit his business. Stella was amazed how big his works were. It wasn't just a case of him showing her around, but also him wanting to show off this beautiful and elegant lady as well. Luckily most things have worked in their favour, and now they can enjoy all the good things that were planned over two years ago. Spending a week in his yacht on that special island that they visited a few years ago, that was off the coast of Bermuda. Also going down to Florida Keys for a few days was well worth the time, and there were lots of other places that they had found interesting. But there was a slight problem, Stella needed to be involved in doing something, something that would occupy her mind.

She just did not want to sit around all day, especially when Clark was at work running his business. Alain didn't need round the clock attention, as he was now getting that little bit older. After trying to think of something that would release her from boredom, suddenly her mind went back to the day when she and Susan were admiring those beautiful paintings in London, which now seems such a long time ago.

Obviously if she decided to do paintings with the intention of getting them into Museums or similar, she would be living in cloud cuckoo land. To get them into someplace where they could be sold, that alternatively could be her way of raising money for Charities.

She couldn't wait to tell Clark when he came home, of her intentions. When after dinner she told him of her idea, he thought it was a brilliant idea and was well worth the try. Next day she went into Miami, in her Bugatti Veyron sports car that Clark bought for her. I must mention that anyone who was now thinking that she had a meal ticket thru life, simply because she was now the partner of this very wealthy man, have simply got their figures wrong, as she herself is a millionaire in her own right. She bought a DVD, and a book that gave her all the information she required to get started, plus all the brushes, paints and of course an easel. Now almost at once she had something to give her an alternative interest for when Clark wasn't at home.

One day when she was sat at the side of the pool, painting a picture of Florida Keys that she could visibly see in her mind's eye, she could hear the Phone ringing in the house. Arnold the butler must have been out somewhere, so she transferred the call from the house to her mobile that was at the side of her. `Hello, Stella Delray speaking` `Hi Stella this is Peter Clay, how are you getting on in your new surroundings?` `Really, really well thank you Peter, and you?` `Top of the world, all thanks to you` `Me, why me, what has happened for you to say that?` `C'mon Stella you must know why, have you forgotten the film we made recently, like "Joan of Arc"?` `Oh my God, I do apologise Peter, but with such a lot of things happening just lately it had left my mind completely, so has the film been a success for you?` `Totally, and I mean totally, I honestly can't believe how well it has done, the film critics love it, Variety magazine loves it, everybody loves it`. Stella could tell by his voice, just how happy he was.

`Oh I am so happy for you Peter` `Thank you Stella, but I am equally happy for you too` `Why is there some other good news that you have for me?` `Yes there most certainly is, because you my most glamorous, and favourite film actress of all time, you now have an excellent chance to win your first Oscar, how does that grab you?` suddenly there is no response, `Hello, hello are you still there?` Peter at last hears a voice `I'm alright now` `Why what happened? you sound as though you have been crying` `I must admit I have, I feel so happy and yet I am crying` `Don't worry I understand, I know it has been a lifelong ambition of yours, and what you have been thru in the last few years, believe me you deserve it` `So what happens now` `Let me explain just what happens now, you have been nominated for an Oscar which means that you will be up against three other actresses, just like when your friend Susan was nominated. Hopefully you will be presented with the Oscar just like she was three years ago, this will be sometime in March. I personally will let you know a month before, okay` `That's fine Peter` and thank you very much for letting me know. Stella can hardly wait to tell Clark the good news. She has suddenly lost her concentration to paint her picture, as a result of the phone call.

Clark is delighted when she tells him about how well the film that she starred in had been very well received by the media. `I hope you are going to come with me to Los Angeles, when Peter lets me know`.

Now putting his arm around her, he answers `You bet your life I am, I know just how much that Oscar means to you, and I want to be there if and when you collect it`. Stella is looking into his handsome face, when she said to him `Do you remember a couple of years ago, when you asked me if I loved you?` and I said at the time I liked you, because you can't just love someone more or less overnight' `Yes I do remember` `Well I love you now` she now gave him a hug and a kiss to prove it. During the following weeks, it was nice to see Clark getting involved and showing affection towards Alain, and who was now teaching him how to swim in their massive pool.

Tony and his girlfriend Jenny who had known each other since school days, would take him down to the beach so he could build sand castles. Bryony as well bought him a big rocking horse. Cheryl and Lee came to visit on a few occasions with their young daughter Grace. As the months are passing and being torn off the calendars, everything in their lives is being lived to the full, as you probably would expect being a mega-rich family.

Things get even better when Stella receives a letter from Peter in Los Angeles, telling her that the date for the Oscars ceremony will be held on March 2nd in Hollywood, and told her to prepare herself for the biggest night of her life, which according to her calculations is about six weeks from now. All her newly adopted family are very excited for her and want to be there just in case she wins it. Clark has his personal representative book a complete suite at the best hotel in town, for the entire family and the circle of close friends for a week, as well as a private plane to get them there.

We will now fast forward to that very special day in Los Angeles. Altogether there are fifteen family and friends streaming off that plane. Later when they have all now been accommodated into their hotel. Stella now rings her best friend Susan to let her know that she is in town again. `Hi, it's me Stella, and I'm here!` and I am absolutely speechless what to say, I really am, all I can say at the moment is that I love you` Susan replied with

`And I love you too, I am in total amazement at the way you have bounced back, somehow I don't know why, because knowing you like I do, it was always going to happen and I am very proud to have had you as a big part of my life, but anyway you are going to visit us on Sunday aren't you?"We certainly are, although I hope you know that there will be about sixteen of us` `That's okay, there is enough room, and tell them to bring their swimsuits as well, the best day to come would be on the Friday about 2 o'clock` `No problem see you then`. There was just one more phone call to make. `Hello` said a ladies voice, `Is that Irene Tennyson?` `Yes, who is speaking?` `Don't you recognise my voice?` `Yes I do now, it's Stella, where are you speaking from?`

`From here in Los Angeles` `What are you doing over here?` `You remember the film I made about six months ago?` `Of course I do "Joan of Arc" `That's right, well I could possibly be getting an Oscar for best actress` `My goodness that is wonderful news, I always remember the people that were responsible for making that film telling me that you were a great actress, you really were` `Oh, that is lovely you telling me that mum, but anyway before that will you and Chris come to Susan's house on Friday as we are having a big get together` 'I will tell Chris tonight when he comes home, I know he will be very happy to come; I definitely will` `I think 2pm would be the best time, see you, okay`

We now jump to Friday at Susan's. I have never seen so much hugging and kissing of fresh air in my life at just one function. I think the most tearful moment of the day, was when Alain spotted Irene coming up the drive. He made a sudden dash towards her, as she bent down to him he threw his arms around her and gave her a big kiss on her cheek, he also held hers and Chris's hand as they walked up to the house.

It turned out to be a wonderful day for everybody. Clark was introduced to Susan by Stella, where he told her that she and her family must visit them in Miami, and he would not accept any excuses whatsoever for them not to come. She promised that they would definitely come.

Peter Clay turned up with a new girlfriend. Alain had a playmate in Silvi (Susan's daughter) also there was Daniel's daughter Helen who was now seven years old, and walking normally, thanks to a successful operation paid for by Susan over two years ago. Cheryl, Lee and baby Grace were also present.

Susan told Stella that she had seen a special viewing of "Joan of Arc" only last week and that both her and Daniel had thought she was brilliant. Which earned her a kiss from her best friend.

Sunday night is here, and as usual the search lights are scraping the skies. Stella is looking more beautiful now than when she stepped off the plane that brought her to Los Angeles almost five years ago.

The same tall slim figure, her natural blond hair that had now grown back substantially, which was now half way down her back, that elegant walk that altogether gave her that "Wow" factor. As well she had a silver necklace that surrounded her throat. She now sat next to Clark who is overawed by this special occasion, he really is. Dotted around this vast arena are her now new family and friends who are crossing their fingers, that she will triumph.

We must not forget as well that there are three more nominees in exactly the same nail biting situation. Anyway the time has arrived, and one of the older stars of yesteryear Tim Carlyle, who himself won an Oscar in the eighties had the golden envelope in his hand. When after showing a few clips from each of their films, he now tells the world that it goes to Stella Delray for "Joan of Arc". All of a sudden, it's as though everybody in the building knew what she had been thru in the last few years.

She now stood up and turned around to all the people who were clapping and cheering at the same time. She now got a kiss and a hug from Clark who was the proudest man in Hollywood without a doubt. She was now ushered on to the stage, blowing kisses to the four corners of this massive arena. Tim had been patiently waiting for the celebration to simmer down before he gave her the biggest reward of her life.

At that precise moment that she was given her Oscar, to her it was the longest moment in the history of the world. Simply because from being an ordinary young woman, she rose quickly thru the ranks of Hollywood's top film stars. Later thru no fault of her own, she found herself being immersed into a nightmare existence. But seeing a chink of light at the end of this long disastrous tunnel gave her the impetus to fight her way back. That is why she is on this stage tonight. She notices her best friend Susan clapping at the front of the stage. Stella beckons for her to join her on stage, which she does. These two tall beautiful ladies, who both went to the same junior school together, almost 25 years ago now have their arms around each other's waist, with Stella holding the Oscar aloft.

There is plenty of flash photography now illuminating the stage, as more of her friends and family join her on stage. The time has come for her speech, and at the moment she isn't feeling nervous as she is telling everybody, `I feel so honored to be here tonight, with all my family and my friends. Going back to my schooldays, I always remember the boys of the class telling the teacher that when they got older, they wanted to be a train driver or a fireman, even a soldier. But Susan and I insisted that we wanted to be film stars and live in Hollywood. Of course, it was just a childish dream that could never be achieved surely. Then one fine sunny day something happened and it came straight out of the blue. It was meeting a man who was the kindest, most warm hearted and caring person that I have ever known.

I am not just saying that because he gave me and Susan the chance of a lifetime, I am saying it because he really was that kind of person that I have just described, and it breaks my heart that he is not here tonight, I really do miss him. I would also like to mention someone else, Kelly Baxter who while she was alive had such a wonderful outlook on life and every minute that we were together was fantastic, and is another person I will never forget.

There are so many people that have been a part of my journey, most of them good, decent and helpful. On the other hand, there have been a few dishonorable associates that have got in the way, but doesn't that happen in each of our lives anyway? Lastly, I would like to thank everybody who voted for me` She is now leaving the stage followed by her family and friends. That basically is the end to this story, apart from the fact that she has been thru every emotion that life has to offer. And as someone said to her later in the book `There was nothing left in life for her to ever come back for`.

It's now twelve years since we were at the Duvall mansion, where everything was as it should be; a happy environment and a sun that doesn't know how to hide behind a cloud. Tony and his then girlfriend Jenny, now his wife have found a new home in Fort Lauderdale and have been blessed with one girl and a boy. Bryony has opened a new fashion shop in down town Miami that she shares with her boyfriend, which now leaves her dad Clark, Stella and their children Damon 14 and Sabrina 13 and finally her first son Alain. Alain is now 19 and is at University studying Economics, he at the moment has no girlfriends, the last one he had who he really liked dumped him for some other guy, which for the last few weeks has left him quite miserable. Up to that point everything in his recent life had been `hunky dory and ticket boo` (great). He deeply loves his mother who has told him to simply get on with his life and to forget about silly fickle girls, who at this time of his life are unimportant. His stepdad who had overheard the conversation between mother and son backed up his wife Stella by reminding him that had a great future in his Construction company. For the moment it seems as though what he has been told has struck home, and is now smiling and hugging his mum and at the same time shakes Clark's hand.

If anybody at the moment needs advice it's Stella. Unfortunately, at the moment there is much confusion as to know just who was the father of her son Alain? There is just nobody who she knows who can help her remove this misery from her mind. Every day it gets worse. I will now explain the situation. As it stands at the moment, Alain is her son, his supposed father was also called Alain. The simple fact is that both men are not related at all.

Question: Have you any evidence to prove what you are saying is true?

Answer: There isn't any, believe me, the only evidence is in her mind.

Question: So then, who is the man that's in her troubled mind that she inwardly knows for certain who the father is?

Answer: Stella told me that she would never reveal his name.

Question: Is it someone who the family knows?

Answer: There is only two people on the planet who knows who it is and that is me and Stella!

Question: It seems to me that Alain's real father is a bad person am I right?

Answer: Put it this way...He was

Question: Do you mean, he is dead?

Answer: Yes, he was found guilty of rape and being the murderer of six women, who was then duly hanged within the week.

Question: If he is then out of the way, why is she going out of her mind with worry?

Answer: It's her knowing that this wicked man is the father of her grown up son, who is beginning to look more like him every day that passes, which as you can imagine is deeply disturbing to her.

Question: Is she 100% sure that this monster was definitely the biological father of her son?

Answer: More likely to be 120%. I have seen photos of Stella stood with Alain Schadeck at the Paris Motor Show, to me there is no similarity whatsoever between the two Alain's. What I have told you in our conversation is correct. Whatever, Stella will have to do a U-turn with her troubled thoughts, and to just get on with the good life that she has already made for herself.

STELLA›S PROBLEM IS NOW SOLVED

Usually about once. a month Stella would drive down to Miami to visit her friends, then take a stroll thru Martell Park, as well just call into a few shops. On this particular day the weather was not its usual self, there were heavy showers forecast. A casual walk thru the park was now omitted, so she took a different route to the shops. She is suddenly caught in a heavy shower and is now forced to stand in the doorway of a building that looked very old, which I would imagine it to have been built when George Washington was President of the United Sates

While waiting for the shower to stop, she could hear Gospel singing coming from behind her, which was coming from one of the adjoining rooms. She was so impressed that she opened the door and went in. There she was suddenly surrounded by children of all ages, in the background were grown men and women looking on. 'Carry on singing don›t let me stop you` Stella was quick to get the message across to them. She now sat next to a friendly old lady, who was saying to her 'I've never seen you here before, have you come to the right place`? `Actually` said Stella after looking all around her `I have only come in to escape the rain, but on hearing the singing I just wanted to hear more`. The old lady replied 'You haven't come to choose a child then`? Looking rather mystified Stella asks `What do you mean choose a child, that is something new to me I'*m afraid 'now looking at the old lady to give her more information.* First of all, she tells Stella that her name is Rosanna and that she comes here once a month to monitor couple who have not (who have lost their own children) yet been interested enough to take any of the present orphans into their homes. Showing some concern Stella asks `How long have these children been waiting to be brought into the real world? Rosanna replies `Some have been here for two years but with no luck` Looking around the room again Stella sees a young girl stood on her own, who at the moment is looking at some parents who seem to be interested in one or two of the other children, she herself was shabbily dressed, also with hair that has not been attended to recently, which could be the reason why she has been ignored.

But Stella can see that underneath all of her pathetic appearance, she can see that there is a girl of eventual beauty.

The name Kim Trollope age 9 has been written down on a preliminary form that could be the start of proceedings that would allow Stella to adopt her.

That is providing that her husband Clark agrees; he does.

After a private meeting between the two, Stella is more convinced than ever that she is the girl she wants.

You may be wondering where Lady Luck came into the story. Although not intended, it was the cancellation of the usual walk thru the park, and the heavy shower that made her seek shelter in this old building that houses orphans, plus being drawn to choosing and adopting a girl who would enter a world that would be beneficial to the girls future ambitions. The annoyance of the Arnaud Belgard escapade has now gone forever thanks to the excitement of having this new addition to the family. It has also made Stella realize just how lucky she was to always have Alain Jr under her wing, and never in an orphanage.

An afterthought:

Kim Trollope soon became Kim Duvall. By the time she was eighteen, you simply would not believe or recognize that it was the same shabby girl that was given a chance (just like her adoptive mother was in Hollywood) to be successful in whatever she wanted to do. After studying at a top University, she later won the job of being an adviser to the Secretary of State in the White House in Washington.

YouTube: You can listen to Jerry Vale singing
MIRACLE IN THE RAIN

EPILOGUE

Probably the saddest episode to emerge from the Oscar Awards ceremony was that somewhere back in London, there was a little old lady sat alone in her bedroom at a hospice for Dementia sufferers, watching the TV and looking at this beautiful young woman on stage collecting her award, totally oblivious that she was in actual fact Stella's grandmother. Who had been her parent and guardian thru her childhood years and beyond?

Would James Danvers who was probably watching the Awards presumably with his wife, suddenly have his breath taken away, and now realizing just who that girl was that he took to Germany for a weekend, and who he had shared a shower with, as well as a bed.

What about Graham and Martha Ogden, what was going thru their minds as they watched Stella lift that prestigious prize above her head.

With a properly thought out approach she could easily have been their adopted daughter they had always wanted. Alain had now inherited another auntie when introduced to Cheryl not long after their permanent arrival to Miami. In the four intermediate years since arriving from London, Stella and Clark had a rethink and decided to get married after all, but with the same stipulation that Clark's will would remain as originally intended, as Stella was already a self-made millionaire in her own right. Also, in that time they have brought into the world two children Damon and Sabrina. With Stella now already having achieved her dream she felt as though it was time to concentrate on her family. Alain who was now seven went fishing with Clark his step father a few times. He was also a pageboy at Tony's wedding to Jenny. As well Stella had now slowly but surely become a very accomplished painter, and had some of her works shown in various exhibitions around the U.S.A.

One of her paintings was of herself looking down on to New York thru a window twenty storey high (which was created from an emotional situation she found herself in while filming `Miracle in the Rain'). She and Susan still visit each other twice a year. One last piece of information that has been left to this last section of the book. It is that Ethan Byrne would not have been able to see Stella receive her award on TV simply because he was now lying in a pauper's grave. The reason for that is because of an association he had with a local business-man's wife, who had decided that living with the filthy degenerate Ethan Byrne in that squalid bedsit was at least better than living with a man who's business had recently been wound up, and who had started to regularly beat her up as a result of his misfortune.

`When told where his wife was and who with, he obviously flipped, where he now took his sawn off double barrelled shotgun to Ethan's bedsit. Where he burst in to find that they were both naked in bed, with Ethan's penis stuffed half way down his new girlfriends throat. He now blasted them both with the sawn off shotgun, Ethan was killed instantly, thankfully his girlfriend did survive. Rather than go into the street where the police marksmen were now waiting, and the thought of going to jail for life, he now turned the gun on himself.

THE END

ABOUT THE AUTHOR

J.E.T. COLLINS is a relatively new author, he won't disclose his age because he says that age is just a number and nothing else. To him it's how you feel in yourself today; tomorrow could be different. Going for long walks helps him to concentrate and work out solutions for problems which sometimes applies to writing.

He himself is not an avid book reader, he prefers to be on the other side of the fence—writing

Leisure time allows him to enjoy music Modern Jazz 1930—50 and old films which include `Twelve Angry Men`/ The Shining`

Favourite actor Kirk Douglas and Favourite Sportsman Lee Trevino.

When I write my books, I am always alone which makes me a true Author. People who rely on a full playground of helpers to give them advice to write their books then how can they be classed as real Authors

www.ingramcontent.com/pod-product-compliance
Lightning Source LLC
Chambersburg PA
CBHW071410200726
48294CB00002B/342

* 9 7 8 1 9 6 0 9 3 9 4 9 4 *